# Kiss And Tell

Printed in the United Kingdom by MPG Books, Bodmin

Published by Sanctuary Publishing Limited, Sanctuary House, 45-53 Sinclair Road, London W14 0NS, United Kingdom

www.sanctuarypublishing.com

Photographs courtesy of Sheila Stewart, Jean Allan, Dexter Gordon, Alistair Mulhearn, Gary Paczosa, Sue Storey, Allan Titmuss and the author's private collection

Front cover photograph by Allan Titmuss. Author photographs courtesy of Sue Storey and Future Publishing

Visit the Martin Taylor website: www.martintaylor.com

ISBN: 1-86074-315-3

# Kiss And Tell

## Autobiography Of A Travelling Musician

## Martin Taylor

### with David Mead

I would like to dedicate this book to all my fellow travelling musicians out there on the road. May you never run out of clean socks...

# *Acknowledgments*

To my family: Liz, Stewart, James, Rhoda, Bob, Sue and Oscar.

To my manager, James Taylor, and everyone at P3 Music, including Alison Burns and Marcus Ford.

For their support and belief: Adam Sieff, Paul Burger, Brian Yates, Chris Black, Sharon Kelly and Geoff Collings at Sony Music (UK); Jeff Jones, Adam Block, Tom Cording and Stefan Moore at Sony Music (America); Kieven Yim at Sony Music (Asia) and Shigeto Saitou, Kozo Watanabe and Ryoko Obukuro at Sony Music (Japan); Allan Titmuss for taking wonderful pictures and Dave Bellwood for being a great sound engineer; Mark Rowles and Jenny Redman at MRM and Mark Wilkins at Edmonds Bowen and Company Solicitors.

Judy Lipsey at JAC, Don Lucoff at DL Media and Cliff Gorov.

Phil Hobbs at Linn Records.

My friends Jack Emblow, David Grisman, Bill Wyman, Tony Clark, Steve Buckingham and Danny Godfrey.

Everyone at Sanctuary Publishing, including Penny Braybrooke and Jeff Hudson.

John Spencer at WL Gore and Associates and Udo Rosner at AER.

With special thanks and much appreciation to David Mead for his hard work in putting this book together, and to Carol Farnworth for transcribing my wild ramblings from the many hours of tape.

# Contents

# Forewords

When David Mead first suggested to me that we collaborate on a book about my life, I was somewhat taken aback. I was very flattered that someone should think my life was interesting enough to write a book about, but at the age of 43 I felt that maybe I was too young. At first I declined, thinking that it's a good idea, but something I should do in maybe 25 years' time.

It wasn't until I started to tell my family and friends about the idea that I changed my mind. I've always enjoyed telling stories and, the more I thought about it, the more I realised just how many stories I have to tell. I didn't realise that perhaps my life has been a little unusual because I've been too busy living it. So, with a lot of encouragement, I decided to have a go at this writing lark.

For months I carried a small notebook around with me, scribbling down thoughts and anecdotes whenever a memory resurfaced in my mind. Other musicians who had heard about "my book" started to call me and remind me of shared experiences, although many of them are unprintable for various reasons!

However, when David and I finally got together and locked ourselves in a room for days on end with a tape recorder, I wasn't prepared for the roller-coaster ride of emotions that I was going to have to put myself through. I found the process of talking about my life deeply painful and, by the third day, I was prepared to quit. Like most people, I have had my share of hard times. But it wasn't just recalling those that hurt so much – it was also the memories of good times that have gone and memories of close friends and loved ones who are no longer here. I don't live in the past. I try to live in the present, with a keen eye on the future. I am not ashamed to say that I shed a few tears while I put myself through this agony, but most of the tears actually came from laughing. Jazz musicians are a funny lot – just ask any bank manager.

I would like to thank David for asking me to do this, and for sitting, for hours on end, listening to me pour my heart out. David, you'd make a great shrink.

Martin Taylor
Scotland
Summer 2000

I've known Martin for about ten years and in that time he's told me many stories about his life as a jazz musician, so much so that I've known for ages that this book simply had to be written – all I had to do was convince him. In the end my gentle nagging was successful and the collaboration you now hold in your hands was born. My own part in this joint literary venture is merely one of scribe – to instigate, collate, prompt, cajole, buff and polish – every word is Martin's own and his story is as unique as his own singularity as a musician and performer would suggest.

I am myself a student of jazz guitar – at least I can tell a flattened fifth from one which still has a few lumps left in it – and recently Martin thrilled me to bits by giving me a guitar which had belonged at one time to Ike Isaacs. Anyone reading this book will know what a marvellously generous gesture that was and I thank him from the bottom of my heart.

David Mead
Bath
July 2000

# 1 *The Carrot Cruncher*

I was standing in the wings at New York's Carnegie Hall, waiting for my name to be announced and thinking of the times I had played there before, with Stephane Grappelli. This was a special night, a memorial concert for Stephane that had brought together a number of musicians, each with a close connection to the great French jazz violinist who had passed away just six months previously.

I was about to go onto the most famous stage in the world and play completely on my own, something that most musicians dream of and many would have nightmares about. But I didn't have a nerve in my body. I was just looking forward to getting centre-stage and playing my guitar, as I always do.

I had toured a lot in America with Stephane and he always announced me, in his distinctive French accent, with, "On guitar, from Scotland – Martin Taylor!" I never bothered to correct Stephane on the fact that I wasn't really Scottish, so I just went along with it.

I heard the lady on stage announce me: "From England – Martin Taylor." There was a lot of applause and I walked up to the mike and, after the applause had died down, said, "I have to correct you – I'm from Scotland." That got even more applause and quite a bit of laughter, and I started to play.

To put the record straight once and for all, I'll start from the beginning…

I was born at five o'clock in the morning on Saturday, 20 October 1956, at 5 Collins Meadow, Harlow in Essex, which is about 30 miles north-east of London. My dad, mum, brother and sister had just moved there from Carshalton in Surrey, where my mum's family lived. In those days there was a kind of pioneer spirit, with families moving to the so-called "new towns", and we were part of that. I was a "mistake" – I wasn't supposed to happen. My dad was quite devastated when he found out my mum was pregnant because they were struggling enough as it was to make ends meet.

And for a while, I think he was quite upset about it, no doubt thinking, "Oh God, another mouth to feed."

My brother and sister were both born in St Helier's Hospital in Sutton, where my dad's family lived. I was the only child to be born in Essex so my dad always referred to me as "the carrot cruncher" as a kid, which was his term for a country boy.

We came to Harlow because my dad had come out of the Royal Navy and got a job as a postman – there were loads of jobs about in those days. He and Mum had been living in a single room in my mother's father's house with my brother and sister. One day, Dad saw this poster advertising jobs in new towns, like Crawley and Welling Garden City, and he saw there was a job in Harlow. Neither Mum nor Dad knew where Harlow was, but a house went with the job because they were trying to get families to move out there, which was a great incentive if you were homeless. So that's how my family ended up moving out to Essex.

I was born in our front upstairs bedroom, which was Mum and Dad's, and it was one of those all-night things. Sorry, Mum. My dad managed to get a midwife and she came out on her bicycle.

We lived in a council house and there wasn't much money about, so I never had a proper cot as a baby. Instead, they used to open a drawer, line it with soft material and use it like a crib.

As for the rest of the household, my dad was called Bill, but as a musician he was known as "Buck" Taylor. My mum's name is Rhoda and I have a brother called Robert (but we all call him Bob), who is six years older than me, and a sister called Sue who is four years older.

My parents were born in south London. My father was born in Lambeth, just off the Wandsworth Road, and my mother was born in Battersea, although their family backgrounds were miles apart.

In Lambeth during the middle of the 19th century, there were a lot of Irish people who had come to London looking for work during the potato famine, although most crossed the Atlantic to America. So both of my father's grandmothers were Irish, Amy Connell and Mary Flaherty. That same part of London, centred around the Wandsworth Road area, also had one of the largest populations of English Gypsies, Irish and Scots Travellers and various nomadic and semi-nomadic people. The English Gypsies called this area of approximately two acres, "Kekkeno Mushes Puv" which, translated from the Romany language, means "no man's ground". There were lots of families there, including the Lees, Boswells, Coopers and Taylors, who all lived close together in caravans and tents. I don't know too much about the Taylor side, although I believe we originated from the New Forest area in the south of England, moving to London to find work.

The families on this "no man's land" had a variety of occupations, including chimney sweeps, which in those days was almost the exclusive domain of Traveller people. Among the sweeps was my great-grandfather, Bill Taylor. In fact, there is a photograph, which sadly I don't have any more, of my dad as a very young child, sitting on a horse and cart with "W Taylor, Chimney Sweep And Carpet Beater" on the side.

My great-grandfather was like a character from a Dickens novel. He made his living, as many did back then, by going round from house to house with his horse and cart, offering his services sharpening knives on a grinding stone and so on – they'd do anything they could to make a crust.

The women had a very hard life, too. They would go round to the houses of wealthy people and clean the steps outside, making what money they could to swell the family coffers. A lot of my dad's uncles also worked on the street markets as "barrow boys", selling fruit and veg.

From what my dad has told me, my great-grandfather was something of a likeable rogue. Apart from his work as a chimney sweep and knife grinder, he also had a very unofficial scrap-dealing business, principally nocturnal, which involved removing lead from church roofs. In fact, sometimes my dad was called into the "scrap" business as a little boy, being instructed to "bring the wheelbarrow round the back of the church" on occasion. Of course, as a youngster, he innocently thought it was all some sort of marvellous game, but I understand that my great-grandfather spent a little time at His Majesty's Pleasure in Wandsworth Prison, as a result of his rooftop activities.

Because of those various stays at the "Wandsworth Hotel", the responsibility for looking after the family often fell to my grandfather. From a very early age he was highly respected among the family for seeing to their needs, and was a very hard-working young man.

My fondest memory of Grandfather Taylor is of my brother and me sitting on his knees while he rolled his cigarettes. He had a silver tobacco tin with a horse's head engraved in the top. He also had a horse's head in a horseshoe tattooed on his chest. He used to show us the tattoo and joke, "'e was just a foal when I got 'im!" I've got the same

"Taylor tattoo" on my right arm.

On my paternal grandmother's side of the family there are the Stewarts. My branch of the family travelled down to London from Scotland during the latter part of the 19th century, because there was plenty of work to be found building the London Underground system. The Stewarts brought with them something that the Taylors didn't have – music. One distant relative of my grandmother's, piper Jock Stewart, has been immortalised in a traditional Scottish song called 'Jock Stewart'. He was the champion piper in Scotland for nine years in a row, and was piper to the seventh Duke of Atholl. He won the gold medal for the pibroch, which is the classical music of the Highland bagpipes, and received it from King Edward at Holyrood Palace in Edinburgh. As the King handed Jock his medal, he asked the name of the piece Jock had played. "It was called 'The Kiss Of The King's Hand', Your Majesty," Jock replied, and this amused the King to such an extent that he said to Jock, "Well, Stewart – you should kiss my hand, then," which Jock did. The story has been passed down through the various family lines and, even before I made contact with my relatives in Scotland, I knew the story about Jock.

Another relative of my grandmother's was the famous singer, Belle Stewart, who wrote a song that has become a standard in traditional Scottish music, 'The Berry Fields O' Blair'. Belle's daughters, Sheila and Kathie, carried on the tradition and Sheila is still travelling the world as a ballad singer and a traditional storyteller. She's actually lectured at Harvard and Princetown in the USA and has worked tirelessly for the cause of Traveller families in Scotland, working with the Secretary of State for Scotland as representative for Travellers and Gypsies. Sheila and I still meet regularly and we hope to actually work together some time soon. She is an extraordinary woman, whom I respect and admire tremendously. She has sung before the Pope, on his visit to Scotland in 1982, had tea in The White House with President Ford and even became a blood sister of the chief of the Comanchi Indian tribe.

So my grandfather, Bill Taylor, married my grandmother, Hettie Stewart, and around that time the Wandsworth Road was full of Stewarts and Taylors. There were the Condons, Flahertys and Tooheys – to whom we're also related – there, too, and they all lived together in a tenement building in Pascal Street, and that's where my father was born in 1928.

Between April and September every year, the family would travel around potato- or berry-picking, and end up hop-picking in Kent. During the hop season they worked on Moat Farm at Ivy Hatch, near Sevenoaks, for the owner, Mr Thomas Barnes, who they all had to address as "Master Tom". They worked in the fields from seven-thirty am until five pm – and the children worked, too. It was very hard, back-breaking work. They would be away for a good part of the summer, but lived out the winter in London.

I can remember going down to Ivy Hatch as a kid in the early 1960s, and seeing my grandmother outside, cooking a stew in a pot over a stick fire. My grandmother lived in a council house in Sutton and her cooking was notorious – it was so bad – and we all thought that she couldn't cook. But she'd learned to cook on a stick fire and this stew was incredible – she just couldn't cook on a conventional oven and so, when you went round to see her at home, it was a different matter. She would cook us something and we really had to struggle to eat it and so, wherever possible, we'd try to leave as much as we could. She would tut tut and tell us, "There's children starving in Africa would do with that." But I've always thought that my grandmother's lumpy custard wouldn't have travelled that well somehow.

My family was hop-picking down in Kent during the Battle of Britain in 1940. Dad was twelve and it was a glorious summer, with clear blue skies. He told me how they used to watch the dog fights: when a British plane was hit, everyone would boo, and when a German plane was hit they cheered. If a plane went down nearby, they would run into the field and find it, although usually there was only the tail-end sticking out of the ground, with the poor dead pilot about eight feet down in the earth. Sometimes they would save bits of the plane as mementos. The Luftwaffe had 1,350 bombers with 10,000 crew. The RAF had 650 planes and 3,080 pilots, so it was an amazing victory, really, for Britain.

During the Blitz, something happened that had a devastating effect on the family and almost ended the musical connection on our side. My father's family were bombed out of five houses in total, all in the same area. When the sirens sounded, they would go down to the Anderson Shelters, but my great-grandmother Flaherty didn't like the idea of that at all. She was a bit of a party animal, I suppose, and loved to sit around with the rest of the family and sing. My grandmother and great-grandmother were good singers and encouraged the whole family to join in. One night, when they

were all in the middle of a sing-song with a crate of beer keeping the pro-
ceedings going, the air raid sirens sounded. My grandmother said, "Ah, I'm
not going in that damn shelter – we're having too much fun here singing,"
with her free Irish spirit to the fore. But the house received a direct hit that
night and nearly all of the family were killed. After that, my grandmother
never sang again and never encouraged music in the house. So the only
member of the family who retained a strong interest in music was my
father. He wanted to have piano lessons, but since that was considered to
be a thing that only middle-class children did, he wasn't really encouraged
to pursue his interest at all.

Both sides of that family were very good boxers. My great-grandfather Stewart's brother was a very well-known bare-knuckle prize fighter
called Ginger Stewart, and my dad's uncle, Johnny "Bugler" Stewart,
was the British Army Champion in India. In the summer, the boxers in
the family used to travel around with the fairgrounds and fight in the
boxing booths. They would get into the ring at the beginning of the
evening and put on an exhibition of fighting, before taking on the local
lads. I remember saying to my dad that it must have been really tough,
going from town to town, taking on all the local hard cases, but he told
me that the hardest part was making the local lads look good in front of
their friends before they finally knocked their lights out. I come from a
pretty tough breed.

My dad used to hang around with a young lad who was a few older
than him and who was much admired for his boxing skills. His name was
Don Cockell and he later went to America where he fought – and lost –
against Rocky Marciano at Madison Square Garden. I've seen the
footage of the fight and I'm afraid Uncle Donnie looked like a lamb going
to the slaughter.

Although my mum was born in Battersea, her father's side, the Guilfords,
came from Brighton. My great-great-grandfather was a saddler and had a
large family, as was common back then. His son, my great-grandfather, left
home when he was eleven and walked to London and started working for
a fishmonger. He was a hard-working young man and did very well for
himself, eventually opening his own places and becoming involved in property. It got to the point where he owned a number of houses on Clapham
Common which were converted into flats, and he did so well that he retired

when he was only 40 years old. He sold all his property in London during the Blitz, fearing that it would be destroyed – I can't help thinking what they'd be worth today. He went on to live well into his 90s.

My great-grandmother's name was Anne Rowe and she came from the Isle of Wight. Her family had been there for a long time and they owned the George Hotel on the island.

When my great-grandfather retired, he bought a house in Carshalton, at 45 Poulton Avenue, and that became the family home. His son, George Guilford (my grandfather), married my grandmother, Grace Pashley, and they also stayed on in the house.

There was music in that side of the family, too; my great-grandfather Pashley was a very keen amateur classical violinist and he was very good friends with the Goosens, a very famous family of musicians. His son, my great-uncle Eric Pashley, became a professional musician, playing cello and saxophone, and was resident for many years at London's Windmill Theatre. This was the theatre which was to become infamous for having the first naked women dancers – although they weren't allowed to move, they had to stand still in vaguely classical Greek poses, covering themselves with feather fans to keep the censors happy. Then, during the war, he joined the RAF and was one of the crew of a round-the-world flight on a Lancaster Bomber to celebrate the end of the war. I have newspaper cuttings of them landing in New Zealand. After the war, he didn't go back into professional music. Instead, he went into business with his brother and opened a hardware store.

Eric's sister, Grace, married my grandfather and, in October 1931, my mother Rhoda was born in Taybridge Road, Battersea. She was a twin, but when she was born she weighed only two pounds and they didn't think she would survive, so they put her aside to concentrate on her more robust brother. Sadly the brother died and they thought they had lost both of the children, until they heard my mother begin to cry. She was only the size of a milk bottle, but she survived.

My mother inherited a love of music from the Pashleys and, because of her, I grew up to the sounds of Nat "King" Cole, Frank Sinatra and Tony Bennett. All those wonderful orchestrations by Nelson Riddle and Billy May somehow got under my skin and resurfaced years later when I started playing solo guitar.

My grandmother had been born with a heart problem and, sadly, when my mother was only eight years old, she died. So my mother was left pretty much on her own, being taught to cook by my great-grandfather. My grandfather, meanwhile, was so devastated by his wife's death that I don't think he ever fully recovered. He never spoke about his wife; he certainly never mentioned her to me. He was a baker's roundsman, back in the days when they used to carry bread on a cart and pull it along. Unlike his businessman father, he was happy just to get by and earn enough to pay the bills and socialise with his friends at their club in London at the weekends.

He had served in the British Army in India and had been attached to an Indian regiment in Punjab, which was predominantly Sikhs. Many of his Sikh comrades had emigrated to England after the war and he spent much of his spare time with them.

I never really got to know him; he seemed quite detached and distant, but when the local paper wrote an article on me when I was eight years old, he got a copy and framed it, and it had pride of place in his front room. He was obviously proud, but not the kind of man to tell you so. A very old-fashioned, Victorian Englishman.

When we used to go and visit my grandparents while I was still very young, we had to go through the centre of London and I can remember the Thames, in those days, being full of ships. Back then the riverside was all warehouses, whereas now it's all very expensive apartments. On one occasion I remember my parents telling me off for running my hands along the walls, because they were all black with coal dust from the smog that London was renowned for in years gone by. I was always very interested in the City of London as a child, little knowing, of course, that I would one day be made Freeman of the City. But I can clearly remember the river, the boats and the policemen, who all seemed about seven feet tall.

My Taylor grandparents were pretty set in their ways. Their house in Sutton didn't have an inside toilet – they had one down the bottom of the garden. In the late '60s the council put extensions on the back of all these council houses and put bathrooms in them, but my grandparents wouldn't use them. They still went on using the toilet in the garden because they considered it to be dirty using the bathroom in the house.

Grandad Taylor kept chickens and had a shed with a small workshop in it with saws, chisels and a work bench with a big vice on it. He used to sharpen people's kitchen knives on a grinding stone, to make "a bit of beer money", but he was very bad at it and people would get very angry when he returned their knives with big chunks missing from the blades. As we say in the music business, he got very few return bookings.

My grandmother (Hettie Stewart) didn't believe in education. She would say, "Too much education and your head will blow up." She really believed that, and I think my brother going to college and becoming a school teacher was a bit of an embarrassment to her. She couldn't understand it. On the other hand, my sister and I had a very sparse education and kind of hustled our way through life, and that she could understand. I remember the first time I did a radio broadcast on BBC radio. I told her what time I was on and she sat up and listened to this jazz programme that was on really late. She got a real thrill when the presenter said my name, but after that, whenever she heard a guitar being played on the radio, she thought it must be me. She would say, "I hear you on the radio all the time, you must be doing well." She thought I was *the* guitarist on radio. I never corrected her, it seemed to make her so happy.

As a child, my dad always had a great love of boats and he made his mind up that, when he left school, he was going to go to sea. He actually left school when he was 14 – just walked out one day and didn't go back. He found his way to Grimsby, knowing that this was a huge fishing port, and signed up on a trawler and became a deep sea fisherman. It was an incredibly tough life – more so for someone so young. They fished off the coast of Norway, the Shetlands, Iceland and the Faroe Islands and Dad hated every minute of it. But he didn't want to run home for people to say, "I told you so," so he stuck it out for a little while. This was at the end of the war and being a trawler fisherman was still considered to be an occupation essential to the war effort, so you pretty much had to stay put once you were signed on. But by the time he was 18 he'd had enough of deep sea fishing, jumped ship and went to Lincoln and joined the Royal Navy. He sailed all over the world, eventually becoming Leading Cook aboard the HMS Glasgow. Dad was a far better cook than his mother, but on the rare occasions he cooked for my brother, sister and me, he always made enough to feed the entire Royal Navy. He didn't understand measurements like grammes and kilos, he only understood bucketloads!

It was when he was on shore leave in 1946 that he met my mother. He was in Carshalton and needed directions and so he stopped this pretty young girl to ask her the way to a friend's house. They got talking and, in the end, he asked her out. They were both still very young at the time – Mum was only 15 – but they used to write to each other and whenever he was on shore leave, they would meet up.

Dad was still in the Navy when, on 12 August 1950, he and Mum were married at All Saints Church, Carshalton, where most of my mother's family are buried. They started married life living with my mother's father and grandfather. In 1951 my brother, Bob, was born in St Helier's Hospital, Sutton, followed by my sister, Sue, three years later.

# 2 It's Arrived, It's Arrived...

One of my earliest memories from Harlow concerns a guitar arriving at the house. It was the late '50s so I can only have been very young, maybe two or three, but I remember my brother was quite excited – something was happening, something was going on. This was a time when we didn't have a television or a telephone or anything like that, so it was quite a simple kind of living, and when someone came to your door, other than a neighbour, it was quite an event.

On this particular day, a van turned up and I can remember Bob saying, "This is it, it's arrived, it's arrived," and calling my dad, and my dad saying, "All right, OK, yeah," and coming downstairs. A man came in and delivered a couple of packages which turned out to be a guitar and an amplifier that my dad had ordered out of Bell's catalogue.

I remember Dad opening the case and that was the first time I ever saw a guitar. It was a Hofner President, with a small Watkins amplifier, and it looked really luxurious. The case had a red velvet inlay. I'd never seen velvet before and I can still remember the smell of the guitar. Then my dad started to play it – he couldn't actually play guitar, he was just learning.

The next real memory I have is sitting on the draining board in the kitchen. It was an old-fashioned, wooden affair and I was waiting for my weekly post-World War II kid's bath. With rationing having only recently ended, parents of that generation just got used to being frugal and so they still rationed water. Being a little kid meant you didn't have a bath, you sat on the side of the sink and were just given the once-over with a flannel. It wasn't even that you sat *in* the sink, you perched on the edge and received a wash-down from Mum.

Being a postman, Dad would often be home by late afternoon. I can remember that, if it was raining, he used to drive my mum mad by coming through the kitchen door and cleaning his glasses on the curtains. Then he'd have a cup of tea. In those days, everyone drank tea from a cup and saucer – you don't see it now so much because most people use mugs, but back then everyone drank out of a cup and saucer. All my dad's family used to get the cup, pour the tea into the saucer and drink it out of the saucer because it cooled it down. It used to really annoy my mum, hearing Dad slurping. Her upbringing had been far more genteel than his.

Anyway, on this particular day, while I was waiting for a scrub from Mum, she must have seen my dad coming up the garden path and she said to me, "I think your dad's got something for you." He had a parcel underneath his arm and he pulled it out and it was a little ukelele guitar. It was red with a palm tree on it and I thought it was fantastic. He gave it to me but he didn't show me anything on it, so I just started strumming away on it and making a racket. Looking back, I think I must have shown an interest in his Hofner guitar and so this was his way of diverting my attention away from it a little bit. But I loved the ukelele and played it most of the time.

One evening I was walking around strumming away and I can remember very clearly my mum saying, "Bill, for God's sake show him how to play it – he drives me mad, playing it all day and all night." I was just playing open strings on it, so my dad showed me the chords C, F and G, and taught me how to play 'My Old Man's A Dustman' and 'Hang Down Your Head, Tom Dooley' – skiffle was very big in England at that time.

For some reason I picked it up instantly; once he showed me a chord and I knew where it was, I just played it. It wasn't like a big thing, I didn't really think anything of it. In fact, later on, friends of mine would come round and they'd pick up the guitar and say, "How do you do so-and-so?" and I'd show them and not be able to understand why they couldn't play it too, because it came so naturally to me. I'd say, "All you do is you just play it and that's it." I just couldn't understand why they didn't have it, but I've always had an aptitude for stringed instruments.

Across the street from us at that time lived the Coe family. One night, I was already in bed, and my mum came into the bedroom and said, "Come and have a look at this." Mum and Dad had been over there because they were friends with the Coes, and Mum wanted me to see a guitar that Pam and Tom had bought for their son. They'd bought it in Petticoat Lane in London's East End and he was having a go on it.

I remember it being really nice and cosy in their house because there was a fire, and I had my pyjamas on and my mum was holding me and I had a blanket round me. Pam said, "Give Martin a go on it." They must have heard me play the ukelele, I suppose, and so I had a play on it and I just loved the way it felt. I was probably about four by this time and I can remember I said that I'd like a guitar just like it. Bearing in mind our financial situation, it must have been like asking for a weekend yacht or something, but somehow my parents got me one. It had metal strings which were really high off the fretboard – it was a real instrument of torture.

That guitar was actually quite ridiculous when I think about it, but I didn't have anything to judge it by then. I played until my fingers were bleeding, but I just couldn't stop. I just got really into it and sat there starting to make little things up. I think it must have been a Saturday when I got that guitar, because I played it all weekend – and I can remember that when it came to Monday morning, Mum had to wrestle it away from me, saying, "You've got to go to school," and me saying, "I want to play..."

That was another thing – actually starting to go to school. It was awful and I hated it from the word go. Mum kept going on about me going, but I didn't really understand what she meant. I don't suppose any kid of that age really knows what's in store for them. She altered all my brother's school clothes to fit me – in those days you'd just have two of everything; one to wear while the other was being washed and, being the youngest I drew the short straw and nearly always had to wear my brother's clothes. But even though I had all these "new" clothes and my brother and sister would keep on talking about school, I really had no concept of it at all.

So one morning we took the short walk to Hare Street School. There was this lady teacher who told me to come in and sit down and offered me the chance to either draw a picture with crayons or have a little wooden-framed blackboard with coloured chalk. I took the chalk and sat down and started to draw, with my mum sitting close by. Eventually, she said to me, "I'll have to go now," and I said, "But I thought you were staying." I thought that school would just be the one day – with my mum. She told me that I had to stay there by myself and left. I cried my eyes out. Maybe it was because I was the youngest of the three kids and so maybe my mum doted on me a bit more. Also, for most of my childhood my brother and sister were at school, so it was like being an only child, really.

So Mum left, I was bawling and the teacher came up to me and said, "Stop crying," took the blackboard away from me and hit me. I'd never been hit by an adult before and it was a terrible shock. I always felt, all the time I was at school, that it was a very violent place.

The teacher was awful. We all sat in rows behind desks with lids and, if you were too slow fetching whichever book out of your desk when she demanded it, she'd go round and smash the desk down on your head. And we're talking about six-year-old kids. At that time it was just part of going to school, but now it's unacceptable behaviour, and rightly so. There really is no excuse for violence against children.

I had asthma as a kid; asthma and hay fever, and sometimes in the summer I used to be quite bad and so I would have to go and see the headmaster's secretary and sit in her office. She would give me an aspirin – whatever good that did, I don't know. One day, I was sitting in the office, waiting for the aspirin to "work" and two six- or seven-year-old lads were brought in for the cane. The head teacher had caned one kid – I could hear the swishes from the next room – but the other kid was screaming, "No, no!" I heard the headmaster say, "Look, *he* took it and you can take it as well."

It was absolutely horrific sitting there. I was never hit by my parents and my father had told me never to allow a teacher to hit me. He came from a pretty "hard" family and, when I had teachers who were bad to me, I would never dare say anything to him. I'd go to a family funeral or something, and I'd see all these hard men, relatives of mine, and they'd ask me how I was getting on at school, often adding, "Just let me know if any of the teachers are giving you a hard time." But I didn't dare tell them. I really believe that, if my father had heard that any of the teachers had hit me, he would have gone round there and knocked the living daylights out of them. So I never said anything.

I never got the cane at school, although I came very close to it completely by accident. There was another kid called Martin Taylor, who was a year below me at Hare Street, and I was sent to the headmaster's office by mistake to get the cane instead of him. I was sitting outside, thinking, "What have I done?" when the secretary came and said, "Oh, it's the wrong one, here's the right boy." I went outside and she gave me a glass of water, while the headmaster sadistically leathered into my namesake in the next room.

There was one kid called Peter Solieux – I think his family came from the Channel Islands – and he was one of those kids who was always bigger than everybody else. He started shaving before everyone else did –

when he was about twelve – and sort of matured very early. Anyway, he went in to get the cane, but grabbed it from the teacher and began hitting him with it instead. He was expelled for his trouble but he became a bit of a hero to me after that.

There was the usual undercurrent of violence and aggression among other kids – the "I'll see you after play time" sort of thing – but the real threat of violence was from the teachers because you witnessed it. It wasn't like it was merely a threat, you did actually see it and were sometimes on the receiving end of it.

One thing at school which I didn't enjoy at the time but I got to appreciate later, was Scottish country dancing. Once a week we used to go into the hall to listen to the BBC Home Service for Schools, and I learned all the traditional dances. I loved the music of Jimmy Shand, but when you're that age you don't want to hold a girl's hand, and so it was all very embarrassing. Years later, when I had moved to Scotland, I was at a wedding anniversary up in Oban and all these dances started up and I knew them all. My wife, Liz, who's from Scotland, said, "How do you know those? You grew up in England."

At school I was very, very bad (and I still am) at anything to do with figures; mathematics, arithmetic and so on. In fact I'm prone to, what I believe is called, dyscalculus, which is like dyslexia, only with numbers. I get numbers mixed up all over the place, which is one of the reasons I had great difficulty learning to read music later on, since written notation is basically just that – mathematics.

So, because I had so much trouble with it, my dad got me a small pocket book and wrote all the times tables out for me. It didn't do me much good, though, because when I took it to school and the teacher saw it, he grabbed it from me and ripped it up. Psychologically that was the worst thing for me; it wasn't like the teacher was giving any help. It's still a major problem for me.

We did have one very good teacher at school, although I can't remember his name. He was a young guy and we thought he was a bit effeminate – I suppose, looking back on it now as an adult, he was a young, gay guy who was well read and actually interested in the kids he was teaching. He was really good because there was no threat of violence from him at all and it was the first time I'd met a male teacher who seemed not to want to give me a good hiding.

One day, I was sitting writing and he said, "You've got very good hand-writing," and he started explaining things about history and English and I thought it was great.

The teacher I'd had before had put me down two classes. I'd started off in the "A" stream and she put me into the "C" stream. Now, this was the class where all the kids were dragging their knuckles along the ground and making grunting noises. So my mum went along to the school and told them that she thought I shouldn't be in that class at all. When I went back the following year, on the recommendation of this particular teacher, they put me back into the "A" stream. But trouble was just around the corner, because the first lesson was mathematics and I didn't know what was going on at all. I went through another terrible time and told the teacher I didn't want to be in the "A" stream at all – I wanted to be with all my thick mates. So I went back down into the dunce class with all the Neanderthal kids.

My primary school wasn't far from North Weald airfield, which is where they filmed *The Battle Of Britain*, which had an all-star cast including Kenneth Moore and Susannah York. While the filming was going on, if the weather was nice, we'd take our desks outside and watch the Spitfires flying overhead. The sunny weather seemed to put the teacher in a better mood, too. There'd be mock dog-fights between the Spitfires and German ME109s, which was absolute heaven for a class full of primary school kids. Strange to think that, around 20 or so years earlier, my father had watched the real thing happening while he worked in the hop fields in Kent.

# 3 It's Not Stanley Kubrick, Is It?

Watching the filming of *The Battle Of Britain* wasn't the only brush my family had with the film world. My mother used to work part-time at the Princess Alexandra Hospital in Harlow, which was where my older son James would be born much later on. Mum was an auxiliary nurse, although in those days they were called ward hostesses. She wasn't qualified, but she helped out on the wards and so on.

She came home from the hospital one day and said, "They're making a film at the hospital at the moment, and there's this funny man called Stanley who seems to be in charge. He's taken quite a shine to me and it's a bit embarrassing. He says he wants to take me out to dinner." My brother, Bob, knew a bit about the film world and so he said to Mum, half-jokingly, "It's not Stanley Kubrick, is it?" Mum said, "Yes, that's his name."

At the time, Kubrick's film *2001 A Space Odyssey* had placed him well and truly in the film director superstar league, and Bob naively spent a lot of time trying to convince Mum to take him up on his offer of dinner, hoping he could go along too – but I don't think Dad would have been too happy about that.

At the time, Kubrick was filming the controversial *A Clockwork Orange* at the hospital, a film which he would later withdraw from circulation until after his death in 1999. But Kubrick's brief encounter with my mum was to be forever immortalised on celluloid. Apparently, he would ask Mum if he could borrow certain medical items for props. They were filming the scene in the film where the central character, Alex, played by Malcolm McDowell, has been "cured" and is being interviewed by a doctor in the hospital. One day, Kubrick sought out my mum and said, "Give me your badge, Rhoda, I need a name badge." So she reluctantly handed over her name badge. Now, if you look closely at the doctor in the movie, you'll see her name's "Taylor" – my mum's namesake.

Fortunately, my life then wasn't all school and I still had plenty of time to go out and have fun with the other kids in the area. In those days

I lived on a kind of council estate, in a "Corporation House". They belonged to the Harlow Development Corporation and were actually very nice – well set out and better conceived than some of the estates you see now. We were right on the edge of the country and so I had a sort of rural upbringing, really.

As soon as I walked out of the house I just went down the road and suddenly I was surrounded by meadows. I used to go down to a place called Cannon's Brook, which was at the bottom of Collins Meadow. There was a small lane that was cut off to the traffic, and there were quite a few Traveller families up there; a whole bunch of Gypsy families and their caravans – even some of the old horse-drawn ones. So the meadow was always full of horses and I used to spend a lot of time there with a family of Smiths. There was one woman who was a real traditional old Gypsy, and she would give me home-made lemonade. I'd also go into some of the old caravans, which were always immaculate and had ornamental plates all over the place. It was really great.

One day, I was up there with a pal of mine, and I saw a horse in the field and it had an erection. Now, if you've ever seen a horse with a hard-on, it's pretty big business and we thought this was hilarious. As a kid, I used to keep a catapult in my back pocket – I always used to carry a knife and a catapult, I was just that kind of country kid. So I got out my catapult, found a stone, aimed at this poor horse's wedding tackle and – *pow*. I'm ashamed to say that I scored a direct hit. Even before the stone had left the catapult's sling, I thought, "Oh no, what am I doing?" I feel terrible about it now because I love horses and have kept them for years. It was an awful thing to do. The poor horse reared up and the old Gypsy came out, but fortunately he didn't see me. It was just one of those things you do as a kid, I suppose. Recently, one of my horses stood on my toe and the pain was unbelievable, but I felt that the horse had at last got its revenge on me and so we're even. A sort of equine karma.

When I was a kid I was always out playing and I would come back with bits of old bicycle frames that I'd found. One day, I met a kid who lived nearby who had an old German Army belt that his father had brought back from the war. The belt buckle had an insignia on it which depicted an eagle carrying a swastika, and I innocently thought it was great. I'd been brought up on comics like *Victory* and so I swapped a bicycle for this army belt and took it home. My parents went absolutely crazy because they'd both been through the war and so it meant something totally different to them. Eventually they let me keep it, but it had to stay in the shed at the bottom of the garden. I wasn't allowed to bring it into the house.

I guess I was mischievous like all children, but I wasn't a bad kid. I remember I went to a shop once, and stole a bar of Five Boys chocolate. I took it back the next day, I just couldn't eat it. Other kids were nicking stuff left, right and centre – everyone was doing it and so I thought that I had to do it, too. But I just couldn't live with myself and I had to take my own ill-gotten gains back.

I've got two cousins who used to work at the fairgrounds. They both worked on the dodgems – they were the guys who used to jump from car to car, giving people the wrong change. My dad used to describe them as "scallywags" and they were harmless enough, but they were always up to something.

There was a place at Old Harlow called Harlow Mill where a guy used to hire boats out by the hour for people to go out on the river. One day, the dynamic duo hired a boat and forgot to take it back, if you know what I mean.

I went round to their house and the boat was in their garden. I'd always liked boats and was obviously taking a lot of interest in it, so my cousins said that I could buy it for a pound. I said, "I'll give you ten bob for it," and the deal was struck. I got my dad to take it back to our house on the roof-rack of his car. I spent a while doing it up, gave it a fresh coat of paint and everything, until it was ready for its maiden voyage on the River Stort. I launched it into the river and was happily rowing up and down when I found myself going past Harlow Mill. It was a Sunday lunchtime and so there were a few people milling about drinking beer. I could see this guy looking at me in the boat. He waved me over to the bank and said, "Can I talk to you, son?" He asked me where I'd got my boat from and I told him the story of buying it from my cousins and he said, "Well, it's one of my boats..." It turned out to be the guy who hired out the boats – I could see the rest of them there. They all looked identical to mine, only I'd painted mine white.

The guy said, "I think we'd better sort this one out," and I was really scared, with images in my head of us all going to prison. The boat man took me back to my house to see my dad. I said, "I didn't nick it, Dad, I didn't nick it." But my dad just said to the guy, "Look, just take it back. The lad's done it up for you and it looks better than those scruffy old boats you've got." He told the guy that he'd give me six of the best later, which was a complete lie because he never hit us. He just said, "Let that be a lesson to you."

There were always loads of kids about when I was young. It was right in the middle of the baby boom of the early '60s and so I was never short of other kids to play with. Sometimes we'd play conkers or cowboys and indians in the woods, or we'd have games of soccer with about 50 a side and the game would last all day. At the end of the match the score would be about 370-242, and on my way home Mrs Smith would give me a glass of lemonade.

One of Harlow's more illustrious residents in those days was the sculptor, Sir Henry Moore, who lived just outside the town in Much Hadham. Harlow boasted many of his works, dotted around the town. A lot of people took them for granted, but I remember looking at them and thinking they were great. There was one near Harlow Town Hall, which I believe is still there, called 'The Family'. As a kid I used to play on them and climb on them – apparently Sir Henry believed they should be experienced up close, but I didn't know anything about Sir Henry Moore, I was just being a kid and having some fun. I didn't realise I was learning about art.

Much later on, I remember being in New York at a penthouse on Park Avenue, and the people there were very much into art. The place contained many sculptures and they had a picture of 'The Family'. I looked at it and said, "Oh, I used to climb on that when I was a kid." That raised a few eyebrows, but I'm sure Sir Henry would have liked the idea quite a bit.

There was another sculpture in Collins Meadow, just by the church where I was christened at Slacksbury Hatch, although I believe it's now been moved to the sports centre. It was called 'The Wrestlers' and it was another popular climbing spot for the local kids. There were all these sculptures around which I remember, and a lot of them were Sir Henry Moore's.

Not far from where we lived there was this little shanty town where people lived in shacks or huts. My dad was friendly with an elderly couple down there, an old Traveller couple. To this day, I've never been able to find out exactly who they were, but my dad would visit them regularly. They were very nice and lived in this little shack next to the River Lee. It was a beautifully-kept place and I used to pay them regular visits. I was still at primary school at the time, but I can remember that there was an old Reading Wagon outside – a traditional, horse-drawn Gypsy caravan. Looking back, they'd probably come off the road at some point and settled there, next to the river. The shack was always immaculate and full of Crown Derby plates, and I would go and play in the caravan quite a lot.

The old man had a little rowing boat and he let me go out on the river in it. He had obviously been a bit of a wheeler-dealer at some point, and one day I went in this old shed he had, and it was full of those old-fashioned irons that you used to have to heat up on the fire. You see them in antique shops now and they fetch a healthy price. This shed must have been at least 10 x 6 feet and it was absolutely full of these irons – from floor to ceiling. They were all a bit rusty and had probably been there for years – maybe it was one of the last deals the old man had done when he was still on the road. I don't know, but, as a kid, I thought it was great and knew exactly what could be done with them. I picked one up, went to the river and threw it in. It made a fantastic splash – so fantastic that I simply had to repeat the process – several times, as it turned out. In the end, I threw the whole lot in – probably about a hundred irons. I think I can vaguely remember where the river was – I might go back with a metal detector one day and make myself a few bob.

The council finally moved the old couple into a council house and I went with my dad to see them, but they weren't happy at all. There was a wall-mounted can opener with a handle in the kitchen and, when my dad asked how she liked living in a house, the old lady said, "Well, it's all right, but I could do without all these mod cons," and she pointed to the can opener.

They died not long after that. I think they would have been better left on their own; they lived a life that some people just couldn't understand, but they were living the life they were born to and "all these mod cons" definitely weren't part of it.

# 4 It's Called Improvisation

After a couple of years, my dad decided that he'd had enough of the post office. It had been steady employment, but all that getting up at three or four in the morning was too much – he couldn't hack it at all. Instead, he went into the building trade. He had a friend called Ernie Walker who was also involved in the building business but was very much into music and could play guitar, too. Ernie had emigrated to Australia once, as a lot of people who lived in Harlow seemed to do. Even my dad took out papers for us to emigrate there at one point, and later on for Zambia in Africa, but was put off by the amount of Brits who seemed to be coming back saying that the life out there just wasn't what they expected. I remember from school that kids would come in and say, "We're off to live in Australia." It was like Harlow was some kind of stopping-off place on the way. Many seemed to settle in Adelaide, for some reason.

Ernie had decided that Australia wasn't for him and so he came back and brought with him a Maton guitar, made in Melbourne, which he'd bought while he was out there. He used to come round to our house on Saturdays and play with my dad, as did many of his musical friends. Amongst these was my "uncle" Dickie Bishop who used to play with Chris Barber, Monty Sunshine and Lonnie Donegan, in the days when skiffle music and trad jazz were both enjoying a lot of popularity. He also played alongside Howlin' Wolf and Big Bill Broonzy, who was the first of the Delta bluesmen to visit Europe, and so he had many tales to tell.

He wasn't really my uncle – although I thought for ages that he was. I called a lot of my parents' friends "uncle" or "auntie", it was just something that was considered courteous for a young kid to do back then. For instance, my mum and dad's best friends were Cis and Steve Tyne, and I was actually 21 when I asked my Aunt Cis which side of the family she was on and was quite taken aback when she told me we weren't actually related at all. I still call her Aunt Cis when I see her, though.

Dad's friends would put on Hot Club of France records and play

'Sweet Georgia Brown' and songs like that. After they'd listened, they'd pick up their guitars and play along – a whole room full of people all playing 'Sweet Georgia Brown'. There'd be one person playing the melody and about 29 others all playing really heavy, loud, chunky, four-to-the-bar rhythm. It must have sounded awful, but to me it was fantastic and I was enthralled.

I must have been about four or five years old by this time, and was really fascinated by it and thought it was fantastic. I can remember very clearly asking my father to show me how to play the melody to 'Sweet Georgia Brown' after one of these Saturday sessions. I think all kids want to please their parents and I was so happy that he was pleased with me for wanting to play the tune.

I was never afraid of my father, but in some ways he was a kind of distant figure during my early childhood, because he always seemed to be out working, so I was always glad to have his approval for anything that I did. I played 'Sweet Georgia Brown' the way he'd shown me and he was so delighted that he patted me on the head with a big smile on his face – it was great. Then he called for my mum to come in and listen to me play and I got the approval I wanted.

I suppose this is something that has really gone through my whole life, wanting my father's approval. After he'd shown me 'Georgia Brown' he sat me down and put this record on by Django Reinhardt. I can't remember what song it was that we listened to, but after Django had played the melody he began a solo and my dad said to me, "He's making that up as he goes along. He's improvising – it's called improvisation." I said, "Well what's that?" and he said, "It's like making up your own melody over the chords that they're playing behind you." I understood straight away, although I couldn't do it – well, I could do it to a degree, but I understood immediately what he meant. Pretty soon, fate was going to see that I had a lot of time to practise the concept to my heart's content.

On my eighth birthday I got a bike. My dad got a friend of his to come round from the market and he brought a couple of bikes with him for us to have a look at. One was a really good one, the other was something that he'd obviously cobbled together himself. Given the choice, I was after the good bike, but kids then weren't quite as outgoing as they are now and so all I could say was, "Well, I quite like that one." Mum pointed to the other one and said, "No, I think this is the one for you." And so I got this fairly dodgy bike that my dad's friend had put together himself.

I went out on the bike straight away and it was fantastic; the freedom and everything felt great to me – it still does. Even today I can still recapture those feelings I had when I was eight by going out on a bicycle. I loved it.

Where I lived there was a pub called the Golden Swift at the back of us, and over the road from there was a swing park, so I headed straight for that. I met one of my friends there and began to show off my new bike. In the middle of the park there was one of those maypole roundabouts that you would see all over England, with chains hanging from the top. I got off my bike to push it around, but before I knew it – *bam* – I broke my leg. It was really painful, absolute agony, in fact. I had to go to the hospital and they put my leg in plaster. The main thing was that I was told I had to stay at home, which meant no school. Which suited me fine.

I was in a lot of discomfort with my leg – it really hurt. I couldn't move about much and so I became bored very quickly. My mum saw this, took pity on me and gave me my dad's guitar – his precious Hofner – to play while he was away at work. It was our secret because sometimes she'd rush in and take it from me, saying, "Your dad will be back soon – don't tell him you've been playing it." It was still a proud possession – but to me it meant I could play on a really nice instrument instead of my own tortuous Russian variation.

It was while Dad was working on building sites that he met a guy who said to him one day, "You're a jazz fan, aren't you?" and my dad said, "Yeah." The other guy told Dad that he was going to live abroad for a while and needed someone to look after his collection of jazz records, and so he gave Dad all these records – and never came back for them. We never heard from him again. There were some great records there. One in particular stuck with me. It was an album called *Travellin' Light* by Shirley Scott, who played Hammond organ. But the guitarist on the album was Kenny Burrell and I played that record like mad. I loved the sound and thought that Kenny had a really cool way of playing. Of course, that style of playing is very fashionable in Europe now, but in the '60s things were different. My contemporaries at the time were all into The Shadows and groups like that and so when I used to sit them down and play them some Kenny Burrell, they'd look at me and say, "Martin, you're weird." But I knew how good it was back then...although I liked The Shadows, too!

My brother and sister didn't share my liking for jazz at all. Bob was really into The Rolling Stones, although these days his big love is classical music. He's always been into music but never took it up. He tried to play the piano once, but lost patience with it. He's very knowledgeable about music, though, particularly classical.

When he was 14 Bob became very ill. He couldn't keep food down and he lost a lot of weight. He was down to about five stone and nobody knew what was wrong with him, and in the end he was rushed into hospital. I can remember hearing Mum and Dad talking in another room and saying things like, "What if he dies?" It was a very traumatic time for the whole family and, being so young, I was scared and upset by it. I used to lie in bed at night and pray for him, with tears rolling down my cheeks.

It went on for a long time and he lost even more weight until there was nothing of him. Eventually, they found out that he had an infection of the lymph glands and he had to have a major operation. Afterwards he made a rapid recovery, but it left him with a big scar on his stomach.

Once when we visited him in hospital, my dad took Bob a book to read, which turned out to be Spike Milligan's *Puckoon*. It's one of the funniest books ever written and Dad had the best possible intentions, but maybe it's not the book you buy someone with about 20 stitches in their abdomen.

A few years later, Bob took me to see Jimi Hendrix at the Albert Hall, shortly before Jimi died. I came home one day and he said, "You've gotta hear this guitar player." He put a record on and it was like nothing I'd ever heard before. I thought, "This is great – I don't know what it is, but it's great." Bob told me it was Hendrix and he was going to see him play and I could go, too, if I wanted. So we went up on the train to London and I just thought it was fantastic. He was great.

As far as music was concerned, my sister Sue's first love was The Beatles. One of the first things we saw when we got a TV was John, Paul, George and Ringo on *The Frost Show*, playing 'She Loves You'. Frost came out and said something about a new sensation from Liverpool, and they came on with these funny hair cuts, going, "Ooooh," and shaking their heads about. Bob and I were on the floor holding our ribs; we thought it was the funniest thing we'd ever seen or heard in our lives. We were laughing about it for weeks and Sue was very indignant and told us, "I think Paul's very nice – he's my favourite." So whenever a Beatles single or album came out, my dad would go out and get it for her. She's got absolutely everything The Beatles ever recorded – the original pressings, too.

I used to dread a new Beatles single coming out because Sue and a friend called Jackie, who also liked them, would get up really early and go to the record shop, come back, put the single on the Dansette and, when the music started playing, they would just stand there and scream. It really was the most bizarre thing I'd ever seen. But I suppose that there were girls up and down the country doing exactly the same thing. They just struck me as really funny and I couldn't cope with it at all.

I really like The Beatles and growing up in that era, all the songs have special meaning to me because I remember exactly what I was doing at the time. Usually, though, it was running away from Jackie, who always wanted to kiss me!

We used to have some neighbours called the Cawthras. Dad knew that the elder boy, John, was interested in music and so he used to invite him round to the house and play him records by Big Bill Broonzy, Lead Belly and Lonnie Johnson. My dad's influence had a great effect on him because later on John went on to change his name to Gypie Mayo and join the rhythm and blues band Dr Feelgood and, later on, The Yardbirds.

At the time, Gypie was one of Bob's friends because they were the same age. One day, I found them both playing down at the brook, which at the time was pretty stagnant and dirty. Bob was climbing this tree that was overhanging the river and he got stuck. The only way out of this predicament was to drop down and land in the brook, which was exactly what he did. He went home covered in nasty, green slime and we had to cook up a story between us about how some older boys pushed him in.

Bob and Gypie had gone down there to smoke a cigarette and they offered it to me. I had a puff and thought it was really horrible and I haven't touched a cigarette since.

As I was beginning to play more and more, I became aware of some of the guitarists who lived in the same area. There was a group in Harlow called The Naturals and their guitar player was called Kurt Kreswell. The group actually had a hit record and were on television in the mid '60s. Kurt was a very good player and I remember that he was the first guitarist locally to have a 30-watt amp. Everyone else had 15- or 10-watt amps and so this was big news in our area. We couldn't work out what on earth

Kurt would need a 30-watt amp for, though – it was much more power-ful than anything we'd heard of.

There was another player called Alan Forsyth, who had a Telecaster and played Chet Atkins, country-style, and a blind guitar player called Tiggy Randolf, who played guitar and sang. There was somebody a little bit older than my dad called Eddy Guy. He played in the Hot Club and Eddie Lang styles and he used to come round the house sometimes and play. Other guitar players were Brian Brooks and another lad, about the same age as me, called Gary Draper.

In one of the bands my dad had, there was a drummer called Roger O'Dell and his wife Lorraine Munden, who sang. In the '70s Roger formed a group called Tracks who later changed their name to Shakatak and had several big hits worldwide. In fact, their guitarist, Keith Winter, once came to me for a lesson.

It's funny thinking back, but we were the first people in our street to get a telephone. This was around 1964; we got a telephone and a TV. My dad was starting to do gigs and so it soon began to be necessary for him to be contactable by phone. In those days, you had to apply to be con-nected and months later someone would come round and get things switched on. So we had this phone in our house for months and months and it wasn't connected. These days, you'd be on to Telecom with a sort of "When are you going to connect our phone?" attitude, but back then you just sat and waited patiently for this piece of cutting edge technolo-gy to arrive in its own good time. People of our parents' generation were more afraid of authority than we are, they didn't like to question things too readily. They must have thought that they'd just switch it on when they were ready.

Before the arrival of the television, evenings would be spent listening to the radio while Mum sat and knitted – that was it. But afterwards there would be programmes like *Sunday Night At The London Palladium* with "Beat The Clock". It was basically British variety on television – they were all variety shows; one minute you'd have a multi-instrumen-talist coming out, then a comedian and then a plate juggler and so on. But there was one programme for me as a kid that seemed like such qual-ity to me, and that was Val Doonican's show. What really attracted me to it, first of all, was I really liked his singing. I'd heard Bing Crosby before and I suppose I just liked that "crooning" style. Val would be on there and he'd sing a lot of songs and he'd also play guitar – that was the thing. He'd also have guitar players on there as guests and it was just a real musical show. I remember thinking that his backing singers, The Ladybirds, were really glamorous.

For my birthday that year, I was given Val's first album, *The Lucky 13 Shades Of Val Doonican*, and on the cover there was a picture of Val wearing one of his famous patterned sweaters and holding his guitar. I can remember saying to my mum, "Oh, I'd love a guitar like that..." and she said to me, "Well, we can't afford one."

At night I'd go to bed and prop the album cover up, just staring at it and wishing I could get a guitar like his. That Christmas, Mum said she had a special surprise for me: "You know how you're always going on about Val Doonican?" And I thought, "Oh great, they've got me a guitar like his." But then she produced a sweater she'd knitted which was just like the one he was wearing on the album cover!

I later found out that the guitar was a Clifford Essex, made in 1958. Val had it made specially for him for the princely sum of £60. I tell audiences the story about my mum's "Val Doonican" sweater and Val himself got to hear about it and thought it was really funny. So, to my absolute delight, he recently presented me with that very same guitar as a gift. I was incredibly touched by this, because the guitar in question is the one Val used all the time for his TV show and recordings. It's become one of my most treasured possessions and I still get a kick out of thinking that I now own the guitar that 'Paddy McGinty's Goat' was played on. Meanwhile, if anyone finds a little red plastic ukelele with a palm tree on it, do let me know!

It's funny how little you actually got for Christmas when you were a kid back then. You got a small present, a bar of chocolate and an orange – and that was just about it. I had a happy childhood. I didn't know we didn't have anything because no-one else had anything either.

The notion of Santa Claus ended very early for me when I asked for a racing car; it was red, moulded plastic, metal axles and plastic wheels, but I thought it was fantastic. Bob asked me what I was going to get for Christmas and I said that Santa was going to bring me this red racing car. He told me that there was no such thing as Santa Claus. I protested, of course, but he was out to prove his point and so he took me up to our parents' bedroom, opened the wardrobe and there it was – my red plastic racing car. I can only have been about four at the time, and it was really hard pretending for years that I still believed in Father Christmas for Mum and Dad's sake.

# 5 Come Back To The Shop – Quick

One day, Bob told me that the Radio Rentals shop in the shopping centre had a colour TV in the window. I didn't believe him, but he told me it was true and you could see that the grass was green and the sky was blue. So Bob, Gypie and I went up to the High, as it was called, and stood and looked at this colour television set in the window. But they were only showing the test card and so Bob went home.

Seeking some other form of amusement, Gypie said there was a sewing machine shop around the corner which had some guitars in and if you gave them a shilling, they'd let you play them. The shop was run by a man called Alan Summers and it was a kind of cross between sewing machines and haberdashery, so Gypie and I went round to see if they'd let us have a play. We didn't have any money on us, but that didn't put us off.

I feel I ought to describe myself as an eight-year-old at this point. We lived at the back of a pub and when the brewer's dray came round I used to like standing there to watch. I used to love the smell of the beer and watching the wooden barrels going down into the cellar. Back then you'd get bottles of light ale and you could take the tops off the bottles and make them into badges by taking them apart and fixing them to your jumper.

I was always filthy as a kid, too. I was always dragging old bicycle frames or prams out of the brook and generally acting like a mud magnet. I was always a bit of an outdoor type, too – as soon as the summer came I didn't live in the house, I'd sleep in a tent in the garden and cook my breakfast outside. I loved it, and what seemed eccentric behaviour to our neighbours seemed perfectly normal to me – "The weather's nice so I'll live in the garden!" So I might not have been exactly looking my best when Gypie and I paid a visit to the sewing machine shop that day – muddy from head to foot with a jumper covered in beer bottle tops.

Alan wasn't at the shop when we rolled in. There was a woman working there, though, and she asked her most unlikely customers what she could do for us. Gypie told her how he'd heard that if we gave them a shilling, we could play the guitars, all the time pointing at a rather lovely Gibson ES335 on the wall. "Who told you that?" she asked us. "Well, all the kids have been talking about it," Gypie replied. She could have chucked us out of the shop there and then, but she was a very nice lady, with wavy red hair and she was sort of glamorous-looking, too.

Apart from the precious Gibson guitar on the wall, there were a few others, too. Gypie pointed to me and said, "He can play the guitar." She looked at me, covered in mud and beer bottle tops and said, "Really?" So I said, "Yeah, I can play." She asked me to play a tune for her. Naturally I wanted to play the Gibson, but she offered me a cheap Spanish guitar and said I could play it as long as I took my jumper off. So I took it off and put my catapult, ball of string, penknife, a compass, my prize possession – a torch with a special button for sending signals in Morse code – and some stones I'd been collecting, on the table for good measure. She handed me the guitar and I played 'Sweet Georgia Brown' for her.

When I'd finished, she asked me to wait a minute and picked up the phone. I heard her say, "Alan, come back to the shop – quick." When he came in, she asked me to play again, this time so that Alan could hear. So I played a second time and he said, "Come around again on Saturday. Quite a few local musicians come in and play then and you should come and play, too. But," he added, "maybe you should have a bath first – and leave the bottle tops at home." So I gathered up my catapult, ball of string, penknife, stones and assorted junk and, as I was leaving the shop, I remembered about the shilling: "I don't have a shilling to give you." But the lady said, "Don't worry about it," and disappeared into the back of the shop. When she came back she handed me a penny whistle. That was the first time I was paid to play.

When I went back on the Saturday, Alan had made a little place for me to play in and he'd obviously been telling some of the other musicians around that there was this little kid who played guitar. Over a very short period of time he started getting more and more instruments in and it became less of a sewing machine shop and more of a music shop. He started having saxophones, trumpets and amplifiers in there and then he hit on the idea that I should go in and clean the guitars on a Saturday. In addition, he made a bit of room in the shop window, put a chair there and I'd sit and play with the amplifier out on the street. I attracted quite a crowd

– to the extent that the police came along and made me stop because I was creating a disturbance.

Every year we used to travel down to the Isle of Wight for a holiday. We went to a place called Whitecliff Bay and stayed in a caravan. One year, hippies were the new thing – we saw lots of kids wearing beads and things like that – perhaps it was the Isle of Wight's summer of love, I don't remember. I went down on the beach one day and saw a bit of a commotion going on. There was a guy in the water who was obviously in trouble – he'd got out of his depth and the currents had carried him quite far out to sea. A couple of men on the beach had gone in after him and managed to reach him, but he was dead when they dragged him out of the water. He looked terrible – all bloated and blue. It was the first time I'd seen a dead person and it affected me greatly. I became very quiet and introverted and I turned to the guitar for comfort and would sit by myself for hours, just playing and ignoring the outside world completely.

To a degree I've always been like that, but that sight triggered something in me and I found salvation in playing the guitar. Even now I always feel happier when I've got a guitar in my hands than when I haven't got one around. Recently, I received the honorary degree of Doctor of the University of Paisley and I had to give a speech of acceptance. I have never been so nervous in my life; I had to get up there in a world I know nothing about – an academic world which was a complete mystery to me. I'd have been much happier if they'd asked me to simply give them a tune. I find it hard to go on stage and talk the way I do without a guitar. Yet I'm very at home on stage playing and talking to the audience.

I don't think about playing because it's just like an extension of me and it was at that point, back on the Isle of Wight, that I really submerged myself in it – not from the point of view of study, because I've never really "studied" the guitar in the accepted sense. But I immersed myself in it and tried to reproduce music I was hearing on the radio and on records, trying to copy the melody and harmony. It was definitely a key moment in my life. By that time I was playing jazz tunes, pop tunes, melodies – anything really. I didn't think in terms of categories. To me, I was just playing music.

When I was learning to play, there weren't the facilities that there are around today. You didn't really see much guitar playing on TV and video hadn't been invented. The only way to learn something was to listen to it and try to play it by ear. I used to get together with some of the other kids that played guitar and that's what we all did. We'd get together and someone would put on a record and say, "Have you heard this tune?" and you'd just try to play it. I remember one recording in particular that really struck me as a kid – 'Marie Elana', which was a big hit for Los Paraguas.

If you had a recording of a tune, you'd just go away and learn it. Next time we'd see each other, we'd find that everyone had learned the tune slightly differently and everyone developed a slightly different style. There have been so many advances in the way guitar is both learned and taught that maybe some of that individuality, which was really brought about by trial and error, has gone. Now it's like, "I've got all the records, the videos, I've been to the masterclass, I've got exactly the same amplifier, same strings, same guitar, same transcription, pedals and so on." It's bred guitar players that are much better than we were, technically speaking, but there are fewer players with individual voices today, in my opinion.

There wasn't the variety of equipment around then, either. You couldn't get American guitars or amplifiers and so we'd all have different types of guitar. Some were made from a bit of this and a bit of that – one of my friends had an amplifier that was made out of an old wireless, and Gypie managed to fix up some wiring so that he could play through a tiny transistor radio. He still got a good sound, though.

There used to be a BBC radio programme called *Guitar Club* during the late '50s/early '60s, which was run by a guy called Ken Sykora. Guitar players like Ivor Mairants, Ike Isaacs and Bert Weedon played on it and it was one of the earliest times I remember hearing guitar on the radio. I used to listen to *Sing Something Simple* which featured The Cliff Adams Singers with Jack Emblow – 1959 and still going strong. There was *Billy Cotton's Band Show*, too – I learned a lot of songs by listening to the radio.

I never was too serious about practising, it was just something I did. I used to play the guitar in the same way I went out and kicked a football with friends. It was just something I happened to do and I pretty much just did it when I felt like it.

Alan Summers had been divorced, although it wasn't really spoken about because it was still actually very unusual at that time and carried a bit of a stigma. I kind of understood that the red-haired lady was actually his girlfriend, even at that young age. He used to run a lonely hearts club and he booked me and Gary Draper, who could also sing a little, to play at the club which used to be held in a place called the Magic Lantern at the Stow shopping centre. It was almost a kind of secretive thing because of outside attitudes towards divorced people in those days. Gary had started playing guitar around the same time as me and was a lot better than I was and received a lot of encouragement from my dad. So the band comprised me, Gary and my dad playing double bass. Dad used to receive a lot of attention from the newly-single women at the club. There was one in particular who kept on coming up to him and asking him to dance with her, but he told her there was no way – he was playing bass.

We played dance band music, waltzes, quicksteps, foxtrots and a bit of rock 'n' roll. So the set list included songs like 'Rock Around The Clock', 'Ramona', 'The Lady Is A Tramp' – that sort of stuff. People were still very much into ballroom dancing and so there was a sequence to the way an evening went. If it was a wedding you started off with a waltz and then a quickstep, a foxtrot – that's the way it was. The tunes were irrelevant as long as they fitted the tempo.

So that was my very first gig. And if you're wondering what I got paid for it, I got a packet of crisps and half a pint of shandy. Many people have claimed to have given me my first gig and it's all nonsense – at last I can put the record straight.

When my dad took up double bass he started playing in jazz and dixieland bands. In Harlow there was a pub called the Greyhound where he used to play and he would take me along to see people. There was the Wake Arms in Epping Forest, Railway Tavern in Bishops Stortford and the Ferry Boat Inn near Tottenham Hale, where Rod Stewart, Eric Clapton and John Mayall's Bluesbreakers used to play. On Sunday lunchtimes they would have a jazz session run by a guy called Freddie Randall. He used to play trumpet and had been a really big name in British jazz. There was a guitar player called Neville Skrimshire who played an old Gibson in the style of Freddie Green, Count Basie's guitar player. Sometimes Kenny Ball would sit in, and that was the start for me, of actually going to hear jazz being played live. On record, the first guitar player I heard was Django Reinhardt and then Eddie Lang, Joe Venuti and blues players like Big Bill Broonzy and then Barney Kessel.

Dad had this band called The Ken Lawrence Band. In fact, there was no such person as Ken Lawrence. The reason it was done is that everyone in the band had day jobs and it offered anonymity so the taxman wouldn't actually be able to track anyone down.

One night, my dad was on a gig and the guitar player didn't turn up. I was sitting at home in my pyjamas, ready for bed, and my dad rushed in and said, "Get your guitar." Mum protested and said I couldn't possibly go with him, I was too young and, what's more, I was all ready for bed. But Dad insisted, saying, "We need a guitarist and he's the best player I know locally." So I put on my Sunday best, a bow tie that my dad found for me, and went with him to play the gig. It turned out really well and so, from that moment on, I was in the band.

The group was my dad on bass, an accordion player called Reg Billing and a drummer called Nobby Clark. We used to do village dances, weddings and social functions and I played in that band from the age of eleven until I was 13.

Of course, by this time I had my first electric guitar and that was courtesy of Alan Summers back at the sewing machine shop. He'd started building up quite a trade in guitars and my dad got some money together and Alan sold us a Framus at trade. It was really nice of him, he really helped us out. So I had my first decent guitar at the age of nine. I was working quite regularly with my dad and, a couple of years after I got the guitar from Alan's shop, I noticed that the strings were getting higher and higher off the neck. I couldn't understand why – I didn't know anything about how guitars were put together at all. One night, we were playing at a youth club and my guitar actually exploded. Its neck and body parted company in a most spectacular way. This was a time when The Who were new on the scene and Pete Townshend was busy smashing up guitars as part of their act. So when the guy who ran the club saw my guitar fall apart, he yelled, "Oi, cut that out." He thought I'd done it on purpose. All the kids were saying, "Wow, that's great..." but I was devastated because my precious guitar had fallen to bits.

The Alex Welsh Band used to have a residency at a pub called the Fishmonger's Arms in Palmers Green. They had a guitar player called Jim Douglas, who had a sort of Charlie Christian style of playing, and my dad used to take me to see him play. Since he and Neville Skrimshire were the first jazz guitar players I heard live, I was being exposed to some really good British jazz musicians. I was also going along to some of the gigs my dad was doing as well and hearing him play with people and then starting to sit in myself.

We were never short of gigs. Harlow had a lot of social clubs back then. Everyone was in work and they used to go out to the clubs at the weekend. Key Glass was one of Harlow's bigger factories and their social club would have regular dances. We played there quite a lot, but we'd also play community centres, village halls and places like that. Some of them didn't have electricity, they were so old. Sometimes there were fights, too, which I enjoyed watching, and so things were never dull.

Once, we were playing a village hall somewhere in north Essex and it was one of those typical wooden buildings with a corrugated iron roof. It was a wedding reception and the place was heaving, people were up and they were having a good time, dancing to the band. At one point, I noticed that I couldn't hear the bass and that it had suddenly turned cold. I looked around and my dad had completely disappeared. It turned out that he had leant against a door at the back of the stage while he was playing, and the door had opened and he'd fallen outside. As he was still holding his bass, he hadn't been able to stop himself from running backwards and he'd run right across a road and down a riverbank, just managing to stop before he hit the water. He had to use the spike at the bottom of the bass to help him climb up the slippery bank. Meanwhile, the door had slammed shut again and we went on playing. He returned to the door and started to knock but no one could hear him, so he had to go round to the front of the hall and made quite an impressive entrance, weaving through the dancing crowd, holding his double bass over his head.

My dad and I were a bit of a double act from very early on. If we had to go somewhere and he didn't want to stay there, he'd tell me that when he gave me a signal (like tapping his knee or something) I had to say, "Ah, Dad, I wanna go home, I wanna go home." At which point, Dad would say, "Oh, these kids…" and he'd drag me out and we'd get outside and he'd say, "Well done, that was great."

I was on a gig once with him, at a wedding at North Weald Village Hall, and it was a rough crowd. The father of the bride was getting very drunk and decided to have a go at my dad. Dad used to play bass with his eyes shut quite often – a trait of many jazz musicians – and this guy told him that he wasn't going to pay him because he was sleeping on the job. Things got pretty nasty and the drunk wanted to take Dad outside for a fight, which wouldn't have been a good idea, because Dad would have knocked him senseless. Luckily, things quietened down and we got paid, but when we got outside the hall, Dad told me, "If anything like that happens again, you crouch down behind the guy's legs, I'll hit him and he'll fall over you and then we'll jump in the car." So, on every gig after that, I used to get all excited, hoping that someone was going to have a go at Dad so he could chin 'im.

I had it all planned: when it came time for the band to get paid, I used to stand and watch the guy and, if things looked like they could get aggressive, I'd be ready to roll myself into a ball like a hedgehog and get into position behind the guy's legs. The thing was, Dad wasn't joking; it was a team thing. We never got to put it into action which really disappointed me at the time, although the thought horrifies me now.

# 6 He Wants To Buy A Guitar

In those days I had a home-made amplifier for my guitar. It stood about four feet high, had two speakers and belted out a throbbing 15 watts. On arriving at a village hall gig in the middle of winter for a party of pensioners, I left the amp in the middle of the dance floor while I went to get my guitar out of the car. When I got back, there were a dozen elderly First World War veterans who had all suffered from shell shock, huddled around the amp, holding their hands out towards it, saying, "Ah, that's better. It's good to get a bit of heat…"

The money was always split four ways when I played with my dad and so I used to get about £3 a night. I saved really hard and after a while I had managed to save £100 from all the gigs I had been doing. After my Framus exploded, I'd been using a black home-made guitar which my father found for me somewhere – it was awful.

It was very difficult to get any decent instruments in Britain then. If you were seriously into jazz then you had to have a Gibson guitar, but you rarely saw them – and if you did, they cost a fortune.

The area of London which was Mecca for guitar players in those days was Denmark Street, Shaftesbury Avenue and Charing Cross Road. There were loads of guitar shops there and I was lucky in that I had an aunt who worked as a cook in Shaftesbury Avenue's fire station. All the firemen knew her as Mrs Toohey, but to me she was Auntie Frannie. So I used to go up to London and spend all day looking around the guitar shops and collecting catalogues. I'd go in the shops just to stand and stare at the Gibson guitars and then I'd go and see Auntie Frannie at the fire station and she'd give me baked beans on toast and an enormous mug of strong tea.

So, once I'd managed to save all this money, I decided to head up to Shaftesbury Avenue again – this time, to buy a guitar. I went with a school friend of mine called Peter Lewis, and we got on the train, went up to Liverpool Street Station, got the Central Line to Tottenham Court Road and went around all the music shops. Then we went to see Aunt Frannie

up in the fire station, before wandering back up to the St Giles area by
Centre Point, where there was a music shop called Giles Music. I went in
with Peter and started looking around but I didn't see anything that struck
me – you've got to remember, we were only twelve years old.

So I was just starting to walk out and this guy said, "Oi, what do you
lads want?" and my friend said, "Oh, he wants to buy a guitar." The guy
in the shop said, "Oh yeah, sure...How much do you want to spend on it,
then?" I told him that I'd go up to £100 and, for some reason, the guy just
got me by the scruff of the neck and the seat of my pants and threw me out
of the shop. It was like something out of a Charlie Chaplin film – I ended
up on the pavement outside the shop with my trousers all torn.

The funny thing was that I used to know the name of the guy – I
remembered it because I thought that, if I ever wrote a book one day, I'd
tell everyone what an asshole he was – but I've clean forgotten it. Maybe
it's just as well.

After I'd picked myself up, Peter and I headed into Oxford Street, still
a little in shock from being jettisoned so brusquely from the music shop. In
those days there used to be a New Orleans-style band called The Happy
Wanderers who busked along Oxford Street, marching up and down in
their uniforms. There was a banjo player, trumpet, clarinet and trombone,
with a fat old boy hitting on a bass drum. There was a guy at the front who
used to have one of those large, colourful umbrellas and I often saw them
on my visits to London. I used to love watching them. In the late '60s, the
Hare Krishna movement opened a temple just off Soho Square, and they
would also go up and down Oxford Street in their saffron robes and
shaved heads, playing Indian drums, clanging bells and chanting their
mantra. Sometimes the two groups would catch up with each other and it
wasn't uncommon to hear them singing, "Hare Krishna, Hare Krishna..."
to the accompaniment of 'When The Saints Go Marching In'.

In any event, the guy in Giles Music probably did me a favour that day,
because the next place I went to was Ivor Mairants' shop in Rathbone
Place, which is just off Oxford Street. I knew about the shop because I'd
looked in the window many times before, on my various pilgrimages to the
guitar shops – and of course I knew who Ivor was, too.

When I went into the shop that day, I was still shaky from the Giles
Music incident and I must have looked a sight because of my torn trousers.
Ivor himself was behind the counter. I recognised him straight away

because I'd seen him on TV, playing in The Mantovani Orchestra. I used to love watching that show, just waiting for the next guitar solo from Ivor.

Anyway, Ivor wasn't nearly as intimidating as the guy we'd just left. He said, "Can I help you, lads?" and, preparing myself to be thrown onto the street again and thinking, "Oh no here we go again," I told him I wanted to buy a guitar and that I had £100. Ivor said, "I've got just the guitar for you," and he took a Guild Starfire Deluxe from the wall and put it into my hands. It was the first really nice guitar I'd ever played – apart from the Gibson 335 back at the sewing machine shop – and so I started playing a few tunes and Ivor said to me, "That's very nice, young man." I said I would like to buy the guitar and Ivor said, "I'll tell you what I'll do. That guitar doesn't come with a case, but I'll give you one with it and I'll also give you one of my tuition books, because you're obviously serious about playing the guitar."

So he went and got a case, which was obviously meant for a completely different guitar. Inside it there were some strings, a capo and some fingerpicks and Ivor told me, "You can have the lot for £90." I didn't have the money on me at that time, because my dad wasn't too keen on me going all the way up to London with £100 in my pocket, but I put a deposit on the guitar and said I'd be back to pick it up the following week.

Before I left the shop that day, Ivor got one of his books out and showed me a few things. He asked me to play one of the exercises and I told him that I couldn't read music. "You can't read music?" he said. "You've got to learn to read music. Promise me you'll learn." I said that I would, little knowing that this particular promise would become quite a feature of our friendship later on.

The following week I went back up to Ivor's shop, this time with my dad. I was so eager to go and pick up my guitar that we actually arrived at the shop before it opened and so, there we were, standing on the pavement outside the shop at about eight am. When I got the guitar home, I just couldn't stop playing it.

My dad was very involved with Harlow Boxing Club. He was one of founders and was an ABA judge and used to put on a lot of boxing evenings.

One summer, when I was about four or five, a boxing booth came to Harlow. My dad went along because a friend of his, Sammy Boswell, who was from a famous Essex Gypsy family, was fighting there and he'd asked my dad to second for him.

It turned out that working at the boxing booth was a guy called Boswell St Louis, a West Indian boxer who was also a friend of my dad's. I think he knew him from somewhere in London, before they moved out to Harlow. It was getting dark when Dad and I got there and, down the side of the tent, there were caravans where the fair people lived, and an old London double-decker bus which the fighters used as a dressing room. My dad shouted up to Boswell, "Hey, it's Bill Taylor," and the boxer called out, "Oh hello, Bill." My dad had to go off and do something else and so he said to me, "Just go up and say hello to your Uncle Boswell."

I went up the stairs of the old bus, which was lit by gaslight, and this man who was dressed in a boxer's robe turned round – it was the first time I'd ever seen a black man. He had a big smile and said something like, "Hello, how are you?" but it frightened the living daylights out of me and I ran down the stairs yelling, "Daaaaaddddddddd!"

It was like something out of a film, the way the bus was all lit up and the windows covered with drapes. I ran down the stairs and found my dad and we went back up together. They sat and talked about the old times and had a drink together, and by this time I really liked Boswell. He was really friendly, always smiling and patting me on the head. He used snuff and I was fascinated watching him. He noticed and asked if I'd like to try some. So, when my dad went out, he got me to hold out my hand and he put a little snuff on it. I was only about five years old at the time and I thought my head was going to explode – Boswell must have been laughing his head off. I've always thought I'd love to see him again, just to see if he remembers.

I actually did a bit of boxing myself a bit later on. I used to go to the boxing club and enjoyed sparring with some of the fighters there. I once sparred with a lad who was the Essex Schoolboy Champion. I don't remember his name, but he was a bit older than I was and his trainer told him to spar with me. Being almost completely naive, I didn't realise that he was going really easy on me – not even getting out of first gear – and so I thought, "Schoolboy Champ, eh? Well, you're not very good," and started to hit him for real. The champ didn't like this one bit and so he clobbered me. I was seeing stars. My nose hurt and my eyes started watering and so I took the gloves off, threw them down and walked out of the ring. That was the end of my boxing career.

My secondary school was Passmores Comprehensive; not a bad place, I suppose, but it did have a PE teacher who was completely psychotic, in my opinion. He could be really heavy-handed with the kids at the school – that's heavy-handed to the point of real violence. I wasn't at all interested in sports and was always getting my dad to write me notes to get me out of PE and games. My tendency towards asthma came in very handy as an excuse, although by this time I had pretty much grown out of it.

The other kids in school knew I wasn't interested in sport and so, one sports day, the jokers in my class put my name down for absolutely everything going. I told the teacher that I hadn't put my name down, but he was insistent that I represent my house in some fashion and so I was stuck. Luckily, I had an ally in another teacher who knew that I was absolutely hopeless at sport, and he offered me a way out. He had noticed that no other house had put anyone down for the javelin and so all I had to do was go out on to the field, throw the javelin and, no matter how far it went, I'd win. I agreed. I didn't even bother to get changed or anything. I just went out on to the field in my school blazer, picked up the javelin and threw it. It landed a few yards away, flat on the ground – it didn't even stick *in* the ground. Suddenly, I was the school javelin champion for the year.

But sometimes my efforts to get out of games backfired. My dad was so used to writing notes for me that he got into the habit of asking me if I wanted one as I was leaving for school in the morning. On this particular occasion, I'd already got a note which he'd written for me the week before but I hadn't needed, and so I said I'd just use that one. When it came time for games, I handed the note over to the teacher, but he noticed the date was out by a week. So he took me in the gym and got me up against the bars, got a medicine ball and started throwing it at my head. He put my head in the bars and started knocking the living daylights out of me.

It was a serious, violent assault and, if it happened now, the teacher would probably have gone to prison. But things were different then; as a kid, you never questioned the actions of a teacher, no matter how unreasonable they seemed at the time. I didn't know what to do – I knew I couldn't go home and tell my dad, because he would have gone round and sorted the guy out and the teacher wouldn't have known what had hit him. So I just thought I'd let it go and try to forget all about it.

At the time, it was a very badly-kept secret in the school that the gym teacher was having an affair with one of the female staff. Everyone knew about it, they used to meet at a pub that was halfway between the school and my house – I'd often see his pale blue Ford Anglia parked down a lane by the side of the pub. They'd meet there some Sunday lunchtimes and often during the week. Now, this Ford Anglia was the teacher's pride and joy. It was always gleaming and so he obviously took some considerable pride in its appearance. One day, I was walking home at lunchtime and I saw the car parked in its usual place down the lane. At the time, there was obviously some building work being done down there because the work-men had left a shovel and a sledgehammer on top of a pile of sand nearby. Something in my mind just clicked; I remembered his terrible assault on me and here was my chance for revenge. At first I thought I'd be clever and smash up the engine and so when he got in the car he wouldn't understand why the car wouldn't start. So I opened the bonnet somehow and started smashing everything I could see with the sledgehammer. I slammed the bonnet down, but thought, "Well, why stop now?" And so I smashed everything I could see; every window and every panel. Nothing was ever said about the incident, but I'd got my revenge and it felt great.

I recently went to a vintage car show and saw a proud owner next to his '60s Ford Anglia. I don't think he'd appreciate this story.

These days, drugs are a serious problem with kids, but when I was at school nobody really had much knowledge about them at all. Taking drugs was almost some sort of intellectual experiment, with people claiming they were expanding their consciousness and quoting Timothy Leary. A police-man came round to the school to give us a talk on the dangers of drugs, with an emphasis on cannabis – very much the drug of the moment. He had photographs of cannabis plants to show us and he told us what sort of effects the drug had on people.

During his talk, he produced this small, dark slab and introduced it as cannabis resin and told us that this would be what the evil drug pushers would be offering us. In order that we could familiarise ourselves more fully with the dark world of drugdom, he passed the resin around the class. By the time he got it back, it had diminished to the size of a garden pea. He stared at the much smaller block of cannabis with some disbelief, and there were body searches all round at school that day. I must add here that I wasn't one of the culprits and have never had any interest in drugs...but more of that later.

Music lessons at school were pretty poor. Usually, they'd get out a box full of broken recorders which they dished out to the class. You'd sit there, hoping that you didn't get one with too many teeth marks on it, and try not to think of all the dribble that had gone down it before it was handed to you. Then we'd all attempt 'Frère Jaques' and that would be pretty much it.

I used to keep quiet about my guitar playing. I didn't say anything about it at all because the other kids would have just taken the mickey. I used to live outside of the general catchment area for the school and so because I didn't live in the same area as a lot of the other kids, it wasn't too hard to keep my guitar playing a secret.

I told one of the music teachers that I played once and asked if I could bring my guitar to school. He said, "Is it a classical guitar?" I told him that it was electric and he said, "No, you can't bring it in."

We had a new music teacher called Dennis Taylor who was in the Salvation Army brass band. The first thing he did was ask everyone in the class who was interested in playing a musical instrument to put their hands up. He really was like a breath of fresh air, because here at last was a teacher who could talk to you without sounding patronising or insulting. You see, I had a problem at school because I was very good at three subjects: music, English and art. In fact, where art is concerned, if I hadn't become a guitarist, I think I would have become a cartoonist or caricaturist.

I loved history, too, but I wasn't particularly good at it. I used to really try hard but just about every other subject was a complete mystery to me. I'd go into a geography lesson and I didn't know what they were going on about – and it was the same in physics, chemistry and so on. Now I kind of understand, but I really wasn't ready for it at that time.

The educational system in those days was really geared to being average so if you were average at everything you did well at school and you coasted through. But I was getting A+ in three subjects and E- in everything else and so they just didn't know what to do with me. Of course in those days they didn't talk about which side of your brain deals with different things. All of us have one side of the brain that works better than the other, I guess.

So, in music lessons, Dennis would play us music and talk about it and it was one of the few lessons that I used to actually look forward to attending. Somehow he managed to raise some funds to buy some new instruments for the school and told us that, if we were interested in playing a brass instrument, to stay after school. I wasn't particularly interest-ed; I'd had a go at playing a cornet when I was younger, but I had to have my tonsils out which meant I couldn't play for a while. When I went to find it again afterwards, Dad had sold it and so that was that. But I stayed behind anyway.

One of the kids in my class was actually Terry Gregory who today plays bass with me in Spirit Of Django. Terry was very good at school, always well behaved and good at all subjects. He was very studious, and in fact he still is. If we learn a new tune in the band these days, he's very good at time management – he'll set his day out, spend an hour doing one thing and then move on to something else in a really organised manner. But, back then, I wasn't organised at all.

Dennis had got cornets, euphoniums, tubas, trombones, flugelhorns and whatever, and he got us to sit there and pucker our lips. He went around the class, looking at our puckered lips, saying, "You're a cornet player, you're a tuba player..." and so on. He just assigned you an instru-ment from the shape of your lips – and he did a great job.

Terry joined the band playing euphonium – little did either of us realise that it wouldn't be the last band we played in together.

My brother had some Jethro Tull albums and so I figured that I might learn to play flute since I wasn't allowed to bring my guitar to school. So I took it up, but I still had a problem in that I couldn't read music. I found out how the flute worked and where all the notes were, so I could busk it quite well, just using my ear like I did with guitar. But I couldn't get the timing from the page.

I had a rough idea and so I could get by by playing very quietly. I played flute in the school orchestra for a while and even took some exams on the instrument, reaching grade six, which wasn't bad for someone who could-n't read music. All the grade exams had a sight-reading test in them and I'd always get terrible marks for that particular part of the exam, which the examiners would always put down to nerves. But I'd somehow make up for it in terms of tone, phrasing and so on and in this way I managed to muddle through. It's ironic that I've recently been invited onto The Associated Board Of The Royal Schools Of Music, putting together a grade course for jazz guitar.

A couple of years after I left school I went back to see Dennis to tell him that I was now involved in professional music, but he was very dismissive, which I found rather upsetting. He told me that what I was doing, which was basically working on cruise ships and doing summer seasons, had no job security, because it was essentially self-employment, which was regarded with undue suspicion by everyone on a salary back then. He told me that he had hoped I would stay on at school and train to be a music teacher. Me, in school for the rest of my life? You've got to be joking!

While I was at secondary school, I continued to play as many gigs as I could find. There was a trumpet player called Ray Crane who had a big band and I played with them a couple of times when I was 14 or so. In that band was a twelve-year-old Guy Barker who played a memorable solo on 'L'il Darlin''. You could tell he was going to be good even then.

In fact, things on that front were beginning to get quite busy. I also used to go and see my dad play in various venues quite often, too. One place that he used to play quite a lot was a pub in St Albans called the Goat. It was quite a well known venue for Sunday lunchtime jazz and it was there that I began sitting in.

I used to play a couple of tunes each week and I think that the other musicians were humouring me to a certain extent. But, to me, I was feeling my way in the territory of jazz. It was around this time I played in a jazz group called The Sonny Dee Jazz Band which was led by a drummer called Stan Daley. But it was a little later before I joined the first group which would provide me with a link to the coveted world of professional music. They had a trumpet player, called Alan Littlejohn, and a sax player, called Lew Hooper, who was very interesting because he used to appear as an extra in films. Funnily enough, he'd worked on *The Battle Of Britain* which I'd watched them filming while at primary school. He was just one of those guys who was in most of the British films made during the '60s and '70s and some of the films from the Ealing and Denham studios in the '50s.

He was a really nice guy and a good sax player, too. He had a part in a film once where he had to play a sax player and so they gave him a sax and he had to mime his part. But the producer said to him, "No, not like that, don't hold it like that – make it look like you really know how to play it."

There was a clarinet player at those Goat sessions, called Dave Jones, who had played with Kenny Ball for a number of years. The drummer's name was Harry Miller and the piano player was Fred Hunt, and he had played in The Alex Welsh Band. It was mainstream jazz and I knew a lot of the tunes, even if I hadn't actually played them before. They'd ask if I knew such and such a song and I'd say, "How does it go?" So they'd start playing and I'd recognise it immediately and I worked my way through using my ears. Those sessions were really my first experience of playing jazz with musicians of some calibre.

The Alex Welsh Band had a drummer called Lennie Hastings. Lennie had a heart attack which put him in the hospital for a while. By the time he got out, they'd replaced him and so he decided to form a band of his own. He had heard me play and, despite the fact that I was still only 14, he asked me to play guitar and a bit of banjo, too. I was a terrible banjo player, though, it has to be said. So I started playing a few gigs with Lennie to the extent that I would sometimes be doing three or four gigs a week and still attending school during the day.

While I was working for Lennie, my dad played in a number of jazz bands. He worked quite a lot with The Bob Wallis Storyville Jazz Band and he played quite a few times with Ken Collier who had one of the first jazz bands in Britain. Ray Webb was the first, followed by Ken.

I was beginning to find it hard to play gigs in the evenings, which often meant late nights, and still be bright eyed enough for school the following day. I wanted to leave school as soon as I could so that I could get more involved in playing, but at that time Edward Heath was Prime Minister and the government was thinking of raising the minimum school leaving age from 15 to 16. The idea was that this would encourage kids to take some sort of exams before leaving school, ensuring that they would have at least some sort of qualifications to face the world with.

I was getting worried because my mum wanted me to stay on at school and get some qualifications. She liked me playing music, but I think she would probably have preferred me to have music as a hobby, rather than as a profession. She worried about the insecurity associated with professional music and, for that matter, she was worried about some of the people I'd be mixing with. She was just being a mum, I guess.

But one day, completely out of the blue, my dad said to me, "You don't want to stay on at school, do you?" and I said, "No, I can't stand it – it's horrible." So he said that I could leave school if I wanted to, continue my playing, but do a bit of studying every day. After all, I could always take my exams later on, if I wanted to. Somehow he managed to talk my mum into agreeing and, to this day, I can still remember the feeling of walking out of those school gates for the last time. For years afterwards, I would wake up in the morning and think, "I don't have to go to school any more." Even now, if I feel a little low, I remind myself that I could still be in school, looking out of the window and wishing I was out in the big world. I couldn't wait to leave school and, despite teachers saying, "You'll look back on it as the best years of your life," I have never wanted to go back for one second. It just wasn't for me.

My sister, Sue, had left school at 15 and gone into the rag trade. It was all she wanted to do, work in a factory making clothes and earn her own money. My brother was very academic, but none of us took our Eleven Plus examination.

Bob really wanted to because even then he was sure that he wanted to go to university. My mum went to the school and told them she really wanted him to take the exam because then he could go to grammar school and on to university. But the school told her that Bob really wasn't university material and yet today he has an MA, a Bachelor of Education with honours and a Master of Education – and was a head teacher at 37. Nobody in our family had ever gone to college or university before and my grandmother was sure it would make Bob's head explode, but luckily it's remained intact – well, so far.

So I left school. I was 15 and doing a few gigs here and there but I wasn't making a living from it. My dad got a gig down in Battersea along with a trumpet player called Terry Meekin. He was from Edinburgh and had long, grey hair, flared trousers, a tight-fitting shirt which was permanently opened to the waist, and a medallion. He looked like the original medallion man but he was a good trumpet player, very much in the Louis Armstrong style. I had the chance to sit in with the band and, during the break, he asked me if I'd ever thought of turning professional. I told him that, technically, I was professional, because I'd left school and was trying to scrape a living through music. He went on to say that he played with a bandleader called Harry Bence and that they played holiday camps, did the occasional broadcast for BBC radio and played on the QE2 in the winter. He said that Harry was looking for a guitar player to do a season in Morecambe and, if I fancied doing it, he'd put in a good word for me. I told Terry that I'd love to do it and, a few days later, I received a phone call from Harry. "Can you read music?" he asked me. "Yeah, of course," I lied. He asked me if I wanted to do the summer season and I said I'd have to ask my dad. So I went and told Dad that I'd been offered a season in Morecambe and he said of course I should do it. My mum was horrified. She didn't want me to go because I was the youngest and both my brother and sister had already left home. I think it caused quite a row, but Dad must have won because shortly afterwards he drove me to Morecambe to start my first professional engagement as a musician. I was only 15 years old.

# 7 Another Bloody Southerner

When I arrived at the holiday camp – Middleton Towers, just outside Morecambe – I was terrified because I'd told Harry I could read music. In the end I needn't have worried because there wasn't really any music to read, just a few chord charts and I was OK with them. I knew most of the material we were playing anyway. The gig consisted of backing the "Bluecoats" during their evening show and then going over to the ballroom and playing for the dancers.

My dad drove me up the M6 and I'll always remember turning up at the holiday camp and thinking, "Oh, God – this is dreadful." But Dad said if I really didn't like it, I could ring him and he'd come back and get me.

I had to go and register and so I went in to the reception area while my dad waited in the car outside. There were a lot of people who were going to work at the camp registering, one at a time. In front of me there was the piano player in the band who came from London. I'd always been told that people from the north were really friendly, but when it came time for me to register, the man behind the desk asked my name and when he heard my Essex accent, turned to his colleague and said, "Another bloody southerner…" That was my welcome to the north.

Anyway, they gave me the key to my chalet – we all had one and they were pretty awful because they had been empty all over the winter and were damp and smelly.

I went off to rehearse with the rest of the band and started going through tunes. That first week was a nightmare for me; I thought the place was really awful, but I didn't want to phone Dad and ask him to come and get me because I would have felt such a failure. One thing I didn't like about the camp, apart from the music we had to play, was that every morning at eight o'clock this racket used to come over the camp PA: "Good morning campers – wakey, wakey!" They'd play loud marching music while all the holiday makers came out of their chalets and went to breakfast. The same thing would happen at lunchtime and I just hated it. When the happy campers went into the restaurant, the Bluecoats made them clap along to the music. One morning, a guy came in who wasn't clapping. One enthusiastic Bluecoat saw this and called out, "Come on, cheer up!" and pulled at his sleeve only to find that the holidaymaker had only one arm. The empty sleeve just whirled around like a windmill.

I didn't stay in my chalet for too long. I got to know a Traveller man who had some caravans and I went to live in one out in a field for most of the season. I couldn't stand living on the site, it was far too noisy. I really didn't like the music we were playing, either.

But after a while, I began to get into life on the camp. I enjoyed the freedom of it. Not having to go to school any more was fantastic. I also enjoyed the social aspect of it, too – the older musicians treated me as an equal and they would invite me out to the pub to drink beer. The bass player in the band, Martin Roach, was about five years older than me. His mum and dad owned a restaurant just outside Blackpool called Hambleton Hall, so sometimes, on our nights off, I'd go and stay there. Martin's dad played double bass the same as mine and I'd really look forward to those nights off. He also played classical guitar and got me interested in playing fingerstyle.

All the guys in the band drank. The older ones had been in the music business for quite some time and I used to like hearing their stories. I'd sit in the pub with them, for hours on end, hanging on to their every word as they told stories about the old days in places like Glasgow Locarno and Bradford Alhambra. It was fascinating for me.

Back then, the pubs used to close at ten-thirty pm and so it was difficult to find somewhere to go and relax and have a few drinks after the gig. There was a place called the Park Hotel in Morecambe and Colin, the owner, really liked having musicians around. You could name any musician and Colin would know him, he was a really nice guy. We would often end up there after our gig at the camp had finished. Although I was only 15 or 16 by this time and couldn't legally drink, I got away with it because I was with the others – Colin probably thought I was just a bit baby-faced or something.

In those days, the idea of the package holiday to Spain was in its infancy. Everyone had work and so they used to take their two weeks holiday in England. Different parts of the country took their two weeks off at different times. The mill towns in the north of England had Wakes week and later on there was Glasgow Fair week. The mining towns had their set weeks, too, so the clubs would always be packed with people, having meals and watching the cabaret.

There was a place called the Morecambe Bowl and it was always heaving. They had people like Bob Monkhouse, Lena Martell, Jack Jones and Matt Monro (with whom I would later tour), and I found myself enjoying the social life more and more. I didn't like the music we were playing at the camp because it was just dance music, in the old-fashioned sense. But I put up with it because I was enjoying myself after hours, socialising with the other musicians and drinking at Colin's place.

The bandleader, Harry Bence, used to do a lot of broadcasts in those days, for late night BBC radio. They used to record them live and so sometimes, on our nights off, we'd drive down to London overnight and do a radio broadcast from the BBC studios in Maida Vale. We used to hire a van which Martin Roach and our drummer, Mike Humble, would take turns to drive during the trip. We were always in a rush and so sometimes they would change over at the wheel without stopping – and we would be doing 80mph down the motorway at the time. Scary. But the radio broadcasts would give me the chance to go back to Harlow for the night and stay with my parents, before going back to Morecambe with the band the next day.

On my first BBC broadcast at the Aeolian Hall in London's Bond Street, Bert Weedon was recording in the next studio. I was so thrilled I rang my dad!

Harry had the idea of splitting the band up into smaller units and said to me, "You do a trio tune with bass and drums." The guys in the band had nicknamed me "Smoky", not because I smoked – I didn't – but because I was into playing jazz and they thought it sounded cooler than "Martin". So my first BBC recording was as the "Smoky Taylor Trio".

This was great experience for me as a musician, especially when you consider that I was still only halfway through my teens. But the real carrot dangling before my eyes during this time was the thought of the winter cruise aboard the QE2. The thought of going to New York and the Caribbean made me stick the season out to the end. I wanted desperately to go to New York – the home of jazz.

Meanwhile, Sue was working in the factory and I was earning a living as a musician, taking £37.50 a week in Morecambe, which was pretty good

My great-grandparents, William Guilford and Anne Rowe, on their wedding day in Brighton, England

Far right: my great-grandmother, Mary Flaherty. Standing next to her is my grandmother, Hettie Stewart. The other people are some of my aunts, uncles and cousins. Taken during their summer travels in Kent in the '30s

My favourite photo of my dad as a small boy, with my grandfather, Bill Taylor. Taken at Ivy Hatch, Kent, where the family went hop-picking every year

My mother's parents, George Guilford and Grace Pashley, on Wimbledon Common, London

My great-uncle, Eric Pashley, playing at the Windmill Theatre in London's West End in the mid '30s. (Picture courtesy of Jean Allan)

The gentleman leaning against the trailer is Piper Jock Stewart. This photograph was taken during the family's travels in Ireland. (Picture courtesy of Sheila Stewart)

The lady sitting on the bow-top wagon is the famous singer Belle Stewart. The gentleman in the centre of the picture is her husband, Alec Stewart. My grandmother comes from the same family. (Picture courtesy of Sheila Stewart)

L-r: Big Bill Broonzy, Lonnie Donegan and Uncle Dickie Bishop. Taken in London in the '50s

My father, William "Buck" Taylor

My mother, Rhoda Anne Guilford

The first picture of me, taken in 1956. "Where's my guitar?"

Harlow, 1958. I'm the innocent little boy on the right. Second left is Gypie Mayo with his brother, David, and his sister, Sarah. Two years after this photo was taken, Gypie and I started playing guitar. Gypie is now touring with The Yardbirds

Struggling to play that terrible Russian guitar in 1960. You can almost see the pained look on my face

Playing guitar with my brother, Bob (r), in our garden in Harlow, 1960

With my brother, Bob, and sister, Sue

# HE'S A GUITAR WIZARD—AT EIGHT

When little Martin Taylor, of 5 Collins Meadow, plays his guitar, people step and stare. This is not surprising for Martin is an accomplished musician at the tender age of eight-and-a-half.

Mr. Bill Taylor, who is a well known double bassist, taught Martin to play the guitar two years ago and now his son is capable of stepping into any dance band in the area. Dance band music is his speciality—'pop' music he hates.

Martin often plays at the music shop in West Walk where the proprietor, Mr. Alan Summers, allows youngsters to 'step in and try the instruments. Other lads much older than Martin hesitate to pick up an instrument alongside him for fear of him showing them up,' says Mr. Summers. And how does he rate Martin? 'What can you say about him. He's the finest prospect I've ever seen and will surely be a brilliant musician in a few years' time.'

Martin is at present trying to form his own trio of under-tens. Already he has a nine-year-old drummer lined up and now he is after a rhythm guitarist. He once sat in on a session with the now defunct Naturals and has had one or two guest spots with a dance band in the area.

He takes his music very seriously and practises nearly every day. He is also learning to read music. And his ambition? 'To play in a famous dance band one day of course.'

A cutting from the *Harlow Citizen*, from 22 April 1966

Playing music with my dad on the Isle of Wight. This was the day that I saw a man drown in the sea

Back from America in 1973. Yes, that suit was actually fashionable at the time

With The Colin Moore Band in the Caribbean, 1974. That's me at the back behind the sax player, struggling to read the charts as usual

With the legendary British drummer, Lennie Hastings, at Camden Lock, London, 1975

With Liz on our wedding day in Glasgow, 1976

Getting into the party spirit in my cabin on the Arcadia during a cruise of the South Pacific, 1977

in 1973. I was earning more money than I could realistically spend and so Sue and I got together to help Bob go through college and, the following year, I gave him the money to put down as a deposit on his first house.

We had some wild times during the season. Harry, his wife Elizabeth Batey, who had been very well known as a big band singer, and Harry's son Freddie, all lived in a house on the camp. Harry came from Wishaw just outside Glasgow and sometimes his elderly parents would come down to visit. One night, we were coming back from the Park Hotel at around three or four in the morning and we'd all had quite a bit to drink. We were walking past the house when Mike Humble said, "I bet they're all in there, snoring their heads off," and he went up and tried the door and found that it wasn't locked – so we all went in.

It became a dare; we weren't to laugh or make a noise, but we went into every room and watched them all sleeping. It was the most bizarre thing to do, but the game was that they mustn't wake up. There we all were, standing over Grandad without his teeth, snoring away...

It soon became quite a regular nocturnal activity, which we extended to include the camp manager, the head of security and a few others who didn't lock their doors. We started leaving things like a box of fish or a wheelbarrow in their room so they would wake up the next morning totally confused, thinking, "Where the hell did that come from?" and believing that they must have had too much to drink the previous evening.

There was another band on the camp as well and one of the guys had a Ford Zephyr, which was the closest thing you could get to an American car – big with tail fins. So, one night, we were coming back and I asked if I could have a go at driving. I couldn't drive, but I took the car all round the site, becoming more and more confident all the time. In the end I managed to mount the kerb and hit a wall, smashing the front of the Zephyr completely. I had to pay for it, of course, but this was the trouble with gigs like those; you'd start doing crazy things because you got bored. There was nothing particularly challenging from a musical point of view and the camp was depressing and so you ended up doing daft things.

There was a cabaret act called The Minitones which was made up of a couple of "little fellahs" called Kenny and Jack. Kenny Baker played the vibes and harmonica and Jack played trumpet and they had a musical comedy act. Jack had one of those big old Rover cars with massive wooden blocks on the pedals so he could drive. So we'd all pile in the car, Jack and Kenny in the front and us in the back, and go off to the Park Hotel for a late night drink. We'd go up to the cocktail bar to visit Colin and to see who else was there. One night, Kenny had downed a few brandies and said that he was ready to go back and so we said, "OK, go on then," but, being only four feet tall, he couldn't reach the door handle. So we stayed put, with Kenny captive behind the bar doors, saying, "Come on, guys, let me out – I want to go home!" whilst he was jumping up at the door handle. Kenny went on to do a lot of acting jobs – including playing R2D2 in the *Star Wars* series and appearing in *The Elephant Man*. But he wasn't the only star in the making that I met there. One of the comedians who worked at the camp was a school teacher called Tom O'Connor, who went on to be a TV game show host.

When the season was over, despite my hooligan antics that summer, the bandleader asked me to do the winter aboard the QE2 – and, of course, I wanted that more than anything.

In those days, if you played aboard the cruise ships, you had to join the British Merchant Navy. I had to go to the Liver Building in Liverpool, where Cunard had an office, and sign all the papers to receive my Merchant Seaman's Card and Discharge Book. The Discharge Book was the document that was stamped after you finished a stint aboard ship. I also had to get my US visa, which was compulsory back then.

I went back to Harlow for a couple of months before it was time to join the ship in November. I was going to be away for six or seven months and, as my dad drove me to Southampton, I was getting cold feet. It was early when we left Harlow and so we stopped on the way to have some breakfast. I suppose I must have been unusually quiet because Dad said to me, "You don't want to go, do you?" I said, "No, I don't." If I had heard there and then that they'd cancelled the trip, I wouldn't have minded, but Dad, having been in the Navy himself, told me that he always felt the same before a trip and that I'd be fine once we were under way.

When we reached Southampton, the QE2 looked enormous and a little foreboding, which made my cold feet a little colder. Dad and I went to meet a guy called Wally, who was the musicians' representative on board. Wally played cocktail piano and had been aboard the cruise ships for years – in fact, I believe that this was one of the last cruises he did. He used to talk about some of the grand old ships of the Cunard line, like the Mauritania, and possessed the sort of cynicism that only comes from being a professional musician for many years.

He had all the charm of a Parisian taxi driver, too. I remember being curious at the fact that Wally was wearing an evening suit, despite the fact that it was only late morning. He was wearing the lot – bow tie and all – and it wasn't even lunchtime. In fact, I never saw Wally in anything but an evening suit the whole time I was on the ship. His hair was greased back, too, very much in the manner of an old time muso.

We went to Wally's office so that he could allocate me a cabin. On the side of his desk he had a tumbler full of what looked like tomato juice, but I noticed that he kept topping it up with vodka every few minutes. I was later to discover that, like many musicians who played aboard ship, Wally was a heavy drinker. After many years of heavy Duty Free drinking, he had a face that looked like it had worn out three bodies.

The process of allocating me a cabin was far from straightforward. Wally said, "We'll put you in cabin 46…no, hang on," then he'd have another drink, "no, I can't do that, er…" another drink, "oh, shit…"

This went on for several minutes until we finally decided where I should go. The next thing was to meet the steward who was assigned to our group of cabins. A lot of the stewards on board were gay and would really take pride in their section of the ship. They'd put curtains up and come up with fabulous flower arrangements to decorate the place. They'd put little rugs down and make sure that you never ran out of ice – things like that. But, as luck would have it, my cabin was stewarded by an alcoholic Irishman called Frank. He had a real attitude to go with it, too; I've since met many bartenders in Ireland and America who remind me of Frank. He had a white shirt, with the sleeves rolled up, and he was going bald so he combed his remaining hair across the top, giving the appearance that his parting was somewhere near his waist.

Frank would only change your sheets if you pleaded with him and sometimes you wouldn't see him for days. Then, you'd wake up in the middle of the night to find him sitting at the end of your bed, swigging from a rum bottle – your rum bottle. It was a regular thing that if Frank ran out of booze he'd raid the musicians' rooms when we were asleep and pinch ours. He hated the musicians on board because we only worked for an hour a night and received £75 a week for it – good money back then. To him, we were just a bunch of overpaid parasites who spent all our time having fun. He was absolutely right, of course.

Before we set sail, Harry had volunteered our band to play in a big hangar at the side of the docks while the passengers boarded. It was like a scene from a film; there was hustle and bustle everywhere and we were playing while people were saying goodbye to each other on the dockside. Then we had to pack up really quickly and sprint up the gangway to get aboard ourselves. My heart sank when the ship pulled away – what had I let myself in for?

The QE2 is so huge that there were five or six bands aboard to play in all her numerous bars. She was like a floating city and it took me ages to find my way around. We left Southampton and sailed to Cherbourg in France, which was the standard route for transatlantic liners on their way to New York. Even Titanic did it. Gulp!

When we were under way it was time for the band to meet all the other acts who would be aboard, working in all the various restaurants and ball-rooms. The QE2 had a cruise director, who oversaw the entertainment side of things, and so we started to work out exactly how we'd fit in.

We were a couple of days out to sea when we started to rehearse for some of the singers who would be working with the band. In one instance, there were charts and I really didn't have a clue. Harry sussed this out straight away and turned to me and said, "You can't read music, can you?" I'd told Harry back in Morecambe that I could read and had managed to fake my way through the whole of the summer season, without him notic-ing that I was busking my way through everything. Now I was caught out.

I decided that the best way was to come clean and so I told Harry that I couldn't read – I figured that, as we were in the middle of the open sea, he couldn't exactly send me home, so whatever the outcome, I was still going to fulfil my ambition to see New York. Harry just smiled and said, "I had a feeling you couldn't. But you really should give it a try because we're going to be getting parts all through the cruise."

So when the singers came in with music, he'd say, "Don't give Martin a part. He'll make something up." So that's what I did. On stage I used to stand between the pianist and bass player and just behind the sax player. I knew where the notes were on the music – I'd covered that when I was learning flute at school – and so when the piano started playing something I knew, I'd look at the sax player's music and work out where it was on the chart and think, "Oh, so that's what it looks like." So I really learned to read in a back to front fashion, looking over people's shoulders on the bandstand. At the end of the six-month cruise, I wouldn't say I was a good sight-reader – I would never become a good reader – but I was an awful lot better than I was when we boarded ship.

# 8 I'm In America – Wow!

Arriving in New York that first time was an experience I'll never forget. The QE2 used to get there around dawn and so I made a point of getting up really early and going forward to watch. There were these huge doors on the port and starboard sides of the ship, which they removed just before docking, and I stood with one of the bandleaders, Jack Sprague, barely able to believe I was actually there. I'm so glad that the first time I went to America it was by ship. I'd love to do it again sometime. I remember looking out and seeing the cars driving along the roads in Manhattan, the Statue of Liberty, Ellis Island – I got a real feeling of how it felt when Europeans came to America back at the turn of the 20th century and before. I was still only 16 and so it was all incredibly exciting.

As we sailed further into Manhattan, the sun started to come up and we were hit by the most famous skyline in the world. Jack knew it was my first time in America and so he started telling me all about it, explaining the grid system and pointing out landmarks like the Chrysler and Empire State buildings.

The immigration guys came aboard and stamped our cards so that we could go ashore and, when I was walking down the gangplank, I remember thinking of Marlon Brando in *On The Waterfront*. I felt like I was in a movie. We went to a place called the Market Diner to get something to eat and, while I was sitting there, still bewildered by it all, a phone rang with that distinctive sound I'd only heard in the movies. At that point it really struck me: "I'm in America – wow!"

I didn't realise it at the time, but I was part of a long-standing tradition among British jazz musicians. Players like Ronnie Scott, John Dankworth and Tubby Hayes – everyone went and worked on the cruise ships because that's how you got to New York, to the home of jazz. This was the hub of things, where you got to hear a lot of the great jazz musicians play.

After our meal, the first place we headed for was Manny's on 48th Street. Manny's is probably the most famous music store in New York and

I was on a mission to buy myself a new guitar and amp. At the time, I was playing a Guild Starfire – not the original one, I'd swapped it for another some time before – and the amplifier I had was a Vox AC30 which I really hated. They're collectors' items now, of course, but mine was really unreliable. When I turned up at a gig, I didn't know if it was going to work or not, and it really wasn't the sound I wanted, either, but it had been all I could afford. Now I had some money in my pocket and thought it was time to invest in some better equipment.

In one of the shops on 48th Street (which is now Rudy's) I saw a 1964 Gibson ES175. I got it down and played it and was so excited that I said I'd have it straight away. I gave them $375 for it and then went across the road and bought a Fender Twin Reverb amplifier, too. I caught a taxi and went back to the ship, still as high as a kite with my new purchases.

I had to get the ship's electrician to rewire the Fender amp because the QE2 works on British voltage and the amp was set up for 110 volts. He was a really nice, helpful guy who played guitar as a hobby, and I sometimes shared a beer with him on the crossing to New York. He put a new transformer in it for me and I was in heaven – at last I had "proper" American equipment.

That evening, when we left New York, I decided I was finally going to get rid of the AC30 once and for all. It seemed only right that I should do so with some sort of ceremony, and so the rest of the guys in the band and I decided that the only thing for it was a burial at sea. So, after we finished playing that night, still wearing evening suits, we went aft and threw the AC30 overboard while the trumpet player played 'The Last Post'. So, somewhere off the coast of New Jersey, at the bottom of the sea, is my Vox amp. It might not work so well now – but then it wasn't very reliable beforehand. Maybe Dr Robert Ballard, the deep sea explorer who discovered the wreck of Titanic, might like to mount an expedition to find it one day. It's probably worth a few bob.

Once out of New York we headed for Nassau, in the Bahamas. When the boat docked, I got up the first morning and walked out on deck thinking, "This is fantastic." I'd never been anywhere that hot before and the feel of the place, with the blue skies, was totally new to me. I went to sit by the pool on the aft deck and ordered a pina colada, thinking that I was a whole world away from Harlow and the school classroom which had held me prisoner less than a year before. I guess it could have been quite a culture shock – I mean, here I was, a 16-year-old lad from Essex, aboard the QE2 in the Bahamas, sipping a pina colada around the aft deck swimming pool of the most luxurious liner in the world. But I just sat there and thought, "I could really adapt to this lifestyle with no problem at all..."

We used to play in the first class ballroom for about an hour a night; never during the day like some of the bands had to. Sometimes we'd back cabaret, but that was really all we had to do each day, the rest of time was our own. Elsewhere, Jack Sprague's band used to play in the other ballroom and a man called Ernie Mellor led one of the other bands. There was a husband and wife organ and drums duo, too. The woman, Monique, used to play drums and sing like Karen Carpenter – The Carpenters were at the height of their fame at this time. There was also a guitar player, accordionist and mandolin player who used to play around the tables in the restaurant.

The QE2 had a theatre and used to bring aboard classical musicians to give recitals. One day, the cruise director said to our piano player that the concert pianist who was to give a recital that evening needed someone to turn pages for him. Immediately Wally, who I think had been aboard every ship since Noah's Ark, jumped in and insisted that it was his job and that he was the only person aboard who was qualified for the job. This we had to see!

Somehow we knew that Wally's liking for Bloody Marys was going to let him down seriously. So every musician on board crammed into the theatre – not to watch the pianist, but to watch Wally. The time came for the pianist to walk out and take the stage to rapturous applause. Right behind him came Wally, lapping up the applause as if it was him they were there to see. The pianist gave a bow, as did Wally, and they both took their places.

To start with, Wally tried to sit on the pianist's right-hand side and we caught the pianist hiss, "No, the other side." The concert began and, while the pianist really was incredible, it was obvious straight away that Wally was totally out of his depth and completely lost. When it came time to turn the page, you could sense that the pianist was starting to panic because Wally was just sitting there, trying to work out where he was up to. The pianist started saying, "Now, now!" and so Wally leant over, knocked the pianist's glasses off with his right arm and turned over about five pages at once. It was a complete disaster. Wally left the theatre in shame and headed for the aft bar, where we left him drowning his sorrows in a sea of Bloody Marys and muttering to himself, "I remember when I was on the Mauritania...mumble, mumble, slurp."

Wally absolutely hated jazz, but a lot of the guys in the band really liked it and played well. Jack Sprague's band were all into jazz and I remember once standing in the aft bar, next to Wally, listening to them play. Despite the fact that it was probably still only eleven am, Wally was kitted out in his dinner suit, with a dusting of dandruff on both shoulders and an alcoholic suntan. He was talking in really bitter tones about the state of the music business, recalling the times when they had string quartets on board ship. Suddenly, Jack's band finished what they were playing with a slightly dissonant jazz chord which set Wally's teeth on edge. "If that band play any more flat fifths and demented 13ths, they'll disappear up their own assholes!" was his appraisal.

Wally's hatred for jazz was well known to all the musicians on board the ship and, whatever we played, we would always try to give it a bit of a jazz slant, which he hated. But if something really bugged him he would never come up to you and say, "I really don't like that." Instead, he would always prefix any complaint with, "There's been a message from the bridge. The captain said..." and whatever musical misdemeanour he was about to charge you with, he'd always try to blame on the captain. If you were a little late starting the set he would come up and say, "There's been a message from the bridge. The captain said could you please make sure you're on time in future." Of course, we all knew it was just one of Wally's funny little ways and we added it to our list of how you could wind him up.

One day, Wally exceeded all expectations with his usual ruse. After I'd finished playing, he came over to me and said, "There's been a message from the bridge. The captain says that the third chord in the tune 'All The Things You Are' is a straight Eb7 and not an E minor seventh with an A7 split chord substitution." He was serious, too, but I couldn't for one moment imagine the captain saying anything like that. In fact, I met the captain on a number of occasions and I don't think he knew who I was or what I did.

A guy called John had been booked to play guitar in Ernie Mellor's band.

He had done some male modelling and was a good singer and a great front man – and a real cockney. One day, he came to see me and asked if I could give him guitar lessons. It was the first time I'd been asked to give lessons and so I asked him what he wanted to know. He told me that he couldn't actually play at all, that he'd bluffed his way into the gig by answering an advert placed by Ernie for a guitarist and singer, but had put his arm in a sling for the audition, pretending that he'd had an accident. He knew his singing and stage presence would get him through, but now he needed to learn the guitar – fast! He'd got by so far by pretending his amplifier had broken down whenever Ernie nodded to him to take a solo.

As a fellow bluffer, having told Harry that I could read, I took pity on John and gave him some lessons, but he was rumbled because we didn't really have enough time to get him playing properly. He never did learn – he wasn't really interested in playing guitar and I'm a terrible teacher. He got to keep the gig, though.

John was a real cockney wide-boy. Almost everything he said was rhyming slang, which was strange at first, but I soon got used to it. One day, we had docked in St Lucia and John and I were going ashore. Suddenly he stopped and said to me, "Hang on, Martin, I've forgotten my wallet and passport," and ran back inside the ship. I stood there for ages thinking, "Wallet and passport? What the hell does that rhyme with?" Then he came running back – clutching his wallet and passport!

We returned to New York two weeks later and I was determined to repeat the experience of watching the sun come up whilst arriving in Manhattan at dawn. This time I was into the party spirit with the rest of the band and stayed up all night before going to the front of the ship. But this time something was different. As I looked portside, towards the Statue of Liberty and Ellis Island, I noticed something going on behind me. A group of guys were pulling on a rope that was hanging over the starboard side of the ship. To everyone's horror, at the end of the rope was my electrician friend. Apparently, when we left New York a fortnight earlier, he had received a letter from his wife telling him that she was leaving him for another man and so he had hanged himself. I went to have a look as they hauled him aboard and it took me back to seeing the drowned man on the beach at the Isle of Wight – it really shook me up.

When we got back to New York, the first thing we all wanted to do was go and hear some jazz being played. Because I was still only 16, Harry Bence had to become my legal guardian for the trip, but that was OK because Harry let me out on quite a long leash. But my problem now was how to get into the Village Vanguard where Elvin Jones was playing that night.

In the US, you had to be 21 to go into a club and I couldn't even pass for 18, let alone 21. There used to be a joke shop up on 48th Street, near Manny's, which sold all sorts of things, like clown costumes and magic tricks – and also wigs and disguises. That night, as we were walking past on our way to the club, John saw the shop and jokingly said to me, "That's what you need…" and pointed to one of the false moustaches in the shop window. I went in and bought one that approximately matched my hair colour and, wearing it, managed to get in to the Village Vanguard. I used that 'tash again every time I wanted to go to a club to hear music.

I was the youngest musician aboard the QE2, but there were some guys who were just a little older and then some much older guys who'd been doing the cruises for years. So there were two groups, really: one young and one older, and the two didn't really mix together socially.

As it turned out, the younger musicians smoked pot and the older guys drank – that was the dividing line. I was seen as belonging to the younger set, naturally, and we used to go to each other's cabins and just generally hang out and spend time together. Being in the Caribbean meant that there was every opportunity for the guys to hop ashore, score some grass and smuggle it back aboard. When it came to smoking it, though, you had to be careful; we'd all huddle together in one of the cabins, put towels around the doors and then cram ourselves into the tiny bathroom where there was an extractor fan which would disperse the smoke from the joints. Then we'd all sit around on the beds saying absolutely nothing until someone would start laughing for no reason.

I joined in because I thought I had to, being one of the younger crowd, but I hated it. It used to make me feel paranoid and, not being a smoker anyway, it just didn't feel right somehow. It wasn't my idea of a good time – I didn't like what it did to me and in the end I didn't like being around people who did smoke it. I stuck it out for a while, but then started hanging out more and more with the older musicians who used to congregate in the crew bar which was called the Pig And Whistle. They used to sit around, drink and tell stories, and I used to find it fascinating to sit and listen. Between them, they'd played just about everywhere and worked with

75

everyone, so the anecdotes and funny stories were never-ending. Bored with standing in a cramped bathroom with my head in a vent, smoking pot with the younger guys, I defected to hang out with "the old boozers".

Once, we did a two-week jazz cruise supporting The Count Basie Orchestra. Basie's band was full of really great players – legends like guitarist Freddie Green on guitar, Al Grey on trombone, Jimmy Forrest on sax and Sonny Payne on drums. I got to spend a bit of time with Freddie Green, who was the master of rhythm guitar. Many years later I worked extensively with Al Grey in Europe.

After the performances we used to jam till the sun came up and so I got to play with the band. Years before, my parents had taken me to see the band at London's Victoria Theatre. On that occasion, they had Ella Fitzgerald singing with them and my dad was really keen for me to see the show. He told me that it might be a once-in-a-lifetime experience – but here I was, actually playing with them, just a couple of years later. It was a very memorable two weeks and I've still got some cassette recordings of those jam sessions – the quality is not very good, but they're personal treasures.

Another port of call on the Caribbean cruise was Haiti, which was a real shock to the system. I didn't like it there – it was just the feel of the place – and our visit didn't pass without incident.

Phil Thomas was the trumpet player in Jack Sprague's band and one of the older generation of players who I used to hang out with. He was a great story teller who had been around and done a lot of things. He knew I was a bit nervous about going ashore in Haiti and so he said that we'd go together – I think he wanted to make sure I was all right. The minute we got off the ship we were descended upon by groups of prostitutes – I couldn't believe it, I was only a kid! It was actually quite frightening, but Phil managed to fight his way through, with me in tow.

We headed for an indoor market and Phil said to me, "I've got to take you to meet the voodoo mask man." I asked him what it was all about but he just said, "Don't worry – you'll laugh your head off, you'll love this." This was the time of Papa Doc and there was a distinct atmosphere to the place which I didn't like at all. But Phil had been there a few times before and knew the place quite well and so I followed him over to a market stall covered in carved wooden masks. Phil told me that the guy who sold the masks threw a fit every time anyone mentioned the word "voodoo" – literally started rolling his eyes, dribbling and talking in tongues – and that this was something I definitely had to see.

So Phil said hello to the guy behind the stall and the guy said, "Hello, I remember you, you've been here before. How are you? Are you still playing in the band?" After they'd finished chatting for a couple of minutes, Phil pointed to me and said, "This is my friend Martin. He plays on the ship as well." The guy smiled at me and said, "Oh, so you're a musician, too?" He was really friendly and amiable. Then Phil said, "Martin would be interested in taking back some presents – maybe one of these masks here," and the guy started to show me some of the masks, telling me he had the best selection in Haiti and that, if I chose one, he'd do me a really good price. Then Phil winked at me and interrupted with, "Are these *voodoo* masks?" and immediately the guy started trembling and his eyes went strange and he started saying, "Ooooo, voodoo, voodoo…" over and over again. This went on for about 30 seconds and then he suddenly returned to normal and took up our conversation from where we'd left off. He indicated one mask and started talking about it and once again Phil cut in: "So would these masks be worn as part of a *voodoo* ritual?" and he's off again, "Voodoo, voodoo…" It really was one of the weirdest things I've seen. I didn't buy a mask because, by the time Phil had finished winding him up, the guy had gone into a trance and was shouting at the top of his voice, running round the market. Nobody was taking any notice of him. I guess they were used to it.

At another place near the market there were some busking musicians, who had a unique way of working the tourists. As they were playing, one of the guys in the band would hand a pair of maracas to someone in the crowd and they'd shake them along to the music for a while. But when it came time to hand them back, the guy would say, "No, no, no. Ten dollars." He'd refuse to accept the maracas back until the tourist paid up out of embarrassment.

We stood watching them for a while and soon the guy tried the trick on Phil. "We're not tourists, we're musicians like you," Phil said, and the band immediately stopped playing. "You are musicians?" one of the band asked. "You are not a musician until you have taken a drink of this," and he handed over a bottle. Phil took a swig and passed the bottle to me. I hesitantly took a sip and suddenly – wow! I haven't a clue what it was, but it was an instant high. Phil and I referred to any drink after that as "voodoo juice". The effects wore off pretty quickly and I still don't know what the stuff was to this day, but it was all part of the general intimidating feeling I got from Haiti. I don't know what it's like out there today, but back then I didn't like it at all. After that, I was glad to return to the safety of the ship. I was even pleased to see Wally.

Occasionally one of the musicians in the bands would go home and, when this happened, another one would simply take his place. This happened to the band that played round the tables in the restaurant. One accordion player left and another joined the ship fresh from his home in Tottenham. The rest of us had all been out there for a while and we had a nice tan – even me – but this young accordion player had just left Britain in mid winter and he was as white as a sheet.

The funny thing was, he managed to keep his ghostly white colour all the time he was on board. In fact, we used to call him "Moonman" because we were sure that while we used to sunbathe, he'd go out on deck at night and moonbathe. We found out pretty quickly that Moonman was a keen gambler and that he'd bet on pretty much anything. If there were two spiders crawling up a wall, he'd have a bet on which one would reach the top first. Soon there were all sorts of scams springing up among the musicians.

One day the sea was really stormy and the ship was going all over the place and a thought suddenly struck me. I asked Moonman, "Want to join our snooker team?" He said, "Yeah, yeah...Do you play for money?" I told him that we did, but he had to put up a $50 stake first. Immediately he counted out $50 and handed it straight to me – but, of course, playing snooker on board a ship would be like trying to play ice hockey in the Sahara Desert. Every so often Moonman would say to me, "When's the snooker going to start, then?" and I'd say, "Oh, soon, soon..." He never did get his money back.

Moonman was really into money-making scams and apparently he had met a doctor in Port au Prince on Haiti and bought loads of cocaine from him. The idea was that, when the ship got back to New York, he'd be able to sell the cocaine on 42nd Street. Unfortunately for him, the Drug Enforcement Agency agents were working in Haiti and he was arrested as soon as we landed in New York.

It had an effect on the rest of the musicians on board because after Moonman's arrest we weren't allowed off the ship. The police and customs officers descended on us and we were all questioned. All of a sudden, if you were a musician, you were immediately suspected of being a drug user.

We were all really shocked by what he'd done. I shared a cabin with one of the pot-smokers and, while all this was going on, two cops walked into the room. "Do drugs, do you?" they asked us and, of course, we denied everything, but they searched the cabin anyway. My cabin mate had been collecting marijuana seeds, unknown to me, and while the cops were searching I could see them in the bottom of one of the drawers. He was going to grow his own and so he'd been collecting the seeds for some time. My life – all 16 years of it – started flashing before my eyes as the police searched the room. I was positive that they were going to find his stash. But they searched everywhere and didn't find anything. I was so relieved but I was really angry with my cabin mate. It turned me even further away from wanting to be associated with the smokers on the ship.

Incidentally, Moonman was deported from America and, about three or four years afterwards, I happened to pick up an English newspaper and he was "Punter Of The Year" – he'd gambled on something and won loads of wonga.

Just like the season in Morecambe, the musician's worst enemy aboard ship was boredom. Since we only played for about an hour a night, that left plenty of time for mischief. Some of the things we got up to then really make me cringe when I think about them now. For instance, some of the cabins had two portholes in them which were quite close together and one of the things we did for a dare in the middle of the night was to climb out of one and crawl back in the other. Obviously we could have been killed – lost at sea – and it scares the life out of me now to even think about it.

When we played in the first class ballroom, we'd usually include some Glen Miller tunes. The music was arranged so that the keyboards and horn section supported Harry's clarinet perfectly – it really did sound authentic and it was a good band. But nobody would take any notice and so the boredom would set in and we'd start doing things like playing the *Laurel And Hardy* theme when someone walked across the floor – but still the passengers wouldn't get it. One night, we raided the female dancers' dressing room, put on their clothes and went on stage in drag. Still nobody noticed; they just thought we were a really ugly female band. They even came up and asked us for requests, although fortunately none of us got asked out on a date.

Another thing we liked to do when the conditions at sea were really windy, was to have a few drinks and then go forward under the bridge and lean into the wind. It was amazing: the wind was sometimes so strong that you could lean over at an angle of about 45 degrees and it would keep you in place. I was reminded of this recently when I saw the movie *Titanic* at the point when they are at the bow of the ship. It was exactly the same – but without Kate Winslet, of course.

A few of the musicians who liked to play jazz would get together after the gig and jam away for hours in the bandroom. I did that a lot and worked hard on my playing. I enjoyed those sessions. We would play until the sun came up and then go for breakfast on deck in the beautiful Caribbean sun. It was more productive than hanging around, drinking beer in the bar and certainly more so than sticking your head in the bathroom ventilator.

# 9 The Engines Have Stopped

I was supposed to be on board for seven months, but one night we were in my cabin, having a few drinks and getting boisterous, when John the cockney said, "Hold on, everyone – quiet, quiet." Even after the "wallet and passport" incident, I still thought that everything he said was in rhyming slang, but he began touching the bulkheads and listening. Finally, he said, "The engines have stopped." We didn't take him seriously at first, but he said, "Go on, touch the walls – there's no vibration."

Then the lights went out.

When we went out of the cabin it was like a ghost ship, with only the emergency lights offering a very pale glow. We found out that the main boiler had blown up – and we were right in the middle of the notorious Bermuda Triangle. It was a news story which went all over the world – "QE2 Adrift In The Bermuda Triangle". A couple of days later another ship came along and took the passengers off. A few key members of the crew managed to get rescued, too – including Wally, our faithful union representative. I still don't know how he managed it. The crew that was left took over the ship, enjoying the benefits of being on a cruise with little or no work to do.

We swam in the passengers' pool, but after three days the water began to look like tea. In fact all clean water was becoming scarce. You couldn't wash or anything, so I decided to go looking for water and scoured the ship in the dark. The heat was incredible, with no air conditioning on the ship, and I spent days literally crawling around, going through pitch black corridors, searching.

Things were beginning to get serious, but eventually I came upon a galley which nobody seemed to have sussed. In it was an urn which was used to boil water for tea and it was still full. I didn't tell anyone where it was. I put the water into small containers and took it back to my cabin. If I had told anyone where it came from, they would have descended on it and it would have been gone in minutes. We take water for granted, but in a situation like this, you really know that it's everything.

With the passengers gone, I thought, "Well, I'm not sleeping in this cabin," and went off and found myself a first class passenger suite, reserved for royalty and international dignitaries.

Meanwhile, though, we were drifting. For the first couple of days it seemed funny, a bit of a laugh and something of an adventure. But when you started seeing sharks alongside because stuff was being thrown overboard, reality started creeping back. It wasn't so bad during the day, but at night we'd sit around talking in the dark and it began to get scary. Eventually, some tug boats arrived from New York and towed us to Bermuda, where we stayed for a couple of days before being towed back to New York.

The story was big news right across the world and when we reached New York, the cameras were there to record us disembarking. My parents were watching on TV in England and saw me come down the gangplank – I was one of the first off the ship. The QE2 went in for repairs and the last couple of cruises had to be cancelled, so I went home about a month early. To say that Harlow seemed dull after that adventure would be something of an understatement. I couldn't wait to get back on the road again.

Although life aboard the QE2 had its ups and downs, and I hadn't particularly liked being left adrift, I really wanted to do it again. Phil Thomas, who lived on the Isle of Wight, offered me the chance of a summer season there, but I decided to stick with Harry and the possibility of further cruises.

This, of course, meant spending the next summer in Morecambe again. The band had a slightly different line-up now – and a few more characters, too. We had a pianist called Colin, who was really into horse racing, and when he'd done all right, he'd come in and buy us all drinks. Pat Eddery was the wonder boy jockey at the time and we all followed his career from the beginning.

Colin was a bit of a wheeler-dealer and had a few sidelines apart from piano playing, including buying and selling second-hand cars. This particular season, though, he had got together with a friend of his on the seafront at Morecambe and they used to take pictures of holiday-makers. They'd got themselves a monkey that they used to dress up in a clown's outfit and sit on people's shoulders, take a photograph, charge the punters ten bob and forward their picture to them later on.

One day, they decided they would give Blackpool a try, but when they went to get the monkey they found it had died during the night. This wasn't the sort of thing to put Colin off. He and his mate managed to do a whole day's trade by photographing the dead monkey, still dressed in the clown's outfit, on people's shoulders. If any of them asked why the monkey seemed a bit limp, Colin would say, "He's just a bit tired." When he came back that night, he said he'd had a fantastic day, but I don't know if the monkey would have agreed with him.

Another of Colin's scams along Morecambe seafront was selling watches, and I used to join him every so often, just to earn a bit of extra money. Obviously the watches were really cheaply made and, if a holiday-maker bought one from us on a Monday, it would probably have stopped working by the weekend. So we only used to sell them on Mondays and Tuesdays, spending the rest of the week lying low in case any irate miners wanted to bring any timepiece-related grievances to our attention. We'd be back on the front by the following week, content in the knowledge that last week's customers were all safely back at work.

I didn't really know if I could take another summer season at Middleton Towers. I liked Morecambe itself and am still very fond of the place, but the holiday camp was pretty awful. It was only the thought of another winter cruise which kept me going.

In Morecambe I met a girl called Marie, who was from Glasgow, and who'd worked in the camp as a waitress the previous year. When she saw me, she said that she and two of her friends were working as barmaids this year and that I should come and meet them. When I went into the theatre bar later on, Marie pointed out her friend, Liz, who was working behind the bar, and it was a really strange thing. I looked over, saw Liz and thought, "That's her. She's the one for me." I really can't describe it.

Meanwhile, Liz looked at me and thought, "Well *he's* different!" I suppose I was, too – at the time I had long hair and a Gypsy earring – and this was before it was fashionable for men to have earrings. I was dressed in my band uniform, with a blazer and bow tie, and so I must have looked a bit strange.

I wanted to ask Liz out, but it was a struggle. I wasn't very good at all that, but eventually I managed to pluck up the courage and say to her, "Do you like dancing?" and she said, "Yeah, in Glasgow we're always out dancing." So I asked her if she'd like to go dancing after we'd both finished work that night, and she said that she would.

A few of the lads had started to go to the Morecambe Bowl, because we had all put some money in and bought a car from one of Colin's mates. I'd paid my share, but I was only just 17 and couldn't yet drive and so I remained a sort of silent partner. The front of the car was a Corsair and the back bit was a Cortina and it had cost us £50. Colin's sales pitch was, "There you go, lads, two cars for the price of one." The thing was a death trap.

Despite the fact that neither of them had a licence, the sax player and trumpet player took it in turns to drive. They hadn't bothered about such niceties as insurance either – and the tax disc was a Guinness bottle label, which looked amazingly similar to the real thing, but was a lot cheaper and more pleasurable to obtain.

So I took Liz out to Morecambe Bowl and I suppose we'd been there for about a couple of hours before she said, "Are we going to have this dance, then?" I said, "I can't dance, I'm a musician." Now this is a funny thing, but it's quite rare to find a musician who *can* dance. I can count on one hand how many musicians I know who can dance, and still have fingers left over. My musical career up to that point had consisted of standing on stage, watching people make complete fools of themselves on the dance floor – although I suppose you could say that they'd spent all their time watching me making a fool of myself playing music!

Anyway, I told Liz that a friend of mine owned the Park Hotel and that I very often went to the cocktail bar and would she like to come with me. She said she would and so we started going out quite a lot after that.

One day I couldn't find her and so I asked Marie where she was. Marie told me that she'd gone back to Glasgow to visit her mum and dad. Liz didn't like it on the holiday camp and I can't say I blamed her – I would have left by this time if I hadn't met her, QE2 or no QE2. I was beginning to get worried that she wasn't coming back so I decided to go up to Scotland to find her if she didn't return. Liz didn't think she'd come back to the camp but she wanted to see me again. It was agony without her around and I remember it was at that point that I thought, "This is who I want to be with."

Liz eventually came back to Morecambe and we decided to stay on and move in together. She came and sorted out my chalet, which looked like someone had thrown a hand grenade in it, and we've been together ever since – we will be celebrating our silver wedding anniversary in 2001. I think me spending time out on the road has had a lot to do with our successful marriage. It doesn't do any harm to be separated for short times; you miss each other and then it's really great when you get back. There's nothing wrong with that – we love each other.

Back in Morecambe, I'd go down to the front to see Colin, who had given up encouraging holiday-makers to pose with dead primates, and had turned his hand to other things. There were several other guys there, plying a trade, and among them was a guy who called himself Johnny Petulengro. He really played up to the Gypsy thing and had a little moustache and earring.

He'd get a crowd around him by saying, "My name is Johnny Petulengro, a true-born Romany Gypsy, and I've inherited psychic powers..." He had a number of envelopes with birth signs written on them – Libra, Capricorn, Sagittarius and so on – and inside they had a set of numbers for the football pools. He'd say, "I don't do the football pools myself because it wouldn't be fair. I have these God-given powers and, if I did, they would be taken away from me." The crowd would stand there, fascinated.

He was a great showman. He'd pick someone out from the crowd and say, "Madam, when were you born?" and the woman would say something like, "January 17th," and Johnny would come back with, "Ah, yes – Capricorn," and he'd say a few things about Capricorns and then carry on: "Well, for just one pound you can have these numbers. Do these numbers every week and they will work for you." All around you could see people getting their pound notes out. I thought it was really fantastic, that all he was selling was envelopes with numbers written in them. They say there's a mug born every minute, but as WC Fields said, "Never give a sucker an even break."

I never really got to know Johnny, although I spoke to him a few times. I suppose that I was just a young lad to him and he didn't take much notice, but I really admired him. I thought his patter was brilliant and spent many hours on Morecambe seafront watching him working the crowd.

Another thing that kept me going that summer, apart from meeting Liz, was putting on a Sunday lunchtime jazz gig at the Park Hotel. The owner, Colin, was a big jazz fan and he suggested we play in the lounge bar every week. It was great to be able to play some good music for a change, just for kicks, and it went a long way towards keeping me sane.

There was another piano player at Morecambe called Eddy, who was an older guy with a serious drink problem. I'd been a professional musician for a couple of years and I'd seen some heavy drinking – I'd even become a part of it myself, because it was all part of that scene – but Eddy was the first alcoholic I'd met. He used to go on benders and, when he did, he would become very aristocratic and book himself into the best hotel he could find, under the name "Lord Farrow". He'd soon run up an enormous bill so Harry would have to find him, asking the desk clerk, "Is Lord Farrow staying here?" They'd all be excited because they thought they had a peer of the realm staying in the hotel.

Eddy was a real character and could charm anyone. He had these funny little sayings which he would use to torment barmaids. He'd say something like, "Tickle your arse with a feather," and they'd say, "*What*?" "I said, 'Particularly nasty weather'," Eddy would say and they'd think they'd misheard him. He'd get away with it every time.

Harry would pay "Lord Farrow's" bill and bring Eddy back. It just seemed like eccentric behaviour to me, but it was really tragic. When he checked into these hotels, Eddy would go to the local off-licence and buy loads of bottles of brandy and beer and just sit up in his room and drink.

I liked Eddy a lot. He was a good piano player, very well read and very intelligent, but the drink had got to him. Once, he disappeared again and Harry went off and found him and brought him back. It was late morning and Harry gave me ten pounds and said, "Take Eddy to the pub. We've cleared him out of money – just buy him bottles of beer as he needs them, but whatever you do, don't let him drink spirits."

I went and got Eddy and sat him down in the pub. He was all shaky and asked me to get him a scotch, but I said, "No, I'll get you a bottle of beer," and he wolfed it down straight away. I kept buying him beers until the alcohol got into his system and he began to calm down.

After a while he started talking and told me that he'd studied classical music. Then he sat down at the pub's piano and played these lovely little preludes, but they were all just slightly wrong because the alcohol had addled his brain. I was quite touched and I really felt for him, because I could see that he was suffering from an illness. Unfortunately, quite a few musicians have gone this way over the years.

The following year he did the same again – checked into the Midland Hotel in Morecambe as Lord Farrow, went to the off-licence, went up to his room and drank himself to death – literally. They found his body the next morning. It was very sad because he was a lovely, gentle guy and a very fine musician.

After that summer in Morecambe I didn't go home. I went to Glasgow, to Liz's parents' house in Springburn, and stayed there for most of the time. I knew I was going to have to go on another cruise in the winter, but now I didn't want to because I wanted to be with Liz.

I'd already signed the contract for the cruise and so there was no way around it. I stayed a week with my parents and then flew out to San Juan in Puerto Rico to pick up the ship. It wasn't the QE2 this time, it was another Cunard ship called the Adventurer. The bandleader was a sax player called Colin Moore, who really liked my playing and encouraged me to play on the more jazzy tunes. He even went to great personal expense to have an arranger do some special arrangements for the band to feature me. Every two weeks they would arrive from England and that made the gig more interesting. I am very grateful to Colin for his encouragement.

I spent my second winter aboard ship, but this time it wasn't the same. I was missing Liz.

After five months, I came back. Once again Phil Thomas, the trumpet player, contacted me and invited me to the Isle of Wight, and this time I took it. It was just what I wanted. Liz and I packed and moved into a flat in a village called Lake.

Phil asked me if I knew a drummer and, back in Morecambe I'd met this guy called Henry who was a really steady player, so I suggested him. Henry came to join us on the Isle of Wight and lived in our flat. He was a bit like something out of the stone age. On the first night, Liz asked him if he took sugar in his tea and he said, in a broad northern accent, "I don't know. Wife does all that…"

Liz wanted to learn to drive and started to take lessons. At the time I couldn't drive myself, but Henry said to me, "Would you let your wife drive, then?" He was a real chauvinist and it started to become hard work just having him around.

After about three months, my dad rang and said that there had been a few enquiries for gigs for me with some jazz bands in London and did I want to go back to Harlow and live there? Harlow was close enough to London and I thought it was my chance to play jazz, so Liz and I moved to Essex.

One of the first things I did when I left the Isle of Wight was join The Alan Elsdon Band on a kids' TV show called *Magpie*. Sometimes, when you're a musician, you're called on to do things which are a little humiliating and, for this show, I had to walk across the bridge at Teddington Lock playing a banjo. It wasn't the high point of my career.

The programme was all about America and so the band then went into the studio to play some jazz. This was to be my first encounter with unions in the studios. As soon as I plugged my amplifier in, the whole place erupted – suddenly the electricians were threatening to go out on strike because it was their job to look after all the electrical appliances in the studio!

A few years later I did another TV show for Anglia, where I was interviewed in a sort of mock-club setting. They'd set up a little table with a cloth over it and there was a bottle of wine and a candle on the table – I'm sure you get the idea. I was sitting there with my guitar and we started doing a few takes and, in between, we were drinking the wine. By the time we'd finished, both the presenter and I had drunk a few glasses each. I leant over to blow out the candle and the presenter looked horror-struck. He mouthed, "No, don't do that!" because they had to get a guy called the fireman to come over with an asbestos cloth and put the candle out for us. A simple thing like blowing out a candle turned into this big ritual and I thought it was all a little beyond a joke. I think things have eased up now, but at one time it was really, really bad.

# 10 *What Do You Want To Do On The Guitar?*

While we were staying in Harlow, my dad took me to see Cedric West, a guitarist from Burma who had grown up with Ike Isaacs in Rangoon. Cedric was the guitarist with the BBC Radio Orchestra and he was a wonderful player. He played with his thumb instead of using a pick, in the same way that Wes Montgomery had done. His style was similar to Wes's in many ways and they were great friends – whenever Wes came over to Britain he used to visit Cedric.

Cedric was playing with a guitarist called Len Argent at a pub called the Lord Napier, in Seven Kings, the night my dad took me to see him. I took my guitar along and got talking to Cedric and he invited me to sit in with the band. I played a few tunes and ended up becoming friendly with him.

We used to meet up every so often and when I got a gig at the 100 Club in Oxford Street, opposite Barney Kessel, Cedric told Ike Isaacs and so Ike came down to the club. I knew of Ike from the BBC radio *Guitar Club* days, but by this time he was working with Stephane Grappelli. After the gig, Ike invited me over to his home in Wembley. Ike's house was well known among guitar players in those days. They'd all congregate there when they were in town – Wes Montgomery, Joe Pass, George Benson, Barney Kessel – it was like a meeting place for all the great players.

Ike and I just sat around and played and his wife, Moira, made a Burmese fish curry. I was astonished at everything he could do on the guitar; his knowledge of harmony was way beyond anything I had ever heard before. I remember Ike asking me, "What do you want to do on the guitar?" and I told him that I listened to piano players and wanted to be able to play guitar in the same way – as a complete solo instrument. So Ike started showing me a few things and it really turned me around. After that I used to go to his house regularly and spent a lot of time there.

It wasn't just musically that Ike impressed me, his philosophy and positive outlook on life influenced me greatly. On the guitar, he opened something inside me – I had always felt that nothing was impossible a would do something and he would laugh and say, "How do you do that?" and I'd say, "I don't know." He told me that the reason I could do it was because no-one had told me that I couldn't, which was true.

That was the thing about never having lessons and learning informally – there are no rules. Ike opened up the door for me and made me realise that the ideas I had were worthwhile and within reach. He really made me into a guitar player. He was my biggest influence and many guitar players will tell you the same kind of story.

Ike gave me his 1964 WG Barker guitar for my 21st birthday – that was the guitar I used exclusively with Stephane on tour and on records. He even started to teach me Hindi and we used to talk together using it. I've pretty well forgotten it all now, although I was quite good at one time.

Ike was born in Rangoon, Burma into a Jewish family who had come from Lebanon a couple of generations earlier. Burma was a very wealthy place which had a huge diamond industry and so there was a lot of prosperity. Ike's father once lent some money to a friend of his who owned a circus, just to keep it going, but it didn't work out and so the circus owner came to Ike's father and said, "I can't pay the money back, I'm really out of business, now." So, instead of repaying the money, he gave Ike's father a Gibson L4 Eddie Lang guitar – and an elephant!

Ike's dad gave the guitar to Ike (he never said what happened to the elephant) and Ike started playing. He began to hear American guitar players on the radio and someone said to him one day, "You know, if you want to play guitar there's a fireman down at the station called Ginger Duncan who plays, he'll show you." So Ike went to see Ginger, who he described to me as being neither ginger nor a Duncan – he was a dark-skinned Indian from Madras. Ginger also only knew two chords: one was C major and the other wasn't. He could strum away for hours on even the most sophisticated Irving Berlin tune, just using one and a half chords.

It was at this time that Ike met Cedric West who shared his love for jazz guitar. When the Japanese invaded Burma, Ike's family had to leave and so they went to Calcutta. Maurice, Ike's violinist brother, went to work for a Maharajah in his private band and so they'd play for dinner at the palace. Ike moved to London in 1948 where he got into session work and started playing with The BBC Radio Showband.

Another major influence on my guitar playing around the same time was going to see Andrés Segovia play at the Fairfield Hall in Croydon. It was one of those major points of my life. At that time I'd already made my mind up that I wanted to be self-sufficient on the guitar and play in the same way that a classical player does, but still have the ability to improvise as well. On stage that night there was just a piano stool and a foot rest and Segovia came out and played. It really planted a seed in my mind. The evening was a very memorable experience and a big guitar lesson.

Meanwhile, the gigs started to come in and so I decided that I had to learn to drive. I applied for the driving test immediately because there was a waiting list and I was desperate to get my licence. I learned to drive by driving to and from gigs. I started driving to gigs with my dad in the car and, once a week, I had to drive from Harlow to south London and back. This meant going through London, which was quite a long way.

The date for the test came through and it was only three weeks after I'd started driving. I took my first test and failed, but immediately reapplied and passed it three weeks later in Bishops Stortford. My first car was a 1966 Volkswagen Beetle, which I paid £100 for in 1975, and which had a hole in the bottom. In order to drive into London I had to go through a ford and I always got my feet wet, so I used to drive in Wellington boots.

Liz and I lived with my parents for a while, but because I had been born in Harlow, we were able to get on the list for a council house and got one pretty quickly. Before we moved in, we were married on 17 July 1976 at St Rollox Church in Glasgow. I was 19 and Liz was 21.

I started doing jazz gigs again, but it was barely paying the rent and so Liz started working in a hairdresser's just to make some money. She is actually a trained hairdresser; working at the holiday camp was just an adventure with her friends.

In the end I gave in and started doing more commercial gigs at the weekends just to make ends meet. I also started doing a little bit of teaching which I was really bad at – no good at all. I looked at doing some day jobs, too. Before Liz and I were married I'd got a temporary job in a rent office at the point where they were computerising the system. I had to get information and put it into code, but the first day I went in to the office there were just loads of people sitting around and talking; just gossip about things they'd read in the newspaper or seen on TV. It felt like being back at school. I couldn't believe that people were prepared to spend their lives in this way. It seemed such a waste – they had such a narrow existence.

I was used to working with musicians and this just wasn't the same at all, but I thought I'd have to get on with it somehow. One day, one of the guys showed me a newspaper picture of Tom Jones' house in Barbados and said, "Wouldn't you like to live in a house like that?" I said, "Oh, I've been there…" and the whole office went quiet. I wasn't bragging or anything, it was just a place I recognised from my travels. One of the singers on the ship was an old friend of Tom Jones and he'd shown me the house when we were out there. But I thought, "Oh no, they think I'm a nutcase." There was a really weird atmosphere in the office after that and I just couldn't take it, so I went out to lunch and never returned. That job lasted exactly three hours.

I had a few musical dates in the diary and I ran a weekly jazz gig at a pub in Buckhurst Hill called the Prince Of Wales, with Mo Morris on violin, Ted Beaumont on piano, Harvey Weston on bass and John Richardson on drums. But I needed something else to bring the money in and so I got a job driving a van.

Every morning I had to go down to Harlow train station in a Transit van and pick up packages from mail order catalogues, and then go and deliver them to places like Broxbourne, Cheshunt and Ware. I quite enjoyed it at first because I felt quite free out on the road and that was fine by me. But the other guys working there must have just seen me as a young lad and decided to make my life difficult. They started giving me impossible loads – there was no way I could deliver them all in one day and so I started getting really fed up with it.

One day, I had a load of footballs to deliver to Woolworth's in Broxbourne. The other guys had loaded the van up so that there were footballs everywhere, including the driving compartment. I drove away, with all of them laughing, and as I got to a roundabout and stopped, all the footballs flew forward, completely filling the driving compartment. I couldn't see out of the windscreen or anything, so I thought, "Sod this," and I switched the engine off, got out of the van and walked home. I'd had enough. I phoned the company and told them where the van was and said I was quitting and that if they wanted their van and footballs back they could come and get it.

That job lasted three days and I was beginning to think that I really wasn't cut out for a day gig. I guess that having been so spoilt travelling around the world and getting well paid to basically indulge myself in my hobby of playing guitar, this was a bit of a shock. But I'd been around long enough and seen enough not to take crap from anybody, even though most people just saw me as a young kid.

In the spring of 1976 they started building houses at a place in Old Harlow called Guilfords – which was strange, it being my mother's maiden name. I had two weeks with nothing much happening and so I thought I'd have a go at working on a building site.

My dad had long been in the construction industry, building roads for Harlow Development Corporation. He loved to see a well-built road and would get quite excited, saying, "Look at that – lovely bit of tarmac – beautiful."

My job on the building site was to wait for a delivery of concrete and then get in a dumper truck, take out a few shovelfuls, put the concrete into square moulds, pound the air out of them and leave them to dry. Then a guy from a laboratory would come along, pick up the samples and test them with a machine to see how much pressure they would take. If they didn't meet a certain standard, he would come back and say, "That batch there, lift it all up."

I really loved that job. The weather was warm and it was like being on holiday. I felt really fit and got myself a good tan and just really enjoyed being out in the open.

Most of the other guys on the site were Irish and I got on really well with them. At lunchtime we'd all go to the pub round the corner and have a pint of Guinness and it reminded me a lot of being with musicians, talking and laughing about things. Every Friday – which was payday – they'd bring a collection tin around and you had to put some money in. If you asked what it was for, they'd say, "It's for the lads back home in Ireland…" or, "It's for the cause…" I never argued with them and just paid up.

Of course, I knew my time on the building site was only for two weeks – if it had been for the rest of my life, I'm sure that would have been another thing. But I really enjoyed it all the same and missed my Irish mates when I left.

In all, my total time working in day jobs amounted to twelve days and three hours!

While I was working on the site, I got the call to do a couple of deps in various West End gigs. One was at the Dorchester Hotel, in the restaurant, playing with an Indian bass player called George de Suza and a drummer from Goa by the name of George de Cruz, who used to sing as well. It was quite a nice little gig and I played there for five months.

We used to play jazz tunes while the people were eating and, being the Dorchester, some of the guests were quite famous. I'd be sitting there playing and Elizabeth Taylor or James Coburn would come up and ask me to play certain tunes. I found it very funny that in the evening I was talking to Elizabeth Taylor at one of the world's most luxurious hotels, and during the day I was driving a dumper truck around a building site. They definitely wouldn't have believed that back at the rent office!

Having left the building site after two enjoyable weeks I went straight back to the Dorchester. The music was good and George had a good voice and so everything was fine. The piano player, Kenny Salmon, packed the gig in after a while and he was replaced by Hugh Ledigo, who now plays with Kenny Ball.

The downside was that we had to wear these truly awful, shiny orange sombrero shirts. They had puff sleeves which meant it was really difficult to play guitar wearing them, but occasional humiliation is all part of being a musician.

I stuck it out for three months and then I got a call to play at the Café de Paris in Leicester Square. I'd done some deps there, too, but I had serious reservations because this gig involved quite a lot of reading and I still wasn't particularly good at it. But I decided to take it on and played with a bandleader called Johnny Joseph, who played drums and sang.

By this time, Liz was expecting our baby. In those days, a lot of pressure was put on fathers to be at the birth, but I didn't want to – I'm a little squeamish – and that was fine with Liz. I come from a family background where men wouldn't attend the birth and the women wouldn't allow them to anyway, but I was still subjected to quite a lot of pressure all the same. Liz and I agreed that I should just carry on working as usual.

In readiness for going in to hospital, Liz packed a little red suitcase which she used to keep by the front door. Every night I'd come home from the Café de Paris thinking, "I wonder if tonight's the night?" and check to see the case still sitting there. One night after I had got home and had gone to bed, the phone rang and it was my mum. She said, "I don't think your dad's well…" He'd gasped in his sleep and woken her up and he was obviously unwell. I went round and took him to hospital where they said he'd had a heart attack.

Luckily it was not a major attack and he was soon back on his feet, but it meant that this particular time was very stressful. What's more, the baby was overdue by a couple of weeks and Liz was getting bigger and bigger and still I'd come home and find the red case sitting there. One night, I was so frustrated that I kicked it all round the hall! Eventually the doctor decided that they would take Liz into the hospital and induce her. And so, on 16 July 1977, Liz went into the Princess Alexandra Hospital – where my mum had lent Stanley Kubrick her badge years earlier – and gave birth to our first son, James, while I played an afternoon session at the Café de Paris.

Shortly after James was born, Liz's father, Jimmy, died of a heart attack at the age of 44. All the family were devastated; he was such a lovely guy. Then Liz's uncle, Pat, died just a couple of months later – also from a heart attack. We had one birth, two deaths and three heart attacks in the family in a matter of months. To say it was a stressful and painful time would be no exaggeration.

When I agreed to take the gig with Johnny Joseph, I knew we wouldn't be playing jazz, but Johnny was writing out parts all the time and I figured that it would be a good chance for me to improve my reading. He'd bring in charts every night and I'd have to sight-read them and that was a good enough reason for me to do the gigs.

At the time I often asked myself why I was doing some of those gigs – I know I needed the money, but looking back now, I can see that it was a period of apprenticeship. Now, you can go to college and learn all this, but I did it the old-fashioned way – on the job.

There were two bands that played the Café de Paris: the one I was in, which was a seven-piece, and a five-piece which featured Don Fraser on guitar. Don had worked with Stephane Grappelli during the war and was Ray Ellington's guitar player for many years. I'd seen him featured in *BMG* magazine a few times and I got to know him quite well.

Don always seemed to be doing home decorating, but everything was always going wrong for him. Whenever I saw him I'd say, "How's it going, Don?" and he'd say something like, "Well, I decorated the hall and I'd just finished and I looked at it and I realised I'd hung the paper upside-down and so I had to strip it off again..." He seemed to spend all his life decorating something or other.

One day he decided that he'd have his whole house re-carpeted. They came to lay it when he was out and, of course, they did the whole house in bright pink carpet instead of the colour he'd ordered.

He'd come out with some great expressions though, like, "I've decorated the kitchen. It's fantastic, it's jet white!"

Don was a really good guitar player and had been around for ages. He'd even played with Django Reinhardt at one point. We often jammed together in the bandroom and I learned a lot about harmony from him.

Although England isn't as renowned for its jazz guitarists as the US, we had our fair share: Albert Harris, who went over to Hollywood and composed music for films – in fact, Barney Kessel studied harmony with him early on; Jack Llewellyn, who recorded with Django; Dave Goldberg, who was one of the first "modern" jazz guitarists in Britain; Pete Chilver, George Elliot, Alan Metcalfe, Billy Bell and Ernie Shear...These were the pioneers of British jazz, from the '20s to the '60s. Many more have come since, but these were the founding fathers. A full list would fill a book in itself, but I feel these guys should be recognised.

When James was just a few months old I got a phone call from a piano player called Art Walters, asking me to do a cruise aboard a P&O ship called the Arcadia, which sailed out of Sydney and cruised around the South Pacific. Although my days at sea were over, I decided to do it because it was only for a month. The band consisted of Art, myself, Paul Carmichael on bass guitar, Norman Leppard on sax and a drummer whose name I've unfortunately forgotten. We did a couple of two-week cruises out of Sydney and took in places like Fiji, Tonga, New Hebrides and New Caledonia, and I had a really great time. But that was my last experience playing on cruise ships.

Some of the commercial gigs I was doing included working for the Sydney Lipton Agency, run by an old time bandleader in the West End of London. I was one of a pool of musicians Sydney had on his books and his secretary would phone up on a Monday morning and book me for the following Thursday, Friday and Saturday. I'd turn up and find myself playing with some of the other guys on his books. After a while I got to know the others quite well and we'd do some society dates together all around London.

One drummer who worked for Sydney was hard work to play with sometimes because he was so bad tempered. There was one date at

Buckingham Palace, for one of the Queen's garden parties, and this particular drummer was booked to play there. A marquee had been set up in the gardens and it was decked out with tropical plants and looked absolutely beautiful. The stage was on the narrow side and so the band had to set up in a long line. After the drummer had set his gear up, there was no room on the stage for the trumpet player, so he asked the drummer to move his kit up a bit so he could fit on the end.

Usually, when drummers set up their kit, that's it; they don't want to move again. As far as they're concerned, they're a fixture. In view of this guy's reputation, everyone was a little nervous as to how he'd take being asked to shift along. He'd obviously been told to behave himself on this occasion, though, since the Queen, Queen Mother, Prince Phillip and the entire first division of the House of Windsor were going to be there, but you could see that he was absolutely seething about having to move. In the end they got it so that the trumpet player could fit on the end of the stage and the band took their places as the guests filed in. An official came over to the band and said, "When Her Majesty and the royal procession comes in, there should be a roll on the drums and then go immediately into the National Anthem." So the band prepared themselves and, at a signal from the official, the lights went up. Unfortunately, the drummer had repositioned his kit over a fountain which immediately sprung to life and soaked him completely. What Her Majesty must have thought when she walked in to find a mad drummer with water coming up from under his kit and him swearing his head off, I don't know...

Around this time I worked with Victor Sylvester and went on a short tour playing at strict-tempo dancing clubs. Victor's musical partner was Oscar Grasso, who played violin with a very distinctive, wide vibrato. I used to sit next to Oscar and double all the violin parts and so I got to know him quite well. I spent a few weeks with the band, standing in for Len Argent, and it was very bizarre – I swear I'll never understand ballroom dancing, I just can't see the point of it.

In the band we all wore jackets which had the letters "VS" embroidered onto them. This meant that if you went into a pub in the small English towns we were playing, everyone would know that The Victor Sylvester Band was in town. It was quite a big thing in some places and people would come up and buy us all drinks. We were all in a pub once, wearing our jackets, and the piano player – a fiery Italian who was also depping in the band and who Oscar took an instant dislike to – said, "It's really embarrassing going into a pub with these jackets on, having 'VS' all over them." I could see that Oscar was getting a bit worked up and that maybe an argument was in the offing, so I said the first thing that came into my head: "It could be worse, we could be working for Val Doonican!" Oscar started laughing and it defused the situation straight away. I got on very well with Oscar. He used to give me a bit of a hard time over my terrible sight-reading – he even shouted at me a couple of times – but he was like a favourite Italian uncle to me.

There was another band who played the tea dances with us and they used to play all tangos. When their guitarist went on holiday he asked me to dep for him and I agreed, although it meant I had to sit there and sight-read tangos. I only agreed to do it because I knew it would throw me in the deep end and make me improve my reading – just as I'd done with Johnny Joseph before.

I'd heard the band play before and I had a pretty good idea of how a lot of the tunes went, but when I got to the parts I didn't know, or if I got lost, I'd just make something up. There was a really nice female Jamaican bass player in the band, who had the most amazing '70s Afro hairstyle, and when she heard me make something up she'd laugh and say, "I like that, I like that – do it again." She thought I was doing it on purpose and didn't realise I was just getting hopelessly lost.

I did a few broadcasts for BBC radio around this time, too. I did some for *Jazz Club*, which was hosted by Peter Clayton, and some for *Night Ride* on Radio 2, and I found it strange because so many of the radio producers then seemed to be ex-RAF officers. They used to sit in the box with their blazers on, which was very curious indeed.

One in particular obviously didn't know a lot about music but felt that he had to say something every so often. You'd record something and he'd say, "That was fine, but could we take the tempo up a bit?" or something like that. I couldn't help thinking that he'd just picked up a few musical terms along the way, but had got his job mainly because of the old-school-tie principle.

Once, the sax player had just played a long, sustained note and the producer said, "That note's out of tune." It wasn't, but he felt he had to say something to justify his salary. "How do you mean?" said the saxophone player. "I don't know," said Biggles. "It's not flat, it's not sharp, it's somewhere in between..."

The same producer was once on a session with the great jazz drummer, Phil Seaman, when Phil was a bit tired from the night before. Feeling a little fragile, when the producer called over the mike, "Where's that Phil Seaman magic?" Phil replied, "Abaracafuckingdabra..."

When I was working with Dave Thacker I met a bass player, called Sam Bass, who used to play at Jewish weddings and Bar Mitzvahs and was part of a whole Jewish circuit of musicians who had been around for years. Despite the age difference, we hit it off immediately. We both had the same warped sense of humour and would tell each other stories. Liz and I had just got married and had moved into the council house and I wasn't doing any residency work at all, just freelance stuff. I had bought an answering machine – believe it or not, I was one of the first musicians in London to have one – and I used to come home at night and find the light on, but nobody would leave any messages because they weren't used to answering machines back then. The machine was actually reel-to-reel, like a tape recorder, and I'd got it on a three-year lease, which had meant me going out on a limb to get it. It was huge and took up one corner of the room, looking like something from NASA. I was starting to panic a little: I'd invested in this machine, I had to find the rent money every month and I had a wife and baby to support. Quite daunting for a 20-year-old. I needed work. Fast.

I'd had the machine for weeks and the first person to leave me a message was Sam Bass who said, "I've got some work for you," and he reeled off a series of dates. At the time, I was getting snow blindness from staring at my empty diary and I can't begin to say how great I felt getting that call. I was soon playing Jewish weddings, Bar Mitzvahs and so on and they were really well paid, too.

I think that Sammy and the rest of the guys sort of adopted me in a way. Other musicians were so used to seeing me do gigs with them that they'd come up to me and say, "I didn't know you were Jewish," and I'd say, "I'm not..."

The guys in Sammy's bands were always a lot older than me, but playing with them took me back to the times I'd enjoyed on the QE2, hanging out in the bar with the older guys and listening to them tell stories. Sammy used to live in Ilford and so quite often we'd share a ride into London to do the gigs. Coming home through the East End he'd point out where he grew up and take me around all of the back streets and show me places from his childhood. He was a great storyteller, too, and had a knack of sitting you down and telling you about six stories at once and intertwining all of them. Sometimes I didn't get in until around three am because Sammy would have taken me for a tour around his childhood haunts. Through his stories he painted a vivid picture of the Jewish immigrants in the East End, how his parents lived and everything. It was wonderful.

Sammy started playing at the Ritz Hotel in London, six nights a week, with a piano player called Norman Percival and a violinist called Joe Rosen. Joe was getting on a bit and he didn't like to play every night and so he needed a dep and they called me. Joe would only want to do four out of the six nights at the most and so he'd call me and say, "Can you do the Wednesday and Thursday of this week and Tuesday and Friday next week?" and I'd go up to the Ritz and do the gigs. They were nice to do and quite early, too – we played from about six-thirty until nine o'clock so quite often I would go on and do a jazz gig somewhere after – like Ronnie Scott's club with The Tony Lee Trio, supporting American artists like Stan Getz and Dexter Gordon.

Sammy became a big influence on me in the same way that Ike was. I used to go to his house quite a lot and see him, his wife Sylvia, and his daughters, Tracy and Lisa, and I became one of the family.

Unfortunately, Sam died in 1998, having contracted cancer. He kept it secret from everyone and I didn't know a thing about it until I received a phone call from Tracy one evening when I was at home in Scotland. She told me that her dad was really very ill and I said I'd fly down, but she said that he was unlikely to last the night. Apparently the family had been try-ing to get hold of me for ages without success. Sammy died that night.

Sammy's wish for his funeral was to have his old friend, Mickey Binnelli, play Italian tunes on the accordion as people came in, and for me to play later in the ceremony. I did it, but it was one of the hardest gigs I've ever done. So many memories came flooding back while I was playing.

# 11 *We Should Make A Record*

At the Ritz, Norman Percival could be quite awkward at times, doing things like not distributing the tips to the band. He would also go from being a nice guy to being quite aggressive very quickly. One night, he was being a real pain in the neck and I thought, "OK, that's it." I was going to thump him, which isn't very elegant behaviour for the Ritz, but fortunately I realised that he was trying to see how far he could push me. Once we got that out of the way, we got on very well and he was very encouraging. I really liked him in a funny way and I actually learned a lot because I'd stand behind him on stage and watch him play. He wasn't a jazz player – not even a particularly good pianist – but sometimes he would just sit and doodle on the piano. I loved the sort of freedom that piano players had and I thought I would love to be able to do it on the guitar, so I began to work at it. It seemed as if, somehow, all the diverse work I was doing, which sprang from me needing to gain experience and make a living, all had a reason to it. It was a musical apprenticeship which has worked out well for me.

I was asked to play in a club just off Leicester Square with a guitar player and singer called Keith Cooper. The club was basically a clip joint and employed glamorous-looking young "hostesses" as companions for visiting foreign businessmen – it was a time when there were a lot of oil-rich Arabs in London. The first night we played there, one of the girls came up and asked us to play a tune and one of the wealthy Arab clientele sent us over a tip for £50 – and I was only on £120 a week then. I thought we were on to a real winner after that, but unfortunately it never happened again.

I got talking to the girls in the club. Most were Irish and found themselves working there for different circumstances. Occasionally the club would put on a stripper and, one night, the girl told us that she wanted a roll on the drums when she took off a certain part of her costume. It posed a bit of a problem because our act only consisted of two guitar players. But the band who had played at the club previously had left a drum machine behind. It was a very crude affair, and nothing like the sort of sophistication you'd find these days, but I thought we could probably work something out. When the time came, I leant over and turned the dial up quickly so it sounded vaguely like a drum roll. Well, sort of. Keith and I would get the giggles every time I had to do this, which really annoyed the stripper, because she thought we were laughing at her tits.

Apart from the normal customers who would be there for the girls, you did get some of the Soho locals coming in. Word spread that we were there and so some jazz fans started coming in to hear us play. Among these was Peter Boizot, the founder of the Pizza Express restaurant chain.

At this time, Peter was already putting on some American jazz musicians like Bud Freeman, Ruby Braff, Al Grey and Frank Foster, at the Dean Street Pizza Express. He came and saw me during the break and said that he had another restaurant, on Hyde Park Corner, called Pizza On The Park and that he'd like to put music on there. Keith was doing other things, but I told Peter that I could do it and I wondered if Ike Isaacs would be interested. I thought Ike was touring with Stephane Grappelli at the time, but it turned out that he'd just finished and so I rang him up and he said he'd love to do it.

Ike and I played that gig every Thursday for two years and it was a real learning experience for me. It was like being paid to take guitar lessons. Sometimes, other musicians would come and sit in with us. One night John Collins, one of the guitarists who worked with Nat "King" Cole, joined us and on another occasion it was Gerry Mulligan. They were great times.

It was Ike Isaacs who introduced me to Stephane. The band were playing a gig in a tiny theatre in Crief, in Perthshire, and Liz and I happened to be up there visiting her family. While we were there we took a ride up to see Ike play with Stephane. The line-up at that time was Diz Disley and Ike on guitars and Phil Bates on bass.

I can remember sitting in the dressing room when Stephane opened his violin case and took out a neatly-pressed flowery shirt. Then he took out his violin which was wrapped in a red "diklo", or silk scarf, that the older generation of Gypsy men always wore. It had violins in the pattern and the music for a Paganini piece in very bright colours. It had belonged to Django and was a gift to Stephane from Django's wife when he died. Stephane treasured that scarf and, when I began touring with him a few years later, I would watch him go through the ritual of unwrapping and wrapping his violin in it. I always found it very touching and Stephane even let me wear the scarf a few times, later on.

One night Ike and I were playing at Pizza On The Park and the bass player, Peter Ind, came in to see us. Peter had worked with the pianist Lennie Tristano in New York and had his own record label, Wave Records. He liked what we were doing and, afterwards, I called Peter to do some dates that came in. There were a few radio broadcasts and things like that and, on one occasion, Peter said, "You know, we should make a record." So we went to his studio in Twickenham and made my first album, *Taylor Made*, with John Richardson on drums. Soon afterwards, we followed it up with another album called *Triple Libra* and my recording career was under way. Sadly the only recording I made with Ike was a limited edition that we did for an amplifier company. It was early days for me, musically, but when I hear those records now I can hear what I was aiming for. I just hadn't got there yet! But, despite my reservations about my early efforts, there is some good playing on those albums.

A guy called Ken Lodge used to put on concerts in Barking, Essex. He would get all kinds of people to play together, and the first night I did it, there was George Chisholm on trombone and the trumpet player, Kenny Baker – veterans of the British jazz scene. That night also had The Tony Lee Trio, with Tony Archer on bass, Martin Drew on drums augmented by Tommy Whittle on tenor sax. There was also a great set by Bob Wilber and Dave McKenna, who were over on tour from the States.

Tony was a regular at the Bull's Head in Barnes, which had been a famous jazz club in London for many years and, I believe, is still going strong. Tony said he'd really like me to do some gigs down there and so I started playing on a fairly regular basis. I managed to stop doing the commercial gigs that I had been doing at weekends and concentrated on playing jazz exclusively.

There was a guy who always came to Bull's Head gigs who was a bit of a cockney gangster type – big and really tough-looking. But when we played a ballad, tears used to run down his cheeks, he was so moved by the music. One night he came up to me and said, "Oi, Martin, 'ow about playing some of that subtle shit?" I think I know what he meant.

Around this time Liz and I decided to buy a hairdressing salon so that it could subsidise me if things became lean later on. I'd already proved myself useless on the day-gig front and so we bought a salon just by

Redbridge underground station in Essex. Liz ran it as a going concern and I would just go in once in a while to make the staff tea and tell the old dears how lovely they looked. We called the salon "Hair by Liz Taylor" and it allowed me to ease off from the other work I was doing.

We continued to live in Harlow, although it was a sort of dormitory for me. Being so near London, it was convenient but I regretted going back. I'd enjoyed my childhood there, but I wanted to move on to somewhere else.

One night at the Bull's Head, Phil Bates came to see me. I'd played a few dates with Phil and I knew that he was currently working with Stephane and he said that there were some dates coming up in Belgium and France and was I interested in doing them? By this time the line-up was Diz Disley and John Etheridge on guitars, with Phil on bass, but Diz had to drop out because he'd broken his wrist.

I said I'd love to do the dates, but there was one problem. Liz, James and I hadn't taken a holiday together and (under pressure) I had already booked a couple of weeks in the Channel Isles for us all – exactly at the time that the dates with Stephane came up.

Liz wasn't pleased, but I said I'd really got to go because it was such a great opportunity. She and James ended up taking my mum with them, but she really wasn't happy about it. We've never booked holidays since, preferring to just go somewhere at the last minute, which better suits my Bohemian nature. Even now, some mornings I'll wake up at home and just hitch up my caravan and take off. I never know where I'm going or for how long. I just know that I have to go somewhere and move on, a bit like Aborigines going on "walkabout".

John Etheridge and I met at Phil Bates' house and we ran over the programme. The following morning I got in the car and drove with Phil to France. John made his own way.

Stephane had an agent called Michel Chaunard who was quite funny because he was very forgetful. Stephane used to say, "Michel's my agent and I'm his manager." Michel would do funny things; he'd ring me up and say, "Martin, eet's Michel…" and then there'd be some mumbling and he'd say, "I cannot speak zee English today," and hang up.

My French is pretty basic and so communication could be pretty erratic at times. Sometimes he'd call and tell me about a gig and say, "I'll send you a map," and a couple of days later an envelope would come through the post and in it would be a piece of paper with a hand-drawn outline of

France with an "X" marking the spot where the gig was.

On this first occasion, Michel had told us that the gig was in Nantes and so Phil and I drove down there. We were meant to be playing at the Theatre Normandie, but we were asking people and nobody knew where the place was. So we called Michel and said, "We're in Nantes. Where is everyone?" and Michel said, "Nantes? Zee gig is een Montes."

Montes is near Paris and we were miles away, in the south-west of France, with absolutely no chance of making the show. So Phil and I went and had a few beers and I thought, "Well, I almost had a gig with Stephane Grappelli, but I blew it." But we met up the next day at a concert in Deauville and Stephane was great about it – I think he saw the funny side – and said, "Well, zees tings 'appen, my dear."

I did a few more gigs with him in France and then we moved on up to Belgium and did some more gigs and a TV show. At the end, Stephane said to me that he had an American tour coming up in a couple of months' time and would I like to do it? And so started eleven years of touring and recording with Stephane Grappelli.

Stephane's agent in the US was Abby Hoffer, who had been the lead trumpeter in Tommy Dorsey's band. Abby had offices on Broadway and he'd booked us a month-long tour which focused mainly on the east coast. After that, we returned to Britain and carried on the tour in the UK. From then on I'd do two UK tours with Stephane a year, usually in the spring and autumn, and two US tours plus a few festivals in France – everything else in between would be my own dates under my own name.

On the second tour of the States, which started on the east coast and ended up on the west, I first met up with David Grisman, who had previously worked with Stephane on the soundtrack for the movie *King Of The Gypsies*. This was to be the beginning of a long and fruitful working relationship between David and me that would result in several successful albums, collaborations and tours of the States.

When I started to play jazz, there was one prejudice in Britain which really used to hold homegrown players back – the notion that you couldn't possibly play jazz if you weren't American. I think it's an idea which has all but been eradicated from popular folklore now, but in those days it was a really difficult thing to get around. I still meet with that attitude sometimes on the Continent, but in Britain things seem to have settled down a bit more. America, though, was so refreshing because I was instantly accepted as a jazz musician with no stigma at all. The fact that I wasn't American didn't mean anything, which was great.

When I first started touring with Stephane in America we were playing in fairly small clubs. Then, over the years, the venues got bigger and bigger and we eventually started playing at places like the Newport Jazz Festival for George Wein. I suppose that during that initial five- or six-year period I'd spend three or four months of the year with Stephane in America or Canada. In fact, I was playing more in the States than I was in the UK.

We had some funny times together on the road. Once, after we'd finished playing a gig in the mid-west, a guy came up from the audience to speak to Stephane. He was an Italian/American and was so emotional, he was practically in tears. He said, "That was so beautiful, so beautiful...I have a country club and I want you to come and play there," and so the following tour, we went to play at his club.

It was an incredible place and the owner was very generous and wined and dined us to our hearts' content. But I had my suspicions about his business connections. His generosity toward us knew no bounds, though; if you complimented him on any item around the place, he'd say, "Take it – it's my gift to you." The audience that night was made up of his family and friends and it was like being on the set of *The Godfather*. The guys all had these wide-lapelled suits, with the long dark overcoats and a blonde on their arms, and they were drinking champagne from enormous ice buckets. Looking around, Stephane turned to me and said, "I t'ink zeez people are gongstare," and I said, "No kidding, Steph." I added that perhaps we might not think about hanging around for too long.

We played the first set and, during the interval, a couple of these really frightening gentlemen came up to me and one of them, who had a scar down his right cheek, said, "Eh, kid – my wife just said that she wants you to take her home and fuck her." My mouth went completely dry and I started laughing nervously. Then I thought, "I bet he thinks I'm laughing about his wife," and began to wonder what would happen next. My laughter turned into a sad whimper and then, just as I was about to go down on bended knee and beg to be allowed to live, he just turned to his friend and said, "Kid's got a sense of humour." Then he patted me on the back and bought me a drink. And I needed one after that.

Once we were in Detroit airport waiting at the baggage carousel and I said to Stephane, "You go and sit down, I'll fetch the bags." As I continued to wait, I heard this guy come up to me and say, in a very polite southern accent, "Excuse me, sir, but is that Stephane Grappelli over there?" I turned round and it was Chet Atkins, one of my all-time guitar heroes and so I said, "Wow, you're Chet Atkins," and Chet replied, "Yes I am, but is that Stephane Grappelli over there?" I said, "Never mind that...you're Chet Atkins – my hero!" and got talking to him.

A couple of years later I went up to meet Chet at his office in Nashville with a friend of mine and I didn't know whether he'd remember us having met in Detroit. But when I walked in he said that he'd been working on my version of 'Old Man River'. Apparently, he'd seen me play in Detroit and had been trying to figure out how to play all the parts together and told me that he was about to give up. I felt very honoured – and I think the friend I was with was pretty impressed, too. So I played it for him there and then in the office.

Stephane's mind sometimes worked in mysterious ways and my first experience of this came after I'd been working for him for about a year. We were staying at a hotel and I got a call from Stephane asking me to go and see him in his room. When I got there, he said, "I 'ave a favour to ask of you. 'As your wife ever been to Paris?" and I said, "Not to my knowledge."

Stephane had a reputation for being careful with money and so I was quite surprised when he offered to pay for a romantic weekend in Paris for Liz and myself. He had a flat in Chelsea, a house in Paris and another in Cannes and went on to explain that he had a suitcase in his flat in Chelsea that he needed taken to his flat in Paris and, if I'd take it across for him, he'd pay my petrol, the ferry and for a nice hotel. He said it would be a nice little holiday for both of us.

Liz thought it was a great idea. When the day arrived, we drove up to Stephane's place and knocked on the door. His grandson, young Stephane, answered and I could see that the long hallway was absolutely full of suitcases. I only had a little car at the time and so I called out, "Stephane, I don't think I can fit all these in my car – you said it was only one suitcase." He said, "I 'ad more t'ings than I t'ought."

He then insisted on opening every suitcase to show me that there was "no funny beeznez", as he put it. Every one was crammed full of cups, saucers, tea pots, tea towels, net curtains and various bits and pieces like that. I said, "All right, OK," and began to load the car up with them. I got Liz to sit in the back seat and managed to cram suitcases either side of her. The next thing I knew, young Stephane had got into the front seat. I said, "What are you doing in here?" and he said, "You're taking me, too." So he was sitting in the front seat with a suitcase between his legs and every single inch of the rest of the car was full, leaving one solitary suitcase on the pavement. I said to Stephane, "The car's full. We can't get any more in," and Stephane looked at me, sighed and said, "Martin, you shouldn't 'ave brought your wife!"

He had a passion for antiques. Once, when the bass player Len Skeat worked with the band, he and Stephane passed an antique shop which had some plates in the window, piled about two and a half feet high. Stephane saw one plate on top which was really nice, so he went into the shop and asked the guy inside, "How much for just zis one plate?" and the guy said, "It's a job lot – 50p, but you've got to take all of them." Stephane said, "But I only want zis one," but it was no good, the guy in the shop wasn't arguing. So Stephane ended up buying the whole lot. He gave Len the job of carrying this massive pile back to the car, having taken the one good one off the top. The rest of the plates were really in a terrible state, all chipped and cracked, so Stephane turned to Len and said, "Perhaps your wife would like zose?" and completely lumbered him with all this useless crockery.

Once, in Cheltenham, I found an antique shop which had a really nice little painting which caught my eye. It was a woman lying on a bed and it was really beautiful. I asked the the shopkeeper what it was painted on and to my surprise he gruffly replied, "Well, it's not silk. If you think it's silk then you're an idiot and might as well clear off!" He was really being unnecessarily aggressive, but as the painting was really cheap, I bought it anyway. I stopped and talked to some people on my way out and they told me that the guy who ran the place was completely mad, totally loopy. He more or less gave the stuff away, it was so cheap, but he would always end up shouting at the customers. 100% certifiable.

When I was walking back to the hotel, I bumped into Stephane and decided to set him up. I thought it would be a great laugh to send Steph into the shop and watch the feathers fly! As I stood outside the shop, I heard the owner yelling, "If you're not going to buy them, put 'em down," and he really started laying into him. I suppose that Stephane and the shopkeeper were about the same age, and Stephane could give as good as he got. He started yelling back. I stood outside, laughing my head off, listening to them both screaming at each other. When he came out of the shop I explained to him that I had set him up and we both laughed about it. He saw the funny side and appreciated the joke.

Although Stephane could speak English really well, he used the singular tense all the time and so "the boys in the band" became "the boy in the band". This could cause quite a lot of misunderstanding – especially when combined with quite a thick French accent – with the occasional amusing consequence.

He told me once that he had gone into Harrods to buy some sheets and went up to the bedding department. The assistant said, "Can I help you, sir?" and Stephane said, "Yes, I want to buy some sheet." She said, "I beg your pardon?" and he said, "I want some sheet." The assistant was quite shocked and said, "Well, there's no need to be offensive..." which only made Stephane angry and so he said, "No, don't be stupid, I want some sheet – sheet, you know?" The assistant called the manager who then escorted Stephane out of the shop, still loudly protesting that all he wanted was "some sheet".

# 12 'Ooever Said Ze Show Must Go On...

On tour in America for two or perhaps three months at a time, we would catch a plane every day – sometimes two or three in one day. By this time, Stephane was already in his 70s and he found it really tiring. But he was an amazing performer. He'd be really tired before a gig and say, "I just want to go back to ze 'otel and go to bed, I'm so tired." Then he would shuffle on stage, start playing and suddenly come alive. He'd almost skip off stage at the end of the evening, it was quite incredible, the energy he had. One time, we had been on tour in America for around three months and playing in different cities every night and I could see that he was really tired, so much so that he looked quite ill. He was sitting in the dressing-room, holding his violin, and saying how tired he was and how he wished he could just return to the hotel and get some sleep. I said to him, "You know, Stephane, there is an old saying, 'The show must go on'," and Stephane just nodded and said, "Yes, you are right, my dear..."

A little bit later, we were standing in the wings waiting to go on stage and play, and Stephane turned to me and said, "'Ooever said ze show must go on was a cont," and then walked on stage and played fantastically.

He had an uncanny way of charming people and would often use his age to his advantage. If we were getting on a plane, Stephane would begin to shuffle and say, "Oh, my leg – I cannot sit 'ere..." and very often they would upgrade him to first class to make him more comfortable. Then he would tell them, "I don't like being up 'ere wizout my grandson, I must 'ave my grandson wiz me." So I'd stay put and then I would see a steward come back and say to me, "Are you Mr Grappelli's grandson?" and I would say, "Oui, monsieur" and I'd get upgraded, too. So we'd both be up in first class, getting stuck into the free champagne and he would continue to charm them: "Have you got any more of zeze bottles?" and we'd get off the plane with our pockets bulging with miniatures of gin, vodka, brandy, you name it.

Stephane used to get a real buzz from doing things like this and the "grandson" trick was one of our favourites.

I used to like being in Paris with Stephane and I remember walking in the area where he lived in Anvers, just up from the Pigalle. He was born and grew up in that area and, if we were walking together, he would point out to me where he was born and the cinema where he first started playing piano for silent movies.

He had lived in London during the war and played at Hatchett's Club with George Shearing, just opposite the Ritz. He lived with a woman then who had an aristocratic background and would often have members of the royal family to visit, among them Queen Mary. Stephane had a trick that he said he had learned from Queen Mary which he'd do all the time, and it always seemed to work. We would be invited round to someone's house and perhaps an ornament would catch Stephane's eye. He would say to me, "Martin, an ornament like that, wouldn't it go well in that little alcove in my flat in Paris?" and I'd say, "Yes, Stephane, it would." Of course, the hosts would give the ornament to Stephane and then spend the rest of their lives telling people that they once gave an ornament to Stephane Grappelli.

Stephane would often tell me tales about Django. At one point, Django was staying with his family just outside Paris where they had the caravans on a patch of land. Stephane went out to visit and, after a while, Django's wife asked him if he was hungry and would he like some chicken? Stephane said that he would and she went outside and Stephane heard the sound of loud clucking followed by dead silence...He said that the food and the hospitality was always fantastic.

Django wasn't only the greatest guitarist in the world, he was good at just about everything he tried. He was a skilled fisherman. One day he and his brother, Joseph, invited Stephane to go fishing with them. They arrived at the river bank and saw a bunch of guys who were "real anglers" – they'd got all the best fishing gear and all the essential paraphernalia – and were sitting there watching their floats for hours on end. Django broke a branch off a tree and fastened a piece of twine on it, then tied a pin on the end, dug up a worm and pulled a fish out immediately, much to the dismay of all the anglers who'd spent a small fortune on equipment further down the bank. Just to add salt to the wound, he repeated the process several times in the space of ten minutes before heading home to cook his dinner.

Another time, Django and Stephane went to a fairground together. There was one stall where you had to knock the lady out of bed by throwing a wooden ball at a target and it was almost impossible to do. Django thought he'd give it a try and so he threw his first ball and – *clang* – the poor girl got thrown out of bed in her underwear. They gave Django his prize and propped the girl back up again but Django threw his second ball and – *clang* – she was out of bed again. He managed to do it five or six times and in the end the girl looked at him and shouted, "Oi, fuck off!"

Stephane was a real city person, unlike me, and he got bored easily. But at least he loved the concept of being in the country. Usually, when we were on tour, we'd stay in a hotel which was in the middle of a city, and Stephane would enjoy walking around and going to restaurants, museums and so on. Just occasionally he would say something like, "Oh, eet's too busy 'ere, wouldn't it be nice to be in ze country?" So once, when we were on tour in England, he said to his agent, Ed Baxter, "I'd really like to stay in a nice 'otel in ze country, it would be lovely." So Ed booked us in to this five star hotel in the country which was miles from anywhere. As we drove up the long, leafy drive to the hotel, Stephane was saying, "Oh, isn't zis nice? Zis is charming."

We were booked into the hotel for two nights and by the second day Stephane rang me and said, "I've had enough of zis, I want to go back to London." I said, "Why?" and he said, "Too many focking tree about."

I travelled all around the world with Stephane. We went to Australia and even played in India for The Jazz Yatra. We did two concerts in Delhi and Bombay which were huge open-air events playing to thousands of people. The Indian violinist, L Subramanian, was also on the bill with Larry Coryell, and Max Roach played a solo set on various percussion instruments. I found Indian people very receptive to jazz, probably because their own classical music includes improvisation.

We played at Carnegie Hall a few times and at the Hollywood Bowl and appeared on TV on *The Tonight Show* with Johnny Carson on a couple of occasions. Most of the time we were in either the UK or America and there was a really big difference in the audiences. In England, the audiences were a lot older and more reserved, but the Americans were made up with much younger people. It was a completely different vibe and it suited Stephane because he liked to be among young people. He really enjoyed playing in America and that's why he went there so often, he just loved the whole atmosphere of it. The feedback we'd get from the audiences was just fantastic and he would really feed on the energy we got from playing there.

Around 1980, in between touring with Stephane and a lot of other things that I was doing, I decided that I didn't want to live in Harlow any more. I'd been spending a lot of time in Scotland and I really wanted to move there. Liz wasn't sure, despite the fact that she's from Scotland herself, but all of my work was touring so it didn't matter to me where I lived – I didn't need to be in London, as long as I was near an airport I was fine.

We decided that we would live somewhere that was within 50 miles of Glasgow but out in the country, and we managed to find somewhere 14 miles outside Ayr. Because we were moving from a council house it wasn't like we were selling up in the prosperous south and moving north, so we had to start from the beginning. We had sold the hairdresser's, but didn't make anything on it.

We found a little cottage at 29 Townhead, Dalmellington and bought it in June 1980 for the princely sum of £10,000. I've lived in Scotland ever since – which is why Stephane would always introduce me as being "from Scotland". It was a lovely little cottage, about 200 years old with a nice view of the hills.

It didn't take us long to settle there and we soon began making friends. There was a place called the Hollybush House Hotel, which was run by Bob and Margaret White, and Liz and I made many friends there, including Alex and Vi Little, and Bob and Margaret's daughters, Holly and Poppy – in fact, I'm Poppy's godfather. The hotel was a wonderful place and Stephane and I once did a charity concert there, which is an evening I'll always remember.

Meanwhile, my mum and dad moved from Harlow in 1980 as well, to live in Caister, just outside Great Yarmouth in Norfolk. My dad carried on his life-long love of the sea by becoming a crew member of the Caister Lifeboat. The motto of the Lifeboat was "Caister men never turn back", because in the 19th century there was a disaster at sea and many of the Caister men on the lifeboat were drowned. At the inquest someone said to one of the surviving crewmen, "If the weather was that bad, why didn't you turn back?" and he replied, "Caister men never turn back."

So Dad was in the Caister Lifeboat for the period of time he lived there and received the Freedom of the Royal Borough of Great Yarmouth. Prince Charles actually came down to present the award to all the crewmen, but my father didn't attend the ceremony because all the men had been told that they must address the prince as "sir" and my dad just couldn't bring himself to do it. He reasoned that the prince was younger than him and no better than he was, so why should he.

I didn't play in Scotland at first, but I got to know a lot of the musicians there. The Glasgow Society of Musicians met at 73 Berkley Street and I started going there through a bass player I knew called Alex Moore. He was in a really good trio with Sandy Taylor on piano and Murray Smith on drums. I got to know Carol Kidd, who wasn't a professional singer at the time, but has recently been awarded an MBE.

I started to be asked to do mini tours of Scotland for an organisation called Platform, run by Roger Spence, and used Sandy, Alex and Murray for them. On some dates I brought in Carol, who is without a doubt one of the best jazz singers ever, as a guest.

I was still going backwards and forwards to America with Stephane and touring the UK and Europe with him too. By this time I'd also recorded some albums with him for Concord Records and I'd made my own album on Concord called *Skyeboat*. I recorded it in San Francisco in 1981 with Peter Ind on bass and Jimmie Smith on drums, but there was no link up with management, tour promotion, etc so the album just came out and basically nothing much happened with it.

Around this time I did a concert in the Queen's Hall, Edinburgh, with Buddy De Franco, the clarinet player. Buddy and I started playing together quite a lot through the early '80s and subsequently put a group together – The Buddy De Franco/Martin Taylor Quintet – and we recorded a couple of albums for Hep records.

I also started working more with other guitar players, too. I had played with Barney Kessel quite a lot over the years and so when Herb Ellis dropped out of The Great Guitars to go and work with Oscar Peterson again, I was invited to take his place and join them. I toured with Barney and Charlie Byrd and the UK promoter Robert Masters also put on a whole series which was like a travelling guitar festival that went around the country. There was Jorge Morel, Bireli Lagrene, Vic Juris, Juan Martin, Antonio Forcione and, of course, Barney. It was great fun – like a travelling guitar circus!

I was touring with The Great Guitars when Barney's divorce from his third wife came through. When he got the news, he was feeling very down and sorry for himself and came up to me and took off his wedding ring and said, "My divorce has come through – you can have this ring if you want it." So he gave me the ring and I put it on, saying, "Oh, Barney – does this mean we're engaged?" which brightened him up a little and made him laugh – and I still have the ring.

I was in Seattle with Stephane in 1982 and his agent, Abby Hoffer, suggested that we went down to a jazz club called Jazz Alley. That night the jazz guitarist, Emily Remler, was playing and she and I got talking. She knew of me because we had both recorded albums for Concord Records.

She invited me back to the club the following night and we played a set together and it was really good, we had an instant rapport. So Abby said, "Right, you two should start working together..." and so for a few years in the early '80s, Emily and I toured the States as a guitar duo.

Once, Emily and I had a concert together in Virginia, which was the last date on that particular tour. Emily was already in Virginia but I was in Atlanta, Georgia, so I hired a car – one of those big old Lincolns – to drive up to the gig. I had only gone about five miles and I found myself driving through one of those one-street southern towns when, from nowhere, a pick-up truck came out from the other side of the road and hit the car side-on.

There was an almighty bang and I hit my head on the window and at the same time felt an incredible pain in my back. The two young guys in the pick-up truck had baseball caps on and looked like they belonged in *The Dukes Of Hazzard* – it was like being in a bizarre TV show. I guess the knock to my head had caused some sort of concussion and suddenly everything went hazy and I couldn't see properly. But things were set to become even more weird...

Some people came out and tried to get my car door open, but they couldn't because of the damage done by the truck. Eventually, they managed to get the passenger door open and I crawled out. The pain in my back between my shoulder blades was getting worse and I suppose that, having hit my head, I was feeling quite out of it. I staggered over to the side of the road and lay down by an old wooden shack. There was an old guy sitting on the porch in a rocking chair and, because I suppose the accident was probably the most exciting thing to happen in town for ages, he came down with his rocking chair and sat beside me where I was lying. He began to talk to me as I was drifting in and out of consciousness and, looking up, he started to look more and more like Jed Clampett from *The Beverly Hillbillies*.

Grandpa looked at me and said, "How ya doin', boy?" in this thick southern drawl. Things were already feeling quite surreal, but Grandpa told me that the police had arrived and when I saw them – two cops: one black, one white – it was Rod Steiger and Sidney Poitier. All of a sudden I'd left *The Beverly Hillbillies* and was in the middle of *In The Heat Of The Night*!

Things were starting to become a bit more lucid for me and I started to see the funny side of being surrounded by all these characters from TV. They told me that a woman who worked as a nurse was coming over to see me and I thought, "Good, I hope it's Elly May," but when I looked up I saw a big-toothed "horsey" woman. "Jesus, it's Mr Ed!" I screamed. I was in complete agony, but I couldn't stop myself from laughing out loud.

Just then, Jed said to me, "I guess they'll take you to the county hospital. I went in there for an operation and they've got some great pyjamas in there…" Then he added, "Yep, great pyjamas. In a couple of hours' time you're gonna be fartin' through silk, boy." I've never taken LSD but I would imagine a trip could be something like this. In my case, it was just concussion. The car never recovered but I did, although I occasionally have to see an osteopath even now.

I missed the last date of the tour with Emily. Of all the guitarists I've played with in a duo situation, Emily was the player I enjoyed working with the most. She was a great accompanist as well as a soloist and that isn't always the case. I've played with some great guitar players who tend to let the accompaniment sag a bit, but with Emily we complemented each other perfectly and swapped solos almost seamlessly.

She was also a very nice person – a lovely young woman. At the time we worked together she was married to the pianist Monty Alexander. It's no secret that Emily fought a battle against heroin addiction, which killed her in the end. I remember once, we were playing in San Francisco and she rang my hotel room and said, "Can I come and talk to you?" I could see that she was all shaky and didn't look well at all. She was sweating and shaking and she asked me, "Can you lend me 50 bucks and I'll send it to you?" She put me in a real dilemma because I knew that she wanted the money to go out and score some heroin and I knew there wasn't anything I could do. You can't wag a finger at someone in that condition and say,

"Naughty naughty, you shouldn't do that," because they have a real problem. So, on several occasions I lent her money and she always paid me back. It was a terrible shame and she fought hard against her addiction and a couple of times I thought she'd beaten it, but sadly it wasn't to be.

I was out in New Zealand on tour in 1990 and I met the pianist Brian Dee at Auckland airport. He told me that he'd seen Emily in Sydney and she'd sent her love and was looking forward to us playing together soon. I said that I'd give her a call as soon as I got back from the tour, but when I returned home there was a message on my answerphone from a friend in Maryland saying that Emily had died.

During the mid '80s I worked as a duo with the Irish guitarist, Louis Stewart. Louis is a great guitar player and we played a lot of gigs together, mostly in Ireland, and we managed to make one album together in Dublin called *Acoustic Duets*.

Louis has a wonderful dry wit. We were staying at a hotel once, enjoying a night off and consuming quite a lot of booze in the bar. The next morning, I managed to drag myself down to breakfast and was struggling away with the bacon and eggs with my head thumping away, feeling a little queasy, trying to keep the food down. Louis hadn't appeared, so I rang his room and asked him if he was coming down for breakfast, to which he replied in his wonderful Dublin accent, "Well, I'm no athlete, but I'll give it a try..."

# 13 Only The Best For You, Mr T

I came to London to work quite often and for a while there was this guy who was a retired policeman – I won't mention his name – who lived in a building just off Hyde Park and had a job as a professional bodyguard. There were a lot of members of Arab royalty who stayed in the building and I guess he was on call most of the time.

Anyway, the ex-policeman used to come and see me play when I was in London and, after a while, started driving me to wherever I was playing. When we arrived at the gig he would get my guitar and amp out, set everything up for me and go and get me a drink in the interval. At the end of the evening he would go and get the money from the club owner, pack all the stuff up and put it into the car. In just a short space of time, he got more and more enthusiastic about it. As I was walking on stage he would walk in front and push people away and wouldn't let anyone near me. It got to the point where, if anybody came up to ask me a question like, "What strings do you use?" he looked like he was about to karate chop them. Whenever I used to say to him, "Aren't you overdoing this a bit?" he'd say, "You deserve only the best Mr T." I'd tell him, "I'm not Sheikh Mohammed, you know, I'm a jazz guitarist and this is just a pub in south London!"

One night he was putting my guitar in the back of the car and I saw a gun in a holster under his jacket. I thought, "This is really taking things a bit too far," but when I mentioned it to him he said, "I always carry a gun – only the best for you." So I had to discourage him from actually coming on gigs, I wasn't convinced about his mental stability – although I'm quite proud to say that I'm probably the only jazz guitarist in the world who had his own armed bodyguard. One night, after a gig with Stephane, we went round to the Redan, a pub in Queensway run by John and Pauline Watkins which was where Diz Disley lived and where Stephane and I would often go for an "after hours" drink after gigs in London. I saw "my bodyguard" standing there next to this Arab gentleman who started talking to me about music and so on. My friend had obviously been assigned to watch over him so I didn't like to ask who he was, but I managed to ask the bodyguard. The Arab gentleman had been one of the top politicians in Iran – this was at the time when the Shah was ousted by Ayatollah Khomeni and so I had this feeling that any minute, guys with machine guns were going to burst through the doors and mow us down. It made me nervous so I made a quick exit.

In fact, I originally met the great French jazz guitarist, Bireli Lagrene, in the Redan. Whenever we were in London with Stephane, we used to stay at the Westland Hotel in Bayswater, which was just around the corner. I went into the pub one night to meet a French Gypsy violinist and he said, "You must hear my nephew play." I wasn't that enthusiastic but then this shy young lad picked up the guitar and played. I was spellbound. Bireli and I have played together a lot since and we are like brothers and I really believe that he is the greatest guitar player in the world.

In 1984, Stephane's UK manager, Ed Baxter, asked me if I would like to record an album of guitar solos that we could sell at concerts along with all the other Stephane Grappelli merchandise. I wasn't signed to a record company at the time, so we agreed to bring out a limited edition album – this was pre-CD days – and had 1,000 pressed. We went 50/50 on the deal and I recorded the album at REL Studio in Edinburgh in three hours. I decided to record tunes that had an association with Art Tatum and called the album A Tribute To Art Tatum, which I hope to reissue on CD soon.

Stephane liked to feature me on a solo tune at every concert and, over the years, that became a regular feature of our performances, along with him playing a medley of old tunes on the piano.

I was also featuring more and more of my solo playing at my own gigs with my band and that side of my playing started to develop and become more popular with the audiences. I would soon be plunged into an unexpected personal situation that would make me develop it even more.

On 13 March 1984, our second son Stewart was born at the Royal Maternity Hospital in Glasgow. Liz wanted to call him Martin but I thought it would be too confusing to have two of us in the house and so we used a name from my side of the family – my grandmother's maiden name. We gave him the middle name of Iain, which is Gaelic for John, after Liz's grandfather.

I'm often asked if we named our elder son, James, after the American singer/songwriter – James Taylor – and here's my chance to set the record straight. James was named after Liz's dad, Jimmy, and although his birth certificate has the formal name of James, we always called him "Jamie", which is the Lowland Scots version of James. However, when he was twelve, he came home from school and told us that, as of that moment, we weren't to call him Jamie any more because it was too young-sounding and so he's been known as James ever since.

Things are not simplified by the fact that my wife is Elizabeth Taylor and I have a cousin called Jimmy Stewart and another called Eddie Condon!

With the new arrival we moved out of our beloved wee cottage and bought a larger house in the same street. All was going well, I was working around four months a year with Stephane and the rest of the year doing my own thing – playing with my band, guesting with other bands, doing the occasional session work and radio broadcast and playing on other people's records.

Liz and I were very happy with our lives in the Scottish countryside with two young children, but then everything started to go horribly wrong. A fortune-teller had told Liz that I was about to go through the worst period of my life and would reach the rock bottom in about a year's time. We both laughed when she told me on the way to the airport, where I was flying out to meet Stephane for a month-long tour. There have been a number of women in my family over the years who used to go from door to door fortune telling, so as far as I was concerned it was all just a scam and not to be believed.

When I arrived at Gatwick airport I got a message from Ed Baxter to say that Stephane had suffered a heart attack in Paris and, although he would be fine, the tour was cancelled. I got on the next plane back to Scotland, disappointed but relieved that Stephane was going to be OK.

Over the following few weeks there seemed to be a strange knock-on effect where I had lots of work cancelled for one reason or another and I was looking at a completely empty diary. Stephane was making a good recovery but wouldn't be able to work for some time.

Around this time some of the major record companies had decided to try and "rock 'n' roll" the image of jazz by signing very young, promising musicians just out of college, put them into Armani suits and market jazz to a wider audience. The problem for me was that, at 30, I was too old to be considered one of the younger ones. I had been around for quite a long time, was reasonably well known and came with a history, which they didn't want. Young kids didn't come with any history and I guess were more of a blank canvas to work with.

I was also too young and hadn't been around long enough to be considered one of the older, established players. I was in limbo land and as a result I couldn't get any record company or management interested in me because of the "youth movement". I was out of work and heading for serious trouble and, to a certain extent, I just buried my head in the sand.

It was a real struggle. Debts were mounting up and I had a young family to support. I got more and more depressed, couldn't see any way out and, as far as I could tell, my career was over. I started selling my guitars to pay bills and began to feel like a total failure – I had failed as a musician and as a husband, father and provider.

I stopped playing completely and withdrew into myself more and more. I just couldn't see the point of anything and without an outlet to play music, something started to die within me.

One year after the fortune-teller's prophesy I realised that I'd sold all my guitars except the WG Barker that Ike had given me for my 21st birthday. I needed money to put food on the table, so I rang a friend of mine and he agreed to buy it from me for £1,000.

When I put the phone down I felt physically sick. I picked up the guitar and just stood there looking at it with tears streaming down my face. As I put the guitar into its case I remembered the thrill I had as a small boy when my dad took his Hofner out of the velvet-lined case for the first time. That was the beginning of my life, and now, as I was putting my most treasured guitar into the case, I felt like I was at the end of it. I closed the lid, went out to my car and put the guitar in the boot, started the car up and began to drive in the direction of my friend's house. I was selling my last guitar; once it had gone I wouldn't be a guitar player any more but maybe I could get a job somewhere doing something – I didn't care any more, I was beaten.

When I got to the bottom of the road I was about to turn right but hesitated for a minute and turned left instead. One of my favourite local places was about seven miles down the road at Loch Doon and I would go there often for the peace and quiet. I took the boys fishing there from time to time and we would have family picnics by the ruins of the loch's eleventh-century castle, too.

I drove slowly down the road, enjoying the scenery and finally parked my car by the loch and switched the engine off. There was total silence. I was looking out at the hills but they were all hazy because I was still crying. I thought, "If I attach a hose to the exhaust and feed it through the window this could all be over very quickly." That thought went through my mind in a split second and the shock of it was like a jolt of electricity. What on earth was I doing? How could things have come to this?

I jumped out of the car and ran down to the loch and washed my face in the water. My heart was thumping and I was shaking. I couldn't believe that I had actually considered taking my own life and I'd really scared myself. I took lots of deep breaths and went for a walk and when I got back to the car I took my guitar out of the boot and walked up to the ruined castle.

I took the guitar out of its case and started to play and I got completely lost in the music. I don't know how long I sat there playing but it started to get dark. I was able to lose myself in music's healing embrace, oblivious to the outside world and all my own troubles.

It's a very difficult thing to describe exactly what happens when I play. People ask me all the time and I think that this is probably the time to try and express it somehow.

Scottish Travellers have a word in the Cant language called Conyach which means "feeling". European Gypsies refer to it simply as Gypsy Spirit. It's very deep and is the very core of the Traveller people. It's something that goes back into the mists of time that has been carried in the genes through generations. It is passed on through the aural tradition where children are taught songs by their parents and learn to sing purely through the heart.

As I began to teach myself to play the guitar, with my father's guidance, I discovered at a very early age that when I sat playing, after a while the music would somehow envelop me, surrounding my whole body. I felt as if I was actually *inside* the music.

A strange thing would happen when I reached this state; I would feel an odd but pleasant heaviness around my body, like being wrapped inside a warm sponge. My tongue would swell up and strangest of all – my guitar would disappear! All that was left was music. No thought, no guitar – just

music, and it felt wonderful. The guitar was somehow able to transport me to a higher level and I have heard of religious people reaching this state through prayer or meditation: for me, though, it's through music.

It is very difficult to describe, it's very powerful, and even as I talk about it now the hairs start to stand up on the back of my neck. It's very powerful and deep. This is why I play music – this is the Conyach.

My relative, the ballad singer Sheila Stewart who gives workshops on Traveller songs, stories and culture, explained it to me like this:

"When I sing, I take the soul, mix it with the spirit and use it in my voice. I am not aware that I am singing, I *become* the song. I'm inside it. I use my heart and bypass my head and the Conyach is what it's all about, it's deep in the soul of the Traveller."

She went on to say something that I always like to quote: "Why the hell use your soul when you're dead when you can use it when you're alive!"

When I am on stage and everything is happening I get the Conyach. I am completely unaware that I am playing the guitar. My eyes close, the guitar vanishes. It's just the music.

It doesn't always happen though, and when it's not flowing I just feel like I'm standing in front of people holding a piece of wood in my hands. That's a horrible feeling because then I just have to shift into professional musician mode and deliver the goods, and that's a very unsatisfying experience for me.

On the rare occasions that I have taught at music schools I have a great problem because students tend to want an intellectual explanation for what I do. There isn't one. The intellect is the wrong tool for the job and it's of no use to you. To make music you must use your heart and miss out your head completely!

Back at Loch Doon on that dark day, I went back to the car feeling as if I had been cured of some terrible illness. I was still stoney broke and in debt up to my eyeballs, but once again my guitar had saved me and made me realise that there was a way out.

When I was a kid my mum would tell me off if she noticed I hadn't played the guitar for a while. She used to say, "God gave you the gift of music. You must use it or He will take it away." With my mum's words of wisdom ringing in my ears, I drove home.

Liz and the boys were back from Glasgow where they had been visiting her mother. When I walked in the door looking dishevelled, my eyes all

bloodshot, she said, "What on earth have you been up to?" All I could say was, "Oh, nothing much." Then I fell about laughing at my lame reply – I had just been through the most harrowing experience of my life and all I could say was, "Oh, nothing much." I gave Liz and the boys lots of kisses and cuddles then went to bed for two days, totally exhausted.

The first thing I did after I awoke from my sleeping marathon was phone my mum and dad. They had been living by the sea in Norfolk for a few years but were getting a little restless, so I said to my dad, "Why don't you and Mum move up here? If we sell our houses we'll have enough money between us to buy a big house in Ayr." They loved the idea, so we sold our houses and Mum and Dad moved up to Scotland.

We bought a large stone-built Victorian house at 6 Park Terrace, right by the seafront at Ayr. We had one of the few remaining houses in the street which hadn't been converted into flats and so there was plenty of room for all of us.

We had two enormous living rooms with high ceilings and fancy cornices and Italian marble fireplaces. There were four large bedrooms, a study, a TV room, two bathrooms, a big kitchen, a dining room and we even had our own bar with adjoining wine cellar.

With the sale of our previous house I had managed to pay off all my debts and put the remaining money into the new house. Dad put his money in and I took care of the relatively small mortgage payments while Mum and Dad lived rent- and bill-free. It was a good set-up.

Now all I had to do was start working again. I set up a desk and a phone in the study and rang everybody I knew. I was so amazed by the response; a lot of people had stopped calling me because they thought I was far too busy and successful jetting all around the world, playing big concerts. So, while I had been to hell and back over the last year or so, they thought I was in America, only returning to Europe occasionally to deposit large amounts of money into Swiss bank accounts. It's a good job I've got a sense of humour.

# 14 Ladies And Gentlemen, Martin Taylor

Since my guitar had saved my life I hadn't been able to put it down and was playing it constantly. I hadn't touched a guitar for over a year, but apart from sore fingers I was playing well and learning new things. I didn't go out that much and so all of my playing was just me on my own and I was really starting to develop my ideas and adopting a solo style.

One day I got a call from a friend of mine called Barry Storey, who, with his wife Sue, promoted jazz in Lincoln. Barry is a marvellous furniture-maker and Sue is an osteopath – who just so happens to be one of the best photographers of jazz musicians in the world – the North Sea Jazz Festival in Holland use all her photos in their festival programmes. They are two of my greatest friends who have supported jazz musicians for years.

Barry asked me if I would like to play a solo concert in Lincoln. I wasn't sure at first. I knew I could play for two hours on my own but I wasn't confident that anyone would want to actually listen for that length of time. He offered me quite a bit of money – something that I hadn't seen very much of recently – so I said yes and looked forward to playing in public again and reuniting myself with some much-needed cash.

I practised like mad for the gig and I drove to Lincoln on the day feeling very nervous. I'd been through a bad time, I'd only just started playing again and wasn't exactly brimming with confidence. I ran through the gig in my mind several times during the journey and prayed that all would go well.

I did a soundcheck in the afternoon and then went to Barry and Sue's house. Sue had prepared a meal for me, but I couldn't eat because my stomach was in knots. I'd never been nervous about playing before, but this was a big one – it was either going to be my comeback or the final humiliation. I drank a couple of large whiskies and felt a bit better.

When I went back to the gig I could see the car park was full, and many people had parked their cars along the street because there wasn't any room. Inside I saw a sight that really turned my stomach over; the place was jam packed with people. There was a tremendous atmosphere of excitement and anticipation and then I saw the most horrifying sight of all – the stage! It had a bar stool with one spotlight on it and, if I could have turned around and run away, I would have done – you wouldn't have seen me for dust.

I downed another large whisky but all it did was dry my mouth up even more, so I drank a pint of beer, followed by another. By the time I started walking up to the stage I'd had three huge whiskies and two pints of beer, but I was still frighteningly sober. I looked out at all these people and thought, "If I mess this up we'll have to give them their money back and send them home" – I had to get it right.

I heard someone announce on the mike, "And now the man you've all been waiting to see – MARTIN TAYLOR!" and a huge cheer rang out. I looked out and saw all these people cheering and clapping, with big smiles on their faces. The first thought that came to mind was, "Oh shit!" but I managed to go up to the mike and say, "It's really nice to be back, thank you for coming along to hear me tonight."

Once I started playing I was away. I can't remember what I played but at the end of the first tune the audience were clapping really enthusiastically and I thought, "That's it – I think I can probably get away with this. All I need to do is keep it going for two one-hour sets and I'll survive it."

At the end of the first set I walked off the stage feeling elated. I went to the dressing room and had another large whisky. This time though it didn't dry up my mouth but gave me a fantastic warm glow. I felt good.

There were more cheers and clapping when I went on to start the second half. I started playing, and again I was away. That moment was back – the guitar had done its vanishing act again and I was right in the middle of the music. I was in heaven, playing music for people with a nice little whisky glow going on in my stomach.

Halfway through the second set I realised that I'd run out of material so I asked the audience if they had any requests. People started shouting out their favourite tunes and I just strung together as many of them as I could remember into a long medley and they loved it. They even liked it when I got things wrong!

After two encores I walked off stage feeling like I'd been reborn. I cannot describe in words how I felt but I had proved to myself that not only could I still play, but that I could play completely on my own and entertain people. That dark day up at Loch Doon started to become a vague memory. It was a tremendous feeling – I wasn't a useless failure after all.

When I got back home I told Liz and my mum and dad how fantastic it had been, and how this meant that I could start working solo. I was sure there must be lots of work – most people like the guitar and I was sure that I could expand my audience.

I got on the phone again and rang around a lot of the jazz festival organisers and bigger promoters that I knew and tried to sell the idea of me playing solo. They didn't want to know.

They all said the same thing: "Who wants to hear a guitarist playing on his own?" I thought, "Here we go again." When I told people as a kid that I wanted to be a professional musician they all said, "Can't be done." When I did become a professional musician then decided to play jazz exclusively, people lined up to tell me it was impossible. Now that I'd made my mind up to go the solo route everyone was telling me I couldn't do it all over again. These are the same people that now tell me how lucky I am to be doing my own thing. Luck has nothing to do with it.

I didn't have a manager, although Ed Baxter had helped me out a few times, so I had to do all the work myself. I decided the only way forward was to go back to the grass roots and slowly work my way up again. By this time I had played some of the most prestigious venues in the world, I had made critically-acclaimed records, appeared on many TV shows in America and Europe, and been a key figure in Stephane Grappelli's career, but I decided to concentrate initially on the small UK jazz club circuit.

Throughout all of jazz's difficult times, there have been enthusiasts running little jazz clubs for no financial gain up and down the country, in hotel function suites and rooms at the back of pubs, just keeping the music alive. It's very fashionable just now to make fun of these people as being bearded guys in sandals and anoraks, but these are the people who have always supported the music and kept it going. Without them it would have died long ago.

When some of the record companies and media decided to try and make jazz sexy in the '80s, they overlooked one important fact: jazz fans are very knowledgeable, they know if someone is good or not, and for a jazz musician to stay the course and win respect they've got to be good. The fans know their stuff. They have a true love for the music and the musicians, and you can't fool them. So I am very defensive of jazz enthusiasts, they kept the music alive – and in my case, came to the rescue.

I'd played some of these small venues in the '70s so spent hours in my study, on the phone, going through old address books and looking these people up. Basically I just offered myself as a solo artist for whatever they could afford. I would establish how much they could charge for a ticket and how many people the venue could hold, and from that I would quote a small guarantee of say £100 against 75% of ticket sales. That way I made money and they made money to put in the kitty and help pay to bring other musicians to their clubs. They all jumped at it. The jazz fans were really happy that they could come and see me play in an intimate setting, and even stand up at the bar and have a beer and a chat with me afterwards. I built up a mailing list and my dad sent out regular newsletters telling people where I was playing. Everywhere I played was packed and gradually the venues started to get bigger because of public demand. I was starting to get back on my feet again.

Even with my abysmal mathematical skills I realised that if I got 75% of 300 tickets at £10 a time, I was going to have a fairly good pay day. Multiply that by 150 solo gigs a year and I could definitely afford to buy myself some silk pyjamas! Things went from strength to strength.

From the clubs I moved on to playing arts centres and small theatres. My solo playing was attracting a wider audience and I was being asked to play at classical music events where I played music from the great American songbook. I was getting a lot of interest from guitar fans and players from other forms of music including classical, folk and rock.

Even some of the promoters who had told me, "Who wants to hear a guitarist playing on his own?" came to me with their tails between their legs to book me. I always added a few hundred pounds onto my fee for them, naturally…

In 1988 my accountant, Derek Hall of WD Hall in Glasgow, came to me and said, "I've been looking at your recent income. What's going on?" I said, "I know, it's good isn't it?" He said it was great, but I'd better register for VAT quick. We were only a few months into the year and I was just about at the threshold, so I registered for VAT and, a little later, Liz and I became a limited company and formed Martin Taylor (Music) Ltd. We were back on our feet…and then some.

During the early years of my solo career I travelled on my own. Liz had to

Playing with Stephane Grappelli in Huntingdon Beach, California, 1980 with the guitar that later saved my life

With Stephane, San Francisco, 1981

With Tal Farlow in Scotland in 1985. I'd more or less stopped playing by this time, but Tal asked me to play a few tunes with him

Charleston, USA, 1983. L-r: Patrice Caratini, Stephane, Martin, Marc Fosset

Backstage at the Wolf Trap Centre For The Performing Arts in Vienna, Virginia, during a special Bastille Day concert. L-r: Martin Taylor, Yehudi Menuhin, Jon Burr, Lady Menuhin, Stephane Grappelli, Michel Chaunard, Philipe Catherine

Rehearsing for our *Reunion* album in Stephane's apartment in Cannes

Receiving the Music Retailers' Association award for Best Jazz Album for *Groovin'*, by The Buddy De Franco/Martin Taylor Quintet at the Café Royal, London, 1986, along with Alistair Robertson of Hep Records. Presented by former British prime minister Sir Edward Heath

Back playing with my good friend Barney Kessel, 1987

The Buddy De Franco/Martin Taylor Quintet at London's 100 Club, with Peter Ind on bass

Recording with Chet Atkins in Nashville, 1987

France in the late '80s with Dutch bass player Jack Sewing

With Charlie Byrd and Barney Kessel on the 'Great Guitars' tour, 1989. I took Herb Ellis's place when he left to rejoin Oscar Peterson

Touring with Gordon Giltrap in 1991

Samois Sur Seine, France, outside the caravan with Django Reinhardt's sister, Victoria, his niece, Nanine, and his granddaughter

At the 1991 Django Reinhardt Festival at Samois Sur Seine, France with Django's son, Babik

In the studio with Steve Howe in 1993. Steve produced my solo album, *Artistry*

The last picture taken with my father, just six months before he died. He didn't like having his picture taken, but I managed to persuade him on this occasion

With my dear friend, Ike Isaacs, in 1993 – the guitarist who has been my biggest
influence

With my two boys, Stewart and James, 1993

A double-bill concert with Joe Pass at the London Jazz Festival, 1993

Out on my own. (Picture courtesy of Alistair Mulhearn)

At home on the farm in Scotland with Dudley

look after the boys at home so she rarely came with me. These days I have two tour managers: Dave Bellwood travels with me with Spirit Of Django and works as my sound engineer; and Marcus Ford is my tour manager for all my solo work. Both Dave and Marcus are excellent guitar players themselves and we get on well together.

It never bothered me to travel on my own at first, but these days I really don't like it. Now that the boys are grown up, though, Liz travels with me more. She gets my stage clothes together for me which is a big help as I am hopelessly colour-blind and get it all wrong if she's not about. For instance, I was playing a solo concert in Newcastle and during the day I went out to buy a jacket to wear on stage that evening. It wasn't until I got into the dressing room that I began to have second thoughts about the jacket, maybe it was a little too loud for a quiet intimate solo performance. In the end I decided to keep it on and went out on stage to begin playing. Then the doubts returned and I began to feel quite embarrassed about my dress sense and felt I had to mention it to the audience somehow by way of apology. So I said, "I'm going to play a tune called 'I'm Old-Fashioned' and you can tell how old-fashioned I am just by looking at this jacket." Immediately a guy down the front yelled back, in a broad Geordie accent, "It's no worse than your trousers..." So much for fashion.

People don't realise that being on the road is actually very hard work. I have to get up very early to travel to the next gig, check in to the hotel, grab something to eat, soundcheck and then actually do the show. The next day I have to do it all again and so it's usually an 18- or 20-hour day. On top of that I have to do a lot of radio and press interviews to promote the concerts, which takes up a lot of time. Some musicians can't handle it but I enjoy it.

One of the things which helps considerably is the fact that I enjoy long drives. I can drive all day long and then play a gig in the evening with no trouble at all. I find driving relaxing and have some of my best ideas in the car. I rarely listen to music on the road, I just do all my thinking and planning while all the scenery whizzes by.

Sometimes, though, I can get a little stir crazy alone in my car. I tend to talk to myself a lot, which Liz says she finds a bit worrying. I once told myself a joke when I was driving along on my own. It was so funny I had to pull over, get out of the car and was howling with laughter in a service station car park, while a group of Japanese tourists looked on in complete bewilderment. Just as I gained control of myself again and was making my way back to the car, wiping the tears from my eyes, it struck me that I'd never heard the joke before and had just made it up. Now that's a weird one, isn't it? The thought of that sent me into even more fits of side-splitting laughter and the Japanese tourists were quickly ushered back onto the bus by their guide.

I rang Liz up and said, "The funniest thing has just happened. I've just told myself a joke I've never heard before. Isn't that the funniest thing?"

"No, you're just daft," was her down-to-earth Scottish reply.

"I went to England once – and it was shut." So goes the old vaudeville joke. But for travelling musicians England does always seem to be shut. Hotels seem to serve breakfast before the sun's even up, restaurants only open during concert hours, and the pubs close five minutes before you get out of the gig. This forces you to go back to the hotel where a female member of staff, chewing on gum, stands by the bar waiting for any stray musicians to come in so that she can pull down the bar shutters and declare with a smile on her face, "The bar's shut, love."

The only hope now is the night porter. In England night porters always have their own supply of whisky, gin and vodka miniatures, along with lemonade, cola and cans of horrible, warm fizzy beer. It's their own little sideline to make a bit of extra money for themselves. They buy their supplies from the local cash and carry store at wholesale prices and hope that some musicians will come back to the hotel after playing a gig and be so desperate for a drink that they are willing to pay five times pub prices for a can of warm beer.

The night porter also always says, "The chef's gone 'ome but I can make you some sandwiches," as he hands you a list of "Various Sandwiches" with his nicotine-stained fingers. No thanks.

It's not as bad as it used to be, but there was one particular occasion when I would have embraced an English hotel night porter and handed over all my cash – it was also an incident which demonstrates the great British reserve.

I was playing a solo concert in the south-west of England. I'd driven all day to get there and was running a bit late so I decided to go straight to the venue rather than go to the hotel first. I like to check out the hotels first because I'm very fussy about where I stay. When you spend as much time on the road as I do, you need to stay in hotels that are at least as good as home and I've refused to stay in quite a lot of places over the years.

I went straight to the venue and played the gig. At the end of the show I was asked to sign some autographs and so I went out to the foyer and a group of people met me with CDs and programmes. There was one elderly gentleman who was hovering nearby and, as I was about to have my photograph taken with a group of people, he put something in my jacket pocket and said, "Here's a little present for you, Martin."

I didn't think any more of it and went back to the hotel – well actually, it wasn't a hotel, it was more like an old-fashioned boarding house but there was nothing I could do – I had to stay there. The theatre manager had given me the key so I let myself in, went up to my room and switched on the light. There was no lamp shade, just a bare bulb, and it was one of those low-wattage bulbs that seem to make the room darker when you switch them on.

I'd had a good gig and was still buzzing so I knew it would be at least another hour before I would come down enough to sleep. There was no bar, no night porter – nothing. I'd forgotten to bring a book to read and there wasn't a TV in the room. I got undressed and lay on the bed, staring at this sad, yellow light bulb. "This is desperate," I told myself.

Then I looked over at my jacket hanging up and wondered what that old boy had given me. I got up, put my hand in my pocket and pulled out the biggest joint I've ever seen. Initially I was quite annoyed – what if I'd left for Singapore the next day? I'd have been executed by the following Wednesday.

Then it struck me as amusing that this frail, innocent-looking old feller was a pot-head. I hadn't smoked pot since the QE2 and it's something I have absolutely no interest in, but I remembered that in the days when I did smoke it, once the wave of paranoia had subsided it always sent me to sleep. So I thought, "Well, if I have just a couple of puffs it will send me to sleep and I can leave this wretched place first thing in the morning."

I'd become used to staying in American hotels where they've got free matchbooks in your room in an ashtray by the bed. On long tours of the States, those matchbooks are sometimes the only way I know what city I'm in when I wake up in the morning, because they always have the hotel logo and address printed on them. I look over from my pillow and see "Holiday Inn, San Diego" or something and it's very reassuring. I usually make sure there's a matchbook on my bedside table when I go to bed – it's quicker than wandering around trying to find out where I am from bemused hotel staff the following morning.

Back in that miserable boarding house, I remembered that I usually kept a book of matches in my guitar case even though I don't smoke. I opened the case but there were none. So there I am, in my underpants, it's midnight and England is closed. I'm going off my head because I've got nothing to do, and all of a sudden, finding a way to light this joint becomes the most important thing in the world.

I put my clothes back on and made my way down the creaky old stairs to the breakfast room. There was no sign of life – in fact it made me realise what it must have been like when they found the Marie Celeste. It was dark, and nobody was about. I looked everywhere, but no matches. Now I've *got* to get this joint lit, and the absurd thing about it is, I don't even smoke! But because I couldn't have it, I *had* to have it – it had become a challenge.

I went back up to my room and got undressed again and sat on the side of the bed. I was getting desperate, and like a total idiot I removed the lampshade from the bedside light to see if I could get enough heat off the bulb, but it was another one of those "dark" 20-watt jobs. Then I noticed a tea- and coffee-making tray in the corner with a big jug kettle, so I got up and poured the water from the kettle down the sink. I figured that I could probably get enough heat from the element to get a light. To stop the element cutting out automatically I had to keep my thumb pressed on the "on" button, which was getting hotter and hotter by the minute and starting to burn my valuable "bass line" thumb.

The element started to glow red hot and the whole kettle started to heat up, so I put the spliff in my mouth and stuck my head in the kettle and made contact with the now white hot element. Finally it lit. Flushed with success and a boiling hot kettle in my face, I sat back, and through a haze of marijuana smoke I noticed a man in a tuxedo and a woman in a long evening gown, standing at my bedroom doorway, watching me. They looked like they had probably been to the local Hunt Ball and had walked into my room by mistake – only to be confronted by a man in his underpants with his head stuck in a smoking kettle. There was dead silence for what seemed like ages then I muttered the only words to come into my head: "I've got asthma…" The man said, "Terribly sorry, old chap," like a true upper-class Englishman, then they left. I never did smoke the joint, which was probably just as well because I don't like the stuff anyway. The point was that I had *succeeded*.

I sat opposite my well-dressed visitors at breakfast the next morning and they made polite conversation about the weather, and would I like more marmalade, etc. They never mentioned the kettle incident. The British can be so polite.

# 15 Notes On Tour

Over the years, I've collected many stories from other musicians which draw a pretty accurate picture of what it's like to be involved in the professional music scene. One of my favourites comes from Bert Weedon, who is a good friend of mine and the man who is responsible for starting the careers of many guitarists through his famous tutor, *Play In A Day*.

Bert was doing a summer season in Blackpool at the theatre at the end of the pier. His cabaret act included playing songs from the shows in his inimitable style, plus a couple of his own hits, including 'Guitar Boogie'. Bert would be on stage playing guitar, accompanied by an orchestra in the pit. There were a lot of young musicians in the orchestra who were studying jazz at Leeds College of Music, and Bert got to know a few of them particularly well. He used to talk quite regularly before the shows to the guitarist, chatting about guitars and different players and, at the end of the season, there was a party for all the acts.

Everyone was there: the comedian, the girl dancers, jugglers, and the guys from the orchestra too. The wine was flowing and the young guitarist had knocked a fair bit back. He went over to Bert and put his arm around him and said, "Oh Bert, I love you man…You've been like a father to me during the season," and Bert was obviously quite touched by all this, and perhaps a little embarrassed, too. The guitarist continued, "There's a question I just gotta ask, man…" and Bert said, "Oh yes, what's that?" He was thinking that it might concern some area of playing, but to his surprise the guitarist said, "Why do you play such a load of crap?"

Bert was quite indignant and so he said, "I'll tell you what, I'll give you a guitar lesson completely free of charge. When I'm playing up on stage, I play the melody on single strings, don't I?" The guitarist nodded. "You're down there in the pit, playing chords, and so you're playing six strings at a time, yes?" Once again, the young guitarist nodded and Bert said, "Well then, you're playing six times as much crap as I am…"

I think that's a great story because you often hear musicians moaning that certain gigs are beneath them in some way, and Bert came out with the perfect riposte. Apparently the young guitarist took it very humbly and I bet it was something that stuck with him for ages.

The great jazz guitarist, Herb Ellis, told me a story about a punk guitarist backstage at the Royal Albert Hall who was trying to tune his guitar. He'd been at it for ages before one of the stage hands went up to him and said, "I've been watching you try to tune that thing for the last 45 minutes. We had Andrés Segovia here last week and he tuned his guitar up in about two minutes." The punk guitarist didn't bat an eyelid and said, "Yeah? Well, maybe 'e don't give a shit."

## Hotels

When a promoter books you to play on a tour, whatever country it is, there are things that you can guarantee are going to happen. First of all, someone from the promoter's office will always pick you up from the airport, but they're always far too busy to drive you back at the end of the trip. It happens nine times out of ten, you can put money on it.

The other thing that happens is that the tour promoter will get some good deals on hotels and, in general, you get to stay in some very nice places. It's an important thing when you're on the road; a hotel is a home from home and it's the one thing I tend to kick up a fuss about. But whenever there's a night off on tour, you can bet that you'll have been booked into somewhere relatively cheap, because you're not making any money for the promoter that night.

Your day off is the one time that you actually get to make use of facilities like a swimming pool or a decent restaurant, and yet it's always the time when you're booked into some hell hole miles from anywhere.

There are a few exceptions to this rule, though. I was on tour in Australia and I had a night off in Adelaide. I was expecting the worst, but to my surprise I found I was booked into the best hotel in town. It had a renowned restaurant, a swimming pool, a leisure centre and was absolutely fantastic. So I was just getting settled in and murmuring words of disbelief, thanks and praise to the promoter responsible for booking me in, when the phone rang. I picked it up and a guy with a Scottish accent said, "Is that Bill Taylor's boy?" and I said, "Yes, it is." "Well, I thought you'd like to hear a voice from Scotland." I said, "That's great – who is it?" and it turned out that it was a guy who used to play with my dad years before and who had emigrated to Australia.

We chatted for a while and then he said, "Well, no boy of Bill Taylor's is going to stay in a hotel. Pack your suitcase and be outside in 15 minutes, I'm coming round with the car. We'll put you up in a proper bed and my wife'll cook some good old Scottish mince and tatties for yae."

I thought, "Oh, no…" I'd booked a table in the hotel's splendid restaurant, I'd got in mind what I was going to order and which wine I was going to have and everything. I'd really got my night off planned and so, thinking on my feet I said, "Actually we've got a rehearsal – I'm on call and so I'll have to stay here." He was adamant and I ended up being quite forceful, but there was no way I was going to be dragged away from all that luxury!

Once, in Aberdeen, the promoters had booked us into a hotel which we didn't check in to until after we'd finished the gig. After the show we all went back there at about one am and sat up talking and having a few drinks until around three. About six-thirty the following morning we were all woken up by this ferocious lady hotelier who was walking along the hotel corridors, ringing a hand bell. It turned out that this was a hotel specifically for truckers and everyone was expected to be up, breakfasted and on their way by seven. Sure enough, by seven o'clock we were all out on the street just as Aberdeen was waking up. Fortunately I haven't experienced a lot of that kind of thing.

Strange things happen when you're stopping in hotels every night. Once I was on a solo tour in the States and I was staying in a motel in Iowa. The room had two doors, one of which went to the outside area where you parked your car, and the other led into the main motel building.

I came back from the gig, parked the car right outside my room and went in to bed as normal. In the early hours of the morning I was woken up by a terrible crash and opened my eyes to see that both doors had been knocked in and that my bed was surrounded by about a dozen of the biggest American cops I'd ever seen in my life. Oh, and they all had machine guns and none of them were smiling.

One of them shouted, "Don't move!" but there was really no need – I wasn't even going to twitch under the circumstances. Someone turned on a light and asked me my name and so, fearing that someone locally might have a serious dislike for jazz and I was going to end up on death row, I gave them my details. To my complete surprise they all turned round and started to wander off, with someone muttering, "Oh, right. OK then…" I asked one of them what was going on and he told me that a murderer had escaped from the local penitentiary and had sworn that he was going to kill his girlfriend. Apparently I was in the room that they had once stayed in together and I fitted his description physically. They also thought Taylor was a pseudonym, like booking in and signing your name "Smith". The management were very sympathetic – I mean, it's probably the sort of thing that happens all the time – and put me in another room and I spent the rest of the night listening for sirens.

Another time I was touring in the mid-west and couldn't get a hotel anywhere. In the end the only place I could find with any rooms was what they call in America an "adult motel". This is a place where men take their mistresses, the rooms have satellite TV with a porn channel and are decorated so that they fall well into the sleazy side of good taste.

The bed had a leopard-skin bedspread and water beds were available at no extra charge. You get the idea – well, perhaps you do. So I checked in, grateful to find somewhere at last that could offer me a bed for the night and probably the only person in the history of American adult hotels to check in on his own.

After the gig I got into bed and noticed that there was a slot machine right at the side. In the end my curiosity got the better of me and I put a quarter in the slot. The bed immediately started moving with a wave-like motion, up and down, and I lay there for a while thinking it was quite funny and wondering to what possible practical use such a machine could be put to. I thought, too, that it would probably stop moving any second, but it didn't. It just carried on and after about half an hour I couldn't take any more and so I took all the covers from the bed and slept on the floor. When I woke up in the morning it was still going strong and so I just checked out and drove on to the next gig. It was certainly one of the strangest nights I've ever spent anywhere.

I think I've experienced just about every level of hotel service during my years on the road and the star rating of an establishment isn't always a good indication of the quality of service you can expect to receive. Some people who work in hotels just shouldn't be there because they don't seem to want to serve you at all, despite being in what is predominantly a service industry.

I was playing at the Edinburgh Festival, staying at a hotel with Jack Parnell and we were a little late down for breakfast. The girl serving obviously wanted to be on her way and was going to make sure that we were in and out in the shortest possible time. She kept glancing at her watch and, when I asked if I could have some more toast, she huffed and puffed her way back to the kitchen with a very disobliging air. When she brought the toast, Jack asked her if he could have another cup of tea. This was obviously a bridge too far and so she said, "Sorry, the kettle's off," and turned heel and sloped off back to the safety of the kitchen's inner sanctum.

## Jack Emblow

Jack Emblow and I have played together quite a lot and once we went over to Shetland, which is an incredible place where everybody plays music.

We were playing at the Shetland Hotel in Lerwick and so we met up there before the gig to decide what we were going to play. We were walking down a corridor and a guy came out of the toilet who I can only describe as the world's most drunken man. He was bouncing off the walls, heading towards the place where we were going to be playing, and all of a sudden he just dropped to the floor, no longer able to stand up. Jack and I rushed to his aid and tried to get him back on his feet and when he saw who we were he said to us, "I've come a long way to see you two, you'd better be good..." which I thought was a bit rich coming from a man who couldn't even stand up!

One of Jack's hobbies is making radio-controlled model aircraft. Some of them are huge and he generally flies them from the back of his house in Amersham, where he has about five acres of land. He made one aircraft which took him ages and he was really proud of it as he took it outside for its maiden flight. He launched the plane and it did a couple of laps around his property before setting off further afield, down towards a windmill which was due north of his house and a little further up the road.

When the plane reached the windmill, Jack decided that it had gone far enough and tried to bring it back, but didn't realise that it had gone out of range of the remote control. He raced after it, but the plane just went on heading north and soon vanished, never to be found, despite Jack's efforts later on with an Ordnance Survey map. Somebody told me the story about the runaway plane and the next time I saw Jack I said to him, "That was terrible about Lincoln Cathedral, wasn't it?" Jack comes from Lincoln and so took immediate interest and said, "What's that?" I said, "Well, nobody knows what happened, but apparently a radio-controlled plane went straight through the south window and smashed it to pieces." Jack went as white as a ghost, thinking it was his plane that had done the damage.

Jack's a very dedicated musician and an incredible sight-reader. Once, he was asked to play for a ballet where the music was by the Argentinian accordionist and composer Astor Piazzola. The score was very complicated and not only did Jack have to play, but he'd been asked to conduct the orchestra as well. When Jack got hold of a copy of the score a couple of weeks before the ballet was to be performed, he went over it and thought to himself, "I wonder how much I'll be able to drink before this gig?" So he went off down the pub and had a couple of pints, came home and ran through the score without any problem at all. So he thought, "Fine – I can have a couple of pints before the show."

The next night, he went to the pub again and had three pints, came home and got his accordion out and found that he couldn't play the score. He knew therefore that this was a "two pint gig" in that he could drink only two pints before going on to play the ballet. Now, that's dedication for you.

Jack was also called upon to play some music written by the American composer Charles Ives. It was a modern orchestral piece and quite "way out". It was to be conducted by the legendary Leopold Stokowski and recorded for BBC Radio 3. Jack's part was quite complicated and difficult to read, but the rehearsal went well, with him keeping a careful eye on Stokowski's conducting. However, when it came to the evening performance, Stokowski became more animated and flamboyant in front of all his fans in the audience and Jack didn't know where he was supposed to be coming in or anything. So he just guessed it, every so often playing a little bit of the part in the wrong place – and yet that evening's performance received fantastic reviews in the press.

Jack used to play with a trumpet player called John McLevy who came from Dundee. In his day, John was a bit of a boy wonder, having worked with George Elrick's band at the age of twelve. George was a very famous bandleader and so it was a remarkable achievement for John.

The first time I became aware of him was on an album that my dad had of Benny Goodman playing live in Stockholm. He played with Benny for a number of years in The European Orchestra and on my dad's album John plays a great version of 'Baubles, Bangles And Beads' with a very distinctive touch and tone. He's one of those players who it's possible to identify from just hearing a single note.

John had a tendency to start every conversation with the line, "I remember when I was working for Benny Goodman..." and also had the uncanny knack of turning any conversation around to the subject of his time with Benny. One day, Jack and John were in the car together and John said, "I remember when I was working for Benny Goodman..." and Jack interrupted him and said, "I've heard it." But John said, "You haven't heard this one because I've only just made it up!"

Another time, John was playing at the Black Bull in Milngavie, just outside Glasgow. The pub is well known as a very good jazz venue for visiting musicians, having a great rhythm section, and was run for a number of years by the drummer Ken Matheson. One night, John was due to play at the venue and before he came on, Ken primed the audience so that when John said, "I remember when I was working for Benny Goodman..." they were all to pretend to fall asleep like they were in some sort of hypnotic trance. So John took the stage and it wasn't long before he came out with the phrase. Immediately all the audience slumped in their seats and even the barman hung over his pumps, leaving John wondering what on earth was going on.

Once a year, Jack and John would tour together, starting off in London and finishing up in Scotland, and they would play with local rhythm sections all the way. This can be a particularly perilous thing to do because you never know who's going to be in the band or the overall quality of musicians you're going to be playing with. For these trips John would always carry a half-bottle of whisky in his trumpet case which he called "The Lifeboat" because it was only launched in emergencies, like when they stayed in a bed and breakfast and couldn't get a drink after a gig.

Once, in Scotland, John was sitting on the bed with his trumpet case, while Jack was shaving in the bathroom, when there was a knock on the door. In came a very loud, boisterous character who introduced himself as that night's drummer. He said, "Oh, I'm looking forward to playing with you lads tonight. I like playing jazz. It's a good job you've got me, because all the drummers in Scotland just tickle the drums but I like to get ma heed doon and gi' it laldy," the latter being a Scottish expression for really going for it.

At that point Jack caught John's eye in the shaving mirror and, without a word being said between the two of them, he got two glasses from the shelf over the sink and John opened The Lifeboat. They knew they were in for a long night.

Trumpet players are a funny breed. Tommy McQuater, who was with a band called The Squadronaires along with George Chisholm during the war, and John McLevy both had false teeth – in fact they both had two sets apiece, one for playing and one for eating and laughing. To a trumpet player, both teeth and lips play a vital role in being able to play. The trumpet is a very physical instrument in that respect and it's a real tragedy for a player if his teeth go – hence the special sets John and Tommy kept in their trumpet cases.

Once, they were on a session together and accidentally picked up the wrong instrument cases and went home with each other's trumpet. Tommy realised the mistake when he got home and phoned John up and said, "Have you opened your trumpet case yet?" and John replied, "Yeah – and you know what? I've tried playing with your teeth in and I can't get a note out of it!"

# Ireland

I love playing in Ireland and try to go over there whenever I can just to soak up the atmosphere. It's a beautiful country and I have many friends there. I met a guy there once called Gerry Drew whose brother, Ronnie, is in The Dubliners. Gerry was in New York once, down on the subway late at night, and was accosted by a pair of guys who were set on mugging him. They said, "Give us your money," and Gerry said, in his wonderful laid-back Irish way, "Now hang on, lads, hang on. Now tell me, just what is it exactly that you're wanting?" The two thugs had never encountered anything like this before, their victims normally just handing over their money with the absolute minimum of protest. So they said, "We want your money – now!" So Gerry said, "OK, look I'll tell you what, let's see what I've got in me pocket," and he put his hand into his pocket and drew out about $12 in change. "Right lads, I've got $12 and so if I give you both $5 each, that leaves me with $2. Now you've got more money than I have so fuck off!" and they ran away.

Another story features Jack Emblow once again. Jack was in Ireland, playing the Cork Jazz Festival and he decided that he'd like to go to Blarney Castle while he was over there. So he got on a coach and went up to the castle and, of course, the thing you do while you're there is kiss the Blarney Stone. So Jack went and lined up and when it was his turn, he knelt down, leant back as a guy held his legs, kissed the stone, and when he came back up again, there was a photographer taking photographs. The idea was that he took your photograph, you give him your name and address and he sends you a picture a couple of weeks later. So Jack paid his punt (an Irish pound) returned home and nothing happened – no photograph appeared. About a month later, a letter arrived for Jack from Ireland which contained a picture of somebody else and an accompanying letter. Jack read the letter, which went something like this:

Dear Mr Emblow

Unfortunately I had a little accident in the dark room while developing your picture and I'm afraid it didn't come out. However, I remember very well what you looked like and I think this man looks very like you.

The photographer had also enclosed a postal order for one Punt – made out to himself. These things can only happen in Ireland.

I went over to Belfast to do *The Val Doonican Show* which celebrated Val's 50 years in the business. It was quite a big production with a full orchestra and everything, and I was the only guest that Val had on. I told the jumper story and played a tune with Val, remembering the times I spent as a kid staring at the album cover.

On that occasion, I actually went over to Ireland a couple of days earlier with my son James and a friend of his. I had my mandolin with me, James had his bodhran, which is a traditional Irish drum, and his friend had a guitar. We went into Donegal town, checked into a hotel and went out looking for music. Ireland is such a wonderful place, you can just go into any bar and ask where the music is happening and you'll find these places where there are a few people in there playing traditional music. So we found ourselves in a pub where we played a few tunes and the landlady brought us over a tray of drinks and we stayed there all night drinking for nothing.

The next day I did the TV show which achieved huge ratings. It seems like most of Ireland were watching their favourite son that night and so there must have been quite a few people wondering if it was me that they'd seen playing mandolin in a local bar the night previously.

# Ronnie Scott

I've played at Ronnie Scott's famous jazz club in London's Soho quite often. The first time I went there was when I was working with The Tony Lee Trio, supporting Stan Getz. Then I did another week supporting Dexter Gordon. Later on, in the '90s, I played there a few times solo and also with Spirit Of Django.

My old friend, Louis Stewart, who played in Ronnie's band, told me that Ronnie was a big guitar fan. Ronnie never let on but he actually played the guitar a bit and took some lessons. He loved flamenco and just wanted to learn a few things that he could play for his own amusement.

The first time I played in the club solo Ronnie sat at the side of the stage and listened to both sets. He did the same on the second night I was there, too. I knew that he usually didn't do this type of thing and was a bit worried that maybe something was wrong, but I went back to his office at the end of the evening and he told me how much he'd enjoyed my playing.

I told him that I'd heard he was a bit of a closet guitarist himself and he told me a story. He said that he had come home late from the club one night – it must have been about four in the morning – and he saw his guitar sitting there in the corner of his flat and, as he wasn't really tired, he picked it up to play. Now, any musician will tell you that once you start playing, you soon get quite tied up in it and time becomes irrelevant. So he was still sitting there when the sun came up and he realised that he'd actually been playing for about four hours or so. A little later in the day, he spotted a note that had been pushed under his door which turned out to be from one of his neighbours. The note said:

Dear Mr Scott

I'm very surprised and quite annoyed that you would choose to keep us up all night by playing the guitar. I would have thought a man of your years would have been more considerate.

So Ronnie sat down and wrote a reply:

I'm most terribly sorry if you were disturbed, but I have Andrés Segovia staying with me at the moment and I can't stop him from practising.

He met the neighbour on the landing a few hours later and the guy was very apologetic, saying, "How is Mr Segovia? Is he happy? Tell him there's no problem if he wants to practise, wonderful, wonderful..."

I played at Ronnie's memorial concert at St Martin's in the Field and it was packed. There were over a thousand people there and a few were asked to play. There was one tune that Ronnie loved called 'Why Did I Choose You', which he'd asked me the music for at one point. I was in the process of finding it for him when he died and so I thought it was appropriate that I play the tune at his memorial.

It was very moving, but also upbeat in a strange way. All these musicians were there and Jimmy Parsons got up and made a wonderful speech which had us all laughing. He opened up by saying that many people had asked him what Ronnie would have thought of the events of that day, in particular that so many people had gathered together for his memorial. He said that he had come to the conclusion that Ronnie would have said, "I wish we could have been on a percentage of the door." Once a club owner, always a club owner.

When I first moved to Scotland, living in a small village up in the hills, I was at home one December just before Christmas and the snow outside was quite deep. I had a fire going in the house, poured myself a whisky and was just settling back to enjoy it when the phone rang. It was Ronnie, phoning from the club to say that Chet Baker, who was supposed to be playing there that night, had been delayed at Amsterdam airport and could I replace him at very short notice. He could see that I didn't have a London phone number and so he said, "How far out of London do you live?" and I replied, "About 400 miles." He thought about this for a moment and then said, "400 miles? I thought you lived somewhere like Wanstead."

Another time, I'd just finished my set at his club and was walking out through the audience when a guy pushed himself to the front and said to me, "Have you got a brother who plays drums?" and I said, "No, you're thinking of Mark Taylor." But the guy was insistent and continued, "No, his name isn't Taylor," so I said, "Oh, I thought you were thinking of the British drummer, Mark Taylor," and he said, "He isn't British, he's Nigerian." I was a little taken aback and said, "I don't know any white Nigerians," and he said, "He's not white, he's black." So this guy thought I have a brother whose name isn't Taylor and he's a black Nigerian…Left me baffled for years.

## Musicians/Characters
Around the early 1980s I was booked to play a week in a jazz club in

Cincinatti. It was a real dive and Abby Hoffer, my agent in New York, who booked me into this joint, would ring me every day and say, "Make sure you get paid every night because the owner is a very shady character and he's not to be messed with."

So every night I would have to go over to this villainous character after I'd finished playing and demand my money. I'd have a few large whiskies for Dutch courage, then go into his smoke-filled office at the back of the club and tell him to give me some dough or I wouldn't show tomorrow night. I wouldn't let him see that I was scared of him and his friends, I would walk in really confidently and just demand the money. Amazingly enough, he always paid up and, despite his fierce reputation, I never had any problems with him. In fact, at the end of the week he gave me a bottle of Johnny Walker Black Label whisky, shook my hand and said, "Enjoy it. I know you Scotch guys are a pretty tough breed." It turned out he was a bit scared of me because he thought I was Scottish and he had heard that all "Scotchmen" were hard fighting men.

My Scottish connection also attracted another guy to the club, which proved to be one of the funniest and strangest encounters I ever had in the States. I noticed him in the front row on the first night. He was really into the music and would applaud loudly after each tune. On my first break he came up and said in a broad American accent, "Gee, it sure is great to meet another fellow Scotchman!" So I asked him exactly what part of "Scotchland" he came from. He said, "I'm from Cincinatti, but I'm Scotch just like you." I didn't want to go into a full explanation of my ethnic background, so I just humoured him, as one Scotchman to another. He bought me a "wee dram" and kept asking me, "So how's the auld country these days, laddie?"

The following night he came in, this time wearing a tartan tie. I had to put up with all his "Och aye, gee – there's no place like Scotchland to be sure, to be sure, begorra laddie, the noo" banter, although it made me cringe just listening to it. The next night he'd added a tartan scarf and I had to put up with even more of his nonsense.

Every night after that he seemed to be wearing more tartan and by Thursday night he was wearing a tartan bonnet with a huge feather in it. He would always collar me as I came off stage and, with a tear in his eye, ask me about his homeland. On the last night he invited me over to the bar for "a farewell dram" and, never one to refuse a free drink, I joined him.

After a couple of large ones I asked him if he'd actually ever been to Scotchland and he said, "No, never laddie – but it sure would be swell to go there one day." I said, "Yeah, you really should. You obviously have a fascination for the place. You would love it. It's a beautiful country, great scenery, great people." He stared into his whisky very thoughtfully before looking up at me and saying, "Where is it exactly?"

I have met quite a few Americans over the years who were a bit vague about where Canada was, but this character definitely took first prize…to be sure, och aye the noo.

Once I was booked to play four concerts in England and I had put together a trio which comprised Alan McPike, who is a marvellous Scottish keyboard player, and my son James on drums. In the middle of this group of dates I had a solo gig at Darlington Arts Centre and so I asked them if they'd mind coming with me and playing a few tunes towards the end of each set. I played for about 40 minutes solo and then introduced Alan and James and we did some trio numbers. We did the same thing for the second half and it went down really well except for one guy who demanded his money back and actually wrote to the local paper saying he was going to sue me under the Trade Descriptions Act for not playing the entire gig solo. I think it was the first time I'd heard anyone complain about getting too much for their money.

There was a great character in London, a piano player by the name of Joe Burns. Joe did a lot of the society gigs and played for a lot of the aristocracy who were all very fond of him. He was one of those characters who was always swearing but he could get away with it, nobody was really bothered by it at all. He had a business card which he gave out to people – Ronnie Scott had one in his office – which was really professionally presented and it said:

For your family listening pleasure, the magical keyboard touch of Joe Burns

"Pissed or stoned, a fucking high class entertainer" – *The Evening Standard*

Stephane told me that he used to play at the Hippodrome in Golders Green with the pianist George Shearing during the war. This was during the days of the blackout in London and Stephane told me that he used to rely on George to take him home because George had this phenomenal radar that many blind people have, where he could find his way about anywhere, avoiding obstacles and so forth.

George has an amazing memory. I met him first when we played a concert in California and many years later I went into the Jazz FM studios in London to do an interview and I was standing at reception, talking to someone and a voice behind me said, "Ah, hello Martin, how are you?" and it was George.

A contemporary of George's was another blind piano player called Eddie Thompson who I worked with on many occasions. He was a wonderful player and I believe that he and George went to the same school. Eddie used to work with a trumpet player called Freddie Randall and they were playing a residency somewhere but they fell out about something and so they weren't talking to each other. Freddie knew that Eddie used to go back to his room each night and read books in Braille, so one night he got hold of an iron and ironed all of Eddie's books so that all the pages were completely smooth. That gives you some idea about the sometimes cruel sense of humour you often come across in musicians on the road, although Eddie saw the funny side of it and often told that story himself.

Being on stage can be a challenging experience. For many it's nerves that are the enemy, but sometimes other, natural and more fundamental forces can take hold. Sometimes you can feel unwell on stage, and if you're playing solo, you've got no one to cover for you. But sometimes it's just a simple matter of wanting to take a leak. Once again, the soloist can hardly just excuse himself and so it's usually a question of gritting your teeth and getting on with it. But there's always room for the occasional innovative idea...

A saxophone player (I know his name but I'm not telling) was playing in a show where the band was on stage with the actors and so he was conspicuous throughout the performance. He liked a few pints of Guinness before the gig – well, seven or eight pints – and when it got about three quarters of the way through the show he was absolutely busting to go to the toilet.

This happened every night, but he wasn't prepared to cut out the beer and so he decided on another course of action. He'd heard about incontinence pants, which are like nappies for adults, designed for people who have lost a bit of control in that department. So, he went to the local pharmacist and bought himself some pants, put them on before the gig, put some baggy trousers over them for camouflage and headed for the pub.

He had his customary eight pints of Guinness and then said to himself, "Well, I've got these things on now," and downed another two. Later on, with about half an hour before the end of the show, he needed a pee, and decided to test out his new underwear. Now, for the audience at home only, incontinence pants are designed to withstand the odd trickle here and there. One thing they're definitely not designed for is a 6'3", 18-stone saxophone player who's just drunk ten pints of Guinness. So, to put it mildly, the result was not exactly what he intended and all of a sudden London had a second major river running through it. To say there wasn't a dry seat in the house would just about cover it.

Another story about a West End show concerns Phil Seaman. It was again one of those occasions when the orchestra wasn't playing in the pit but was up on stage and Phil was playing tuned percussion. Somehow, he managed to fall asleep on stage and woke up in a complete panic, thinking he'd missed his cue. He knew he had to hit this huge orchestral gong at one point and he was sure, in his sleepy state, that this was the point they'd reached in the performance. So he jumped up, grabbed a mallet and hit the gong for all he was worth.

Of course, he'd managed to do it at one of the show's quieter moments, and so the whole orchestra, cast and 3,000-strong audience stared at him in utter disbelief. Phil took a few steps forward on the stage, bowed and said, "You rang, my Lord?" and the whole place just erupted into laughter. It stopped the show for a while and the only person who didn't see the funny side was the show's producer...

There is a British guitar player called Peter Chilver, who was one of the first modern jazz players in this country. He played in The Ted Heath Orchestra and was a very good friend of Django's. He was a very successful musician, but when he met his wife, Norma, in the 1950s he decided to stop playing altogether and join his wife's family business which was principally real estate. He moved to Edinburgh and did very well for himself.

Once, when Ike and Moira Isaacs were over from Australia on a visit, they came to stay at my house in Dalmellington. I rang Peter and told him that Ike was there, but we wouldn't be able to get across to Edinburgh to see him. Pete said there was no problem and that he'd come over to see us. I gave him directions to the cottage, but told him that if he managed to get lost once he reached the village, just ask anyone where "the guitarist" lived and they'd be able to put him right.

Dalmellington was a small ex-mining village and everyone knew everyone else and because of my unusual occupation I had a minor celebrity status – so I was sure he'd be able to track us down one way or another. Peter was much later than expected and about an hour after we were expecting him there was a knock on the door. There was Pete, complete with a bottle of champagne – and a story to tell.

He had two cars at the time, a Porsche and a Rolls-Royce, and he had decided to come over from Edinburgh in the Rolls. He'd found the village without any trouble, but when it came to finding the cottage, he decided to take my advice and ask someone for directions. So he stopped a man walking down the hill and said, "Do you know where Martin Taylor, the guitarist, lives?" The man said, "Aye, I ken where he lives," adding, "I'm going that way myself, I'll show yae." So he got into the Rolls with Pete and they drove all over the place, up and down the village.

After about half an hour, they came back to exactly the point where Pete had picked him up in the first place. The man said, "That's his hoose over there," and Pete said, "But this is exactly where I picked you up in the first place." "Aye," said the man. "That's right enough, but I've never been in a Rolls-Royce before..."

## There's No Business...

Another reason why I started to play solo was because I did a lot of work playing around Britain using local rhythm sections and, if you cast your eyes back to the experience John McLevy and Jack Emblow had a few pages back, you'll understand that some of them were good, very good in fact, but some of them were impossible to work with.

Under those conditions, I would always say that I'd do a few numbers on my own to make things easier on myself and, being a guitar player, I had the luxury to do that – it is a different story if you're a trumpet or sax player. I didn't do that kind of work for very long, but it was the norm in many circumstances, especially for visiting American soloists.

Barney Kessel told me a lovely story about this kind of thing happening to him. This particular story took place in America, where they have a similar convention of providing local rhythm sections. Barney was playing at a club and he recognised the bass player in the rhythm section he'd been booked to play with that night. He'd had a terrible time at the last gig they did together and he wasn't looking forward to the prospect of a repeat performance.

After the gig, which was every bit the nightmare Barney had feared it would be, the bass player sought Barney out, obviously seeking some sort of compliment on his performance that night. "Ah, well Barney…" he said, and Barney came out with this great line which could be taken either way: "Well, you're still doin' it."

I used to work with a trumpet player, I won't mention his name because he's still alive, but he was a great friend of Louis Armstrong's. Whenever he and Louis were in the same town they would meet up for a few hours and roll a few joints together. During one of these sessions, the trumpet player said, "Hey Louis, one of the things that's always fascinated me about you is I've heard you play with so many different bands and sometimes they don't sound good at all. I don't know how you do it, but you still play great and it doesn't seem to bother you."

Louis said, "Well man, it's like this. I've got this band in my head and if I don't like the band on the stage I just play along to the band in my head." The trumpet player took a puff on the joint, passed it to Louis and asked, "So who's in the band?" Louis took a puff himself and, passing it back to his friend said, "I'm not telling you. Get your own band."

I sometimes play classical festivals which I really enjoy doing and I've made some very good friends with some of the classical guitar players over the years. There is a story about a classical singer who landed a major record deal but who had never recorded before.

Now, one problem a lot of classical musicians have is with amplification in general and microphones in particular. Many classical guitarists don't want their guitars amplified or "enhanced" at all and sometimes the result is that you can hardly hear them in a large concert hall. I know for a fact that John Williams has his guitar amplified when he plays with a symphony orchestra and that attitudes in this area are changing, but with some, old habits and attitudes die hard.

I did a concert at London's Queen Elizabeth Hall with Carlos Bonell and he used a mike; similarly, the classical guitarist Simon Dinnigan will tend to use some form of amplification when he performs.

Anyway, this classical singer went into a recording studio for the very first time and met the producer and the engineer who gave her a guided tour of the place, just to settle her in. They took her into the main room in the studio where she would be singing and said, "This is the microphone you will be singing into," and her manager very indignantly responded, "Microphone? She doesn't need a microphone – she's classically trained!"

As I've mentioned a few times already, I'm an abysmal sight-reader but once I was contacted by Robert Farnham, who is a wonderful arranger and used to work for Frank Sinatra on some of those classic recordings. Robert specifically wanted me to play on a recording he was doing with an American opera singer called Eileen Farrell where she would be recording songs by Gershwin and Cole Porter. I must admit that very few singers are able to switch comfortably between opera and show tunes, but this was one of the very few times I've ever really heard it work.

The session took place at CTS Studios in Wembley and consisted of a full orchestra and the rhythm section, if you could call it that, comprising Lenny Bush on double bass and myself. In order to stop any overspill in the studio where my guitar could interfere with the mikes picking up the orchestra and vice versa, I was put in a Perspex box which was like a huge fish tank.

They placed the box on a platform on one side of the orchestra, which raised it two or three feet in the air. I was there, in my own little glass booth, staring out at everything that was going on around me, feeling a little conspicuous to say the least. I looked at the music that was set in front of me and, to my relief, the parts weren't hard at all. But one thing I wasn't used to was the way a classical conductor uses his baton to count in the orchestra – Robert wasn't giving me the sort of down beat I was used to at all. He was conducting the classical way where they don't actually count in like a jazz player would – there was no "one, two, three, four". Instead, I was meant to determine the tempo of the piece from the speed of the conductor's upstroke with his baton. To make matters worse, whereas a jazz musician would take a downwards stroke of the baton as meaning that's the place to come in and start playing, in the classical world the orchestra comes in slightly after the initial downbeat.

The first tune we played had a guitar intro and so Robert tapped his baton to get everyone in their starting position, raised his baton and – I missed it completely. I didn't really know what was happening at all. The orchestra came in where they were meant to, but I was left standing, so to speak. All I could say was, "Oh, sorry. Let's try it again." So the process was repeated and I missed it again. By a mile.

Once again, the orchestra all came in where they were supposed to and petered out when they realised that I had missed it. A whole orchestra's worth of accusing eyes rested on me in my conspicuous glass cage and I meekly apologised and we tried all over again.

The fourth time we tried it, I had given up relying on the music in front of me and just guessed where I was supposed to come in and got away with it, but it was an awful experience and I've subsequently developed a lot more sympathy for goldfish.

My friend, Mick O'Brien, runs a bar in Ayr called Wellingtons and he puts on a lot of traditional music there. One American singer, who's a native Indian, was staying at a B&B round the corner. After a few drinks in the bar, he decided to go back to the guest house and a woman in the bar said to him, "Will you be able to find your way?" and he replied, "Of course I'll be able to find my way, I'm a fucking Indian!"

One of the real legendary figures in Scottish music is Hamish Imlach, who was a real larger-than-life character. Mick phoned him one day and said, "Hamish, I'd like you to come and play at the pub," adding, "How much would you want?" Hamish said, "Well, how much did you pay me last year?" and Mick told him that it was about 15 years ago, but back then it was about £20. Without hesitation, Hamish said, "Oh, that'll do – as long as my drink is free."

So Hamish did the gig and drank a bottle of brandy and quite a few pints of beer. In the morning he wasn't looking too good at all and said, "You know what, Mick? I think I must be allergic to leather," and Mick said, "Well, how do you work that one out?" Hamish replied, "Well, whenever I wake up in the morning with my boots on, my head's thumping..."

My second instrument is mandolin – I don't play well, it's more of a hobby than anything, but I heard one story about the great saxophone player, Al Cohn, which really rings true. Al has a son called Joe who is a great guitar player and he told me that there is this bar in New York where a lot of jazz musicians used to hang out. One night, Al went in there and ordered a large whisky and downed it in one. He ordered another one immediately and the bartender said to him, "Al, what's the matter with you? What's up?" and Al replied, "I've had a terrible day. I've been in a studio doing a session with five mandolin players." The bartender said, "Five? Where on earth did they manage to find five mandolin players?" and Al said, "Put it this way, today you couldn't get a haircut in Jersey City…"

I've played at a few festivals with Alan Randall on vibraphone. A lot of people know of Alan because he's been on TV quite a lot and he also did an act singing George Formby songs and playing ukelele. There used to be a TV show in England called *The Good Old Days*, which used to be filmed at the City Variety Theatre in Leeds and featured an audience all dressed up in period costume, and you would quite often see Alan on there.

George Formby's music still has a very wide following and there's even a convention held in Blackpool once a year where everyone takes along their ukeleles and has a great time. So Alan wrote a serious play about the life of George Formby, featuring himself as Formby, and he pretty much financed the whole thing on his own. The first night played to a full house and Alan walked on stage against a backdrop of a Lancastrian street with a lamppost strategically positioned at one side. The play starts and the mood is set with Alan talking about the life of George Formby: "I was born in Lancashire and…" He walked over to the lamppost to sing Formby's most famous song, 'Leaning On A Lamp Post', but as he started to sing the first line, "'Cos I'm leaning on a lamp…" everyone in the theatre took out a ukelele and began to sing along!

Alan was horrified and had to stop the play and ask the audience not to play or sing along. After that, they had to make a sign to hang in the theatres that said "No Ukeleles To Be Taken Into The Auditorium". People had to hand their ukeleles in to the box office like gun slingers handing in their six shooters in the wild west.

Talking about George Formby, Jack Emblow tells a story about the days when he was playing the music halls around England. Outside one particular theatre there was a huge picture of Formby with a big, toothy gormless smile on his face. This chap was walking along with his young son and he pulled him across the street, pointed to the picture and said, "There you are. That's what you'll look like if you keep playing with yourself."

# Home And Away

I've always admired Jimmy Shand and I think that he is the greatest ambassador that Scotland has ever had. I was so pleased when he received a knighthood, he's done so much to promote Scottish music around the world.

Quite recently, Jack Emblow, my son James and his girlfriend, Alison, who is a music lawyer and also a singer in a group called The Penny Dainties (a sort of a Dinning Sisters/Andrews Sisters vocal group) were on our way to Dundee to play at a guitar festival and we went through Auchtermuchty, which is where Jimmy Shand lives. It turned out that Jack knew him and had played on some of his records, and so he suggested we popped in to see him. We found his house and he invited us in and we had a wonderful couple of hours there with him, his wife and son.

We signed the visitors' book and he gave Jack and me copies of his autobiography and, as we were leaving, he said that, had he felt well enough, he would have come on to Dundee with us and watched the show. He said, "I've got a request, lads. Will you play 'Bonnie Dundee' for me?" This is an old Scots song which became Jimmy's signature tune and so Jack and I worked out a bossa nova arrangement of it in the car and played it that night. We play it quite often now and I often think about the time that we met that day in Dundee. Jimmy said something once which I could relate to myself, being such a poor reader. He was asked if he could sight-read and he replied, "Aye, I can read fine as long as I ken the tune." I thought that was a lovely answer.

It's a bit of a musician's cliché, but I'm always being asked about the worst gigs I've played. Well, I don't like to put places down, but certainly one of the most uncomfortable experiences I've ever had was out in a place called Chittagong in Bangladesh.

I was with some of the guys from Spirit Of Django and we'd played the night before at Dacca and everything was fine. We moved on to the Agrabad Hotel in Chittagong, which is in a very remote part of the country, and I understand that we were the first jazz band to play there. When we arrived, some of the guys decided they would go for a walk, but I was recovering from a flu bug and so I decided I'd go to bed. When I saw them later on I asked how their walk went and they said, "We got stoned." Knowing that none of the band were pot smokers, I asked them what they meant and they told me that they'd walked down the street and people started throwing stones at them merely because they were westerners.

The day after that we were going to Sri Lanka and we had to fly first of all to Calcutta. It was a horrendous journey. We got on the plane and there were people there holding chickens in cages – one guy had a goat with him. As we were sitting on the tarmac, waiting to take off, I saw that there were a lot of people waiting outside the plane. Just as we were set to go, they let them on board despite the fact that there were no seats left. So when the plane took off, there were passengers standing in the aisles, it really was a bit worrying. To cap it all, when we arrived at Calcutta for the stop-over before boarding the flight onward to Sri Lanka, they tried to arrest us because we didn't have visas. We had been told that we didn't need them since we were just in transit, but obviously there had been some sort of oversight.

Eventually we managed to sort things out and were issued with a 24-hour pass and so we went over to check in for the next flight and they wanted an enormous amount of money out of us for excess baggage. We didn't have any at all, in fact we were travelling very light, but I think someone there saw the opportunity to rip a few westerners off.

Terry Gregory said, "Leave this to me," and he took over the negotiations and finally got us all upgraded to first class and the onward journey ended up being splendid. So everything ended well and we had a great trip on Air Lanka down to Colombo, but it's the first thing that usually pops into my head when the subject of "worst gigs" comes up.

The first time I went to India, I was booked to go to Pakistan, Bangladesh and Sri Lanka by the British Council. In between the booking and the dates coming up, the Gulf War began, so we had to cancel Pakistan and Bangladesh because they were Muslim countries, but they gave me the choice of going to India. I agreed to go, but was told that I would have to be issued with bodyguards by the Indian Army.

I arrived at Bombay airport and was met by two soldiers – and they were holding hands. I thought, "This isn't a good sign," but I found out that one of them had eye-glasses on like lemonade bottle bottoms and couldn't see a thing – he looked like one of Benny Hill's characters. So the other soldier had to lead him everywhere.

I didn't feel at all threatened while I was out there. In fact, the only thing that worried me was that both my bodyguards were carrying sub machine guns and one of them couldn't see beyond the end of his nose.

When you travel all over the world, you expect to come up against strange traditions and customs, special foods and drink, and it's only polite to get involved, in my opinion. But when you look around England, we've got some fairly strange customs ourselves. I was driving through the West Country and I passed a farm with a sign which said "Farmhouse Scrumpy", which is a kind of rough cider – and some types of scrumpy are a lot rougher than the rest. So I pulled in to the farm and the farmer came out, looking like one of The Wurzels and I asked if I could buy some scrumpy.

He took me into a barn and said, "D'ya want the sweet or the regular?" and so I asked him if I could try some sweet. He gave me a schooner full of the sweet and I tried it, but it was far too sweet for me and so I tried the other one and decided to buy a couple of gallons. It was 75p a gallon, which is cheaper than petrol, but probably about as effective an aperitif.

I put the two gallon containers in the back of my car and drove off down the country lane. I soon came across a sudden bend to the left but, as I went to brake, I discovered that I couldn't feel my foot at all. It had turned to a sort of numb jelly and I realised that it must be the after effects of my two minute schooners of scrumpy – it must be one of those drinks where you get drunk from the feet upwards. I had to get out of the car and walk around a bit before I felt it was safe to drive on.

I took the scrumpy home and put the containers in a downstairs bathroom that we rarely used and forgot all about them. A few months later I went in there and it was like something from *The Quatermass Experiment*. Both plastic containers had expanded to about three times their original size and looked set to explode. I was terrified that they would blow up in my hands and so I had to get a broom handle and hook them carefully before taking them to the bottom of the garden. Then I went upstairs and fetched an air rifle and ended everything as humanely – and quite explosively – as possible, making a note to avoid scrumpy at all costs in future.

When I worked with The Tony Lee Trio, we sometimes used to bring in a West Indian percussionist who played congas with the band. He was very fond of ganga and was rarely seen without some sort of massive spliff on the go. We were booked to do a broadcast from the BBC studios in Maida Vale once, and while we were setting up, the conga player sat there rolling up one joint after another and lining them up on his congas, ready to start smoking them during the course of the session. When we came back from a break in the canteen, the bass player went over to his jacket and found that someone had stolen his wallet. Then the conga player said, "Someone's stolen my ganga, man. Call the police." I said, "You can't call the police for that," but he was insistent. "It cost me good money, man…" But I said, "You can't call the police and say 'someone's stolen my marijuana' – I don't think they'd be too sympathetic, somehow."

# Stop The World...

I've had my fair share of embarrassing moments on the road – this is another question people ask me about. I guess one of the worst came when I was in St Louis and, forgetting my fear of heights, decided to go up the St Louis Arch. This is a free-standing arch which looks like half a McDonald's sign – only one hundred times bigger. I don't know what I could have been thinking about, it was just one of those occasions where something seemed like a good idea at the time.

I queued up with a huddle of girl scouts before being herded into one of these tiny capsules and being transported up the inside of one leg of the arch. When the doors of the capsule lift opened, I saw that part of the floor was glass that you can walk over – and we were 630 feet off the ground. It was my worst nightmare and all I can remember is a guy saying to me, "Are you OK, sir?" and being able to mumble back, "No, I'm not." I just froze and to my own eternal embarrassment, had to be helped down by two of the girl scouts. When we got to the bottom, one of them said, "Will you be all right now, sir?" and I muttered that everything was fine, now I was back on planet Earth.

Another embarrassing moment occurred when I was in Tel Aviv. I was at the Israel Guitar Festival and was scheduled to play in Bethlehem and Jerusalem, too. I had only just started playing solo gigs and I hadn't yet got into judging a set in terms of how long to play for and so on. Instead, I used to mount an old alarm clock on my pedal board, among my volume pedal and reverb unit, just so that I could keep an eye on the time while I was playing.

Everything was fine until I tried to take my pedal board through airport security – all they saw was a board covered in wires with a clock in the middle and suddenly I found myself surrounded by armed guards. I practically closed down Tel Aviv airport and they gave me a bit of a hard time about it.

Certainly one of my favourite true stories concerns an extremely camp producer who was putting on the pantomime *Snow White And The Seven Dwarfs*. One night, one of the dwarfs was off sick and so he had to find a dep at short notice (no pun intended). During the show, there was a routine where all the dwarfs had to go forward on stage, do a tumble in time with a scored part for the drums. When it came to the dep dwarf's turn, he didn't tumble, but just ran to the front of the stage and stuck both arms out in the time honoured "Da-Daaaaah" fashion. The producer was livid and threw a very camp fit, saying to the dwarf backstage, "Why didn't you tumble? Why didn't you tumble? You've ruined my show, why didn't you tumble?" The dwarf replied, somewhat sheepishly, "I'm sorry, but I can't tumble," and the producer screamed, "Well what's the point in being a fucking dwarf if you can't tumble?"

I once played in Prague with Stephane and, from our hotel off Wenceslas Square, you could see where the Russian Army was setting up the banked seating for the yearly parade through the streets with tanks, missiles and other evidence of military might, celebrating the Russian presence in Czechoslovakia.

I decided to go out and look around the shops and someone recommended that I went to a particular department store. I went in and there was just nothing there at all. In the section where they have the electrical appliances there were a couple of old black and white televisions and a transistor radio and that was about it. I felt very sad because it is such a beautiful city with absolutely wonderful architecture and yet you see people queueing up to buy food and it all seems such a shame somehow.

I couldn't help thinking of Peter Sellers in the film *I'm All Right Jack* where he played a trade union leader called Mr Kite. In one scene he proclaims, "It must be wonderful in the Soviet Union. All them corn fields and ballet in the evening..." I thought about that as I watched people lining up for food and wondered what could have gone so wrong.

We were in Prague to play at a festival and Kenny Ball was there with his band. At that time, Kenny's band included the guitarist, John Fenner, and my old friend from the Dorchester Hotel days, pianist Hugh Ledigo. As a kid I used to go along to a Sunday lunchtime gig with my dad to watch Freddie Randall play and sometimes Kenny Ball would sit in with the band. At the time Kenny was at the height of his career and was riding high with his hit 'Midnight In Moscow'. He would appear on the *Morecambe And Wise* show every week on British TV and was really considered to be quite a big star.

The night of this gig, Kenny was opening the show for us and, naturally, he played 'Midnight In Moscow'. To everyone's horror, a lot of the audience started booing and heckling – it was a time when there was a lot of unrest in Prague and the Czechs were not very fond of the Russians, to say the least.

A couple of years ago I saw Kenny interviewed on a BBC television programme and one of the questions he was asked was, "What was the worst moment of your life?" and he recounted that exact story and so it must have left quite a mark with him.

The day after we left Prague was the day of the Wenceslas Square Uprising which brought about a radical change of politics out there. We got out just in time – if we'd have stayed another day we would have been caught up in all the troubles. But I'd love to go back, it was such a beautiful city.

Sometimes, when you travel around the world, you do stumble into all kinds of political situations or local taboos which, of course, you can be blissfully unaware of at the time. On a much lighter note, I once played in Guernsey in the Channel Islands and, with one of those momentary memory lapses, said to the audience, "It's great to be back in Jersey..." completely oblivious to the fact that there is this rivalry between the two islands. I've never been asked back, either!

There was a violinist who worked for several major orchestras who was very well known for being a bit tight with money. He used to keep this cigarette tin and, whenever he'd finished smoking a cigarette, he would scrape out the tobacco remaining in the butt and make a tiny little cigarette out of it. So this tin would be full of tiny, stumpy little cigarettes. One day, he was doing a rehearsal with Sir Thomas Beecham, who was one person he badly wanted to ingratiate himself with. Halfway through the rehearsal, Sir Thomas asked the orchestra, "Has anyone got a cigarette?" and the violinist saw his chance and he rushed forward with his terrible, tatty tin and opened it under Sir Thomas's nose, saying, "Please, take a whole one, Sir Thomas..."

I have a unique claim to fame which I enjoy telling people about. I was doing an Australian chat show – the equivalent to the David Letterman show – and I was hanging around backstage with all the various people from the TV company who were helping out that evening. Very often, these helpers consist of young girls fresh out of university, and I went over to one girl who was hanging around the tea machine and asked her for a coffee. She said, "OK then, do you take sugar?" and I said, "Yeah," and she said, "Milk?" and I nodded. "Would you like a biscuit to go with that?" she asked and I said, "Oh, yes thanks..." It wasn't until I got on the show that I discovered that it was Dannii Minogue. She was very nice about it, though.

## Postlude

It's a funny thing, but you can do the best gig you've ever done in your life and musicians will never get to hear about how well you played, but the one night you screw up, that goes around like wildfire.

There was a sax player in the Channel Islands – I don't remember his name – who was at a function where he had to play 'God Save The Queen' at the end of the evening. He was half asleep when the moment came, but must have heard the roll on the drums which was his cue to come in. Unfortunately, in his sleepy state he went straight into 'Happy Birthday To You' instead. I just know him as "the guy who played 'Happy Birthday'" which is a terrible thing to have to try and shake off in your career.

There's a story which underlines this kind of thing perfectly. A musician living in London met a clarinet player who he knew from years ago and said to him, "Hello, haven't seen you in a while. What have you been doing?" The clarinet player said, "Well, I've been doing a lot of work in the studio, a lot of film soundtracks and so on." So the musician said, "Really? I didn't know that." "Then I got really interested in arranging and so I started doing some arranging and became quite successful at doing that." "Well I hadn't heard about that," the musician said. "Then I thought that the arranging scene in London was a little small and so I tried my luck in America and landed a couple of jobs in Hollywood, arranging the scores for some blockbuster movies," the clarinet player went on. "Really? Wow, I hadn't heard that," the musician replied. "So then I got into conducting as well and ended up arranging the music and conducting some of the finest orchestras in the world – The Berlin Symphony, Royal Philharmonic, Boston Pops and The Los Angeles Symphony, things like that." "That's amazing – I never heard about any of that!" said the musician, "What did you do next?" "Well, in the end I got fed up with all the stress and red tape that came with doing these things and so I got the clarinet out and started practising again. I really got into it and one day I got a call to do a session and so I went down to the studio, put the music in front of me and I completely screwed it up." "Oh yeah," said the musician, "I heard about that." That just about sums it up.

# 16 Sarabanda

One of the first places I played in America with Stephane was a club in Greenwich Village, New York, called the Bitter End. This was where artists like Joni Mitchell and Bob Dylan played in their early days and it was to become a regular part of our tour itinerary.

A guy used to come along to see us whenever we played there. He was a little bit older than me and a huge fan of Stephane's. He had his own construction business in Georgia and was a keen amateur violinist. Over a number of years we got to know each other quite well and at one gig at the Bitter End he said to me, "You know, I'd like to hear you make a contemporary album," and went into some detail about what album he'd like me to make. He said that I should go to LA, work with a really good producer, use some of LA's finest musicians and he was sure that the result would be really good.

I said I'd love to make another album – especially like the one he was describing – but the main problem was financing a project like that. He said he knew a way of doing it and so I said OK straight away.

He was so into my playing, he organised it for me to go to LA and record an album with David Hungate, who had been playing bass with Toto up until recently, producing. David had never met the guy before, but luckily for me agreed to produce the album straight away. Some of the musicians involved were guys like John Pattitucci and Paulhino de Costa as well as some really great LA players. The resulting album was called *Sarabanda* and nothing happened for quite a while after I recorded it. It was touted around the record companies in the States for a while with no luck, until a company called Gaia Records took the album and brought it out. With next to no promotion it started to receive airplay and reached Number One in the Gavin charts and a couple of other places, too. It was played on radio stations all across the States and still is.

By this time I had returned to Scotland, but from time to time the guy would phone me and tell me that the album had gone up a couple of places in such and such a chart and things were beginning to look really good indeed. I had to go over to the States to do something, but there was no real coordination, no campaign to back the album. I didn't have management and so there was no-one over there who could put a tour structure in place which would allow me to promote the album efficiently.

Just as things began to look really good, the record company fell into financial difficulties and ended up going down the tubes. All was not lost, though, because one of the guys who had worked there went on to work for another major record company and he decided to follow things through with his new firm.

I went over to New York and was met at JFK airport and taken by limo to the Gramacy Park Hotel where I was shown to my suite before being taken over to the record company. It turned out that *Sarabanda* had sold more than 25,000 copies in just a few weeks, with absolutely no promotion whatsoever. It had sold on word of mouth and constant airplay across the US and in a very short space of time, too. I could just imagine how many it would have sold if it had been properly promoted – although I try not to think about it. But it looked very likely that something was going to happen and everyone had very positive feelings about the album gaining a new lease of life.

Around this time, I started having suspicions about some of the business dealings the guy who had arranged the recording was involved in. I received a phone call from him in New York saying that he had a couple of colleagues in the city who were going to call me at the hotel and take me out for a meal.

A little while later, they turned up at the hotel. One guy was a New Yorker, the other was a Colombian, and we went out for a meal together. The guy from New York had quite a lot to drink and was obviously getting well and truly hammered. He said that his mother had just died and that he'd grown up in a project in Queens and he'd like to take me and show me where his mother had lived.

At this point, little alarm bells were ringing in my head and I wasn't at all sure that I liked the idea, but he talked me into it somehow. He had a car with a driver and so we all piled in and set off for Queens. We drew up outside a very run-down apartment block and he said to me, "Come on, I want to show you where my mother lived."

The apartment was completely empty, very seedy and run down and struck me as not being a pleasant place to be at all – those alarm bells hadn't stopped ringing, either.

The only item of furniture in the whole place was a single chest of drawers. It was about four feet high, five feet wide and three feet deep with five drawers in it. He said, "I've got to show you this, man – this is the greatest thing," and he started opening the drawers. Each of them was absolutely full of large blocks of cocaine. There must have been millions of dollars' worth there and I knew immediately that the alarm bells were right. My mouth went completely dry. It was so surreal, like something out of a detective novel – but I wasn't Sam Spade, I was a jazz guitarist with a dry mouth and a very urgent need to get back amongst normal people as soon as I could.

He started saying, "This is great, man. This is a great business we've got going here," and I was trying to fight a rising tide of panic and mumbled something like, "Oh, yeah. Great." He continued very much in the same vein, saying things like, "This is the greatest way to make money, man," and started breaking off bits of cocaine about the size of golf balls, laughing and throwing them at me, saying, "Go on, take some back with you…"

Obviously my suspicions were justified. Eventually, we went back to the hotel and my mind started to race. I didn't tell anyone about what had happened – I couldn't – but eventually, one of the musicians who had played on the album told me that our "friend" had been arrested by the Drug Enforcement Agency and was subsequently sent to jail for a very long time. Both David Hungate and I were shocked and devastated when we found out and I still think I had a lucky escape, but *Sarabanda* never received the exposure it possibly deserved and the masters are still in New York. I receive letters and emails every week asking if that album will ever be remastered. I really don't know – maybe it's best to leave it alone, it could be jinxed. I'm always asked, "What happened to *Sarabanda*?" and up until now I haven't felt able to tell the full story – but now you know.

One of the last things I did with Stephane was a soundtrack for a movie called *Milou En Mai*, which was a black comedy directed by Louis Malle. We went over to Paris for the week to record at the CBS studios there with Jack Sewing, Mark Fosset and an accordion player and pianist. Stephane, being Stephane, couldn't record the conventional way that they work in the film soundtrack world, which means working with a click track. So we had to adopt a way of working which meant receiving directions like, "We need music in this bit here." Louis Malle would come over to the band and say, "We need music from the time the guy puts his bicycle against the wall, walks into the house, goes into the room and looks over there – then you stop."

It was a nightmare. Jazz musicians aren't used to playing the same thing over and over again and getting it exactly the same each time – especially Stephane. It turned into the recording session from hell.

Malle idolised Stephane, but you could sense that things were getting a little frayed around the edges because we were taking so long to record some of the scenes. We were booked into the studios for five days and were being paid very well for our time, but there was some sort of friction between Stephane and Jack at the time, I don't know what it was about. Every time there was a mistake, Stephane would turn to Jack, like it was his fault and this was getting on Jack's nerves, to say the least. Sometimes Stephane would have a go at Jack in between takes and this was making matters much worse. Eventually he did it one time too many and Jack, a fiery Dutchman, said, "Right, that's it, I'm out of here," put his bass down and walked out of the studio. Stephane was very upset and, knowing that he'd pushed Jack too far, started crying and saying, "What have I done? We've worked together so long, I didn't mean to upset him. I'm just nervous about this recording." By this time, Louis Malle must have been wondering exactly what he was dealing with.

I went out, scouring the streets of Paris for Jack and eventually found him having a beer in a nearby bar. I said, "Are you coming back? Because we've got to finish it," but Jack said, "No, no, no – I've had enough." I tried to reason with him and eventually he did come back, but he refused to speak to Stephane for the rest of the day.

We completed that day's recording, but the music still wasn't finished. We were at the end of the allotted time and Louis Malle came up to me and said that there was still some more music to record and would I stay on for another two or three days. I was earning quite a lot of money for the recording, but I had such a bad time I said no – even when I was offered lots more. There was nothing that could tempt me to endure any more time in that studio; I just couldn't do it. The atmosphere had turned bad and I wanted to go home.

Around 1989, I decided to stop touring with Stephane and concentrate exclusively on my solo career. I'd had ten great years with him but it was time for a change. The only thing that would make me tour again was if there was another Australian trip, because that would mean that I could see Ike.

I'd actually tried to quit before, but Ed Baxter would leave things until Stephane was getting near another tour and he'd ring me up and offer it to me saying, "Look, Stephane isn't going to be around forever. Think about it." I'd go away and remember how it was so great to sit next to Stephane every night and watch that magic just pour out of him. I'd remember too how we played great venues, stayed in the best hotels, ate the best food and everything and I'd get tempted back. But in 1989 I decided to make the move. As fate would have it, though, in 1990 Stephane was offered an Australian tour.

So, in 1990 we did our last tour together, in Australia and New Zealand. We played Sydney, Adelaide, Perth, Auckland and Wellington and did quite a few TV shows along the way, too. I saw Ike again, too. I hadn't been to Australia since I was on the Arcadia and the South Pacific cruise and it was great to be back.

I played my last gig with Steph in Auckland. I was sad to go but knew I had to as there were some exciting things on the horizon.

One day, I received a letter from the Inland Revenue telling me that I owed them £38,000. It was just as I was starting to get back on my feet and was the beginning of another saga. There was no way I owed them that much, but I was nonetheless subjected to two years' investigation, funnily enough from an Inland Revenue tax inspector who was a fan of mine and obviously had a personal interest. I was really put through the mangle because practically every day there was a letter on the mat asking me questions which I had to answer. They must have asked every question half a dozen times. It was a difficult two years, and it meant fighting hard with the help of my accountant to prove my case. I've always been straight with tax and have employed an accountant since I was 16 years old.

In the end, we cleared most of it up, but they still insisted that I owed £7,000. I said to my accountant that it would take me even longer to prove that I didn't owe them anything, so I told him to send them the money just to get rid of them. I was fed up with it going on and the psychological cruelty they employed began to affect Liz's health.

All the time I'd been playing with Stephane, I'd been using the Barker guitar that Ike had given me. I'd also managed to acquire a few more instruments after having sold all of them during the mid '80s.

In 1989, I met Martyn Booth, a British luthier who at that time was working for Yamaha in the UK. He was keen for us to design a guitar together which Yamaha would then manufacture. I showed Martyn the Barker and said, "This is the guitar I really like to play."

We looked at that guitar, took some dimensions, came up with some ideas and Martyn drew up some plans and submitted them to Japan. I didn't hear anything for two years and by this time all the staff had changed at Yamaha UK, but one day I received a call from them saying, "We've got this guitar here for you." I'd actually forgotten all about it and so I told them I didn't know what it could possibly be. The guitar had been made by Jackie Minakuchi in Japan especially for me and so Darren Power and Mick Sweeney from Yamaha-Kemble brought it up to my house in Ayr. Yamaha called it the AEX 1500 – not a name that rolls off the tongue, but it was a lovely guitar and credit is due to Martyn Booth for coming up with such a wonderful instrument. I used it nearly all the time until the end of the '90s.

By then, I had begun talking to Mike Vanden, a luthier who lives in Strontian in the north-west of Scotland, about making me a guitar which would encompass everything I dreamed of in an instrument. In the end, we came up with two: an acoustic guitar called The Gypsy which I use for Spirit Of Django gigs; and The Artistry, the electric guitar I use for playing solo.

I picked up my new Vanden "Martin Taylor Artistry" guitar three days before I left Glasgow airport for New York to begin recording *Kiss And Tell*. Now, Glasgow's a funny place – I've heard Billy Connolly say so many times and it's true. The people are very, very funny – I've got lots of relatives there and everyone's a born comedian.

I was going through security at the airport and there was this little Glasgow lady who asked me to open the Vanden guitar case because something had come up on the x-ray machine. When she saw the guitar, she said, in a broad Glaswegian accent. "Och, ma man's got yin just the same as that," and I explained that he couldn't have one exactly the same because this was the only one in the world. "Naw, naw, naw, son," she insisted, "it's jist the same. It was awfie dear, mind, he paid £300 fir it." I said, "Look, this is the only one in the world and it's worth £6,000." But she just shook her head and told me, "Och, the shop saw yae comin', son!" You can always rely on a Glaswegian to put you in your place.

On another occasion I was playing the Theatre Royal in Glasgow with Stephane when the Scottish piano player, Sandy Taylor, decided he'd come to the gig. He went up to the box office and asked the little old lady there for two tickets to the show and added, "Also, could you tell me if Martin Taylor is playing with Stephane tonight?" The lady replied, "Nae, son – she's daen' it all hersel'."

# 17 Hitting The Purple Patch

During the '90s, I recorded a few albums for Linn Records. Linn Products in Glasgow make very high quality hi-fi equipment and they decided that it would be a very good idea to take the whole hi-fi process back a few steps and actually produce their own albums so that they could demonstrate their equipment, keeping "hands on" the whole process.

The first album they produced was by Carol Kidd, who had sung in my band in the early '80s. As soon as they recorded it they knew that they'd got something a bit special. It had Sandy Taylor on piano, Alex Moore on bass and Murray Smith on drums. Linn started putting it into shops and it began to sell. They hadn't set out to be a record company, but due to the success of Carol's album, decided to make more recordings specialising in jazz, classical and early music.

During the '80s I had met a guy in Glasgow called Elliot Meadow, who was involved in various aspects of the jazz business, also working as a music critic for *The Herald*. I got to know him because he came along to my concerts and reviewed some of them.

Elliot knew the people at Linn and told them that I wasn't recording for anyone, although I'd done the occasional album before. So Elliot and I went to Linn's main building in Eaglesham, just outside Glasgow, where we met Phillip Hobbs who was the head of Linn Records, and we agreed that I'd make an album for them. Elliot produced the first recordings and we had some good times in the studio together. He had lived in New York in the late '60s and would sometimes slip into a sort of late '60s, hip jazz-speak that really used to make me laugh.

Elliot has some great sayings. We were recording *A Change Of Heart* and he asked me if I wanted to keep the sessions open-ended from a working schedule point of view. I told him that I usually work from ten till six in the studios and so it probably wasn't worth keeping the studio open any later because I've usually had enough by then. But he said in his transatlantic accent, "Hey man, we'll keep the session open-ended anyway, because you never know when you may hit a main vein and enter into a purple patch." I think I know what he meant but I just cracked up at the time. I was very grateful to Elliot for everything he did. In producing those two albums he was a great help and I really enjoyed doing them.

I had done quite a successful tour in the UK for Jazz Services with a band comprising Dave Newton on piano, Dave Green on bass and Allan Ganley on drums, and so I decided that these were the musicians I'd take into the studios. We went to Abbey Road and recorded my first album for Linn, *Don't Fret*, with Tristan Powell, Georgie Fame's son, engineering and Elliot producing.

By this time, Linn had become a fully-fledged record company. They continued to record other artists, as well as some early classical music, too, which was Phil's speciality.

I recorded my second Linn album a little bit closer to home in Castle Studios, Pencaitland, which is near Edinburgh. The line-up for *A Change Of Heart* was Dave Newton on piano, Brian Sheils on bass and John Rae on drums. Once again, Elliot took the producer's chair, but this album had a few problems during the recording.

The studio had two pianos, neither of which Dave was impressed with, so he had a good old moan about them. There were a few other technical glitches which made recording uncomfortable, but I managed to get through it somehow and the album has some very good moments.

My next album for Linn, *Artistry*, was to be a real landmark for me. It was produced by Steve Howe, who came to fame in the early '70s as the guitarist in the rock band Yes. I had received a call from Yamaha inviting me to their development centre to see a new guitar synthesiser they were producing. When I got there, Steve was there too. We were introduced and got talking, eventually agreeing that it would be nice to work together at some point. We met a few times afterwards, and when it was time for me to make another album, I went to his studios in Devon to record it. I'd been thinking for a long time that I should record an album completely solo and so we started the sessions with Steve producing.

*Artistry* came out and, by now, Linn had much better distribution through Polygram and so the album became better known. It proved to be a significant milestone in my career and it created a lot of media interest.

Around this time, I decided that I needed proper management. I'd never been managed before with any continuity, it had all been a little on-and-off. So I took Ian Middleton on board as my manager in 1993. He'd been involved in jazz quite a lot before, having been director of the Glasgow Jazz Festival, and he was setting up his own management company and so we agreed that we'd work together.

As time went on, Ian's role became more that of agent than manager, due to his commitments with other artists. *Artistry* was just coming out and, for the first time in my life, everything actually coordinated well. The album was released, there was some very good publicity for it and Ian and I put together a 35-date tour of the UK. There were a few club dates, but most of the venues on the tour were art centres and small theatres which were ideal for solo performance. I didn't take anyone out on the road with me, I did the whole marathon alone. It was the first time that there was interest in what I was doing from outside of the mainstream jazz world. People would come along to some of the dates who were just into music, or into guitar. It opened up a new world for me because I was receiving profile from Yamaha and the guitar magazines, like *Guitarist*, were keen to interview me.

*Artistry* made quite a big impact in the classical world. I meet classical guitarists all the time and they all seem to have the album in their collections – often their only jazz album!

I was becoming known to a wider audience as a soloist, touring and doing radio shows, but there was never any TV work in the UK – I don't know what you have to do to get on television in the UK when you play instrumental music. I've done virtually nothing in the UK on TV, but loads in Australia, America and on the Continent, too. There just doesn't seem to be any programming for it here. When BBC Scotland made a documentary on Stephane and me in 1993, called *Meeting Grappelli*, it was shown just about everywhere in the world except England. The best way I can see of getting on UK TV is by getting one of my kids to video me falling down stairs and submitting it to *You've Been Framed*.

Incidentally, I actually did manage to fall down the stairs once, while holding a guitar. I'm sure the guitar players among you will understand, but while I was falling I heard a terrible crack and thought, "I hope that's only my ribs I've broken." As I've already explained, jazz musicians are a funny lot and guitarists even stranger.

Despite the fact that I have only rarely appeared on TV in England, my playing was given its widest ever audience in this country when I was asked to record the music for the Renault Clio adverts. That's my playing which accompanies the "Papa? Nicole!" saga and it all sprang from a phone call I received from Jenkins/Ratledge, a company run by two musicians who used to play in the band Soft Machine – Mike Ratledge and Karl Jenkins.

What they had in mind for the advert was a kind of "Django" style take on the song 'Johnny And Mary' by Robert Palmer. At first I didn't want to do it because there are a few people who can do a better impersonation of Django's style than I can. But we talked about it and, in the end, I agreed to provide a solo which wasn't so much an impersonation, more in the spirit of Django – which was much more up my street, and was later to become the name of my acoustic group.

So I flew down to London and spent about 30 minutes in the studio with Martin Drew on drums, Ron Mathewson on bass, Johnnie Van Derrick on violin and Jack Emblow on accordion, laying down a couple of solos before flying home. I honestly didn't think too much more about it, but then all of a sudden the adverts started appearing on television and the "Nicole" story started to unfold. I recorded another couple of things for subsequent chapters in the series and later included 'Johnny And Mary' on the first Spirit Of Django album. We were originally going to miss the track off that album because I didn't think it was strong enough, but in the end saw that, at least commercially, it was far too good an opportunity to miss.

Interestingly enough, the young lady who plays Nicole in those adverts wasn't French, she was Polish – and, more surprisingly, she couldn't drive!

Since then I've worked with Karl Jenkins on another TV music project called *The Celts*.

When *Artistry* was released, I did my first solo tour of Australia and after that I started going back there roughly once a year. The promoter was Wally Wrightman who had come from London originally and was a contemporary of Ronnie Scott's. He played bass and his story was like something from *Some Like It Hot*, but without the drag...

During the '60s, Wally was playing a gig in London in a place that was run by gangsters and, one night, he witnessed a gangland "incident" around the back of a West End nightclub. Wally wasn't sure if anyone had seen him, but he decided to leave London in any case and wound up getting a job on the cruise ships. He worked on some of the ships that used to take the British emigrants out to Australia – this was in the days when it was possible to emigrate from Britain to Australia for ten pounds and the Aussies used to refer to them as the "Ten Pound Poms". On these trips, Wally found himself falling in love more and more with Australia and so he decided to stay. He stopped playing, but set up a management company over there and started to put on variety shows and things like that.

Wally had many contacts in TV and radio. One of the biggest TV shows in Australia at that time was *Hey, Hey It's Saturday* with Daryl Summers and Wally booked me on the show. The next day I got a call from Tommy Emmanuel, Australia's most famous guitar player. He'd sold a great many albums in Australia and was a very well known musician over there. He was doing a concert at the State Theatre in Sydney – a gig that he told me he'd dreamt of doing since he was a kid – and said to me, "D'ya want to come and sit in on my gig tonight, mate?" So I went to the show and played a few tunes with Tommy which was the start of a long-standing association between us.

Tommy moved to England a couple of years ago and we've played together a few times since. He's played at my guitar festival in Kirkmichael and my son, James, has acted as both UK agent and manager for him in recent years. In 1999, Tommy and I went to New Zealand to play at the World Series Guitar Festival in Auckland, which is quite a major event. We flew out from Heathrow in Business Class on Air New Zealand via Los Angeles and it was really very comfortable. As I've already mentioned, I'm not that keen on flying and so the little extras you get by going Business Class made the long journey to New Zealand that bit easier to bear.

Tommy is a great player and always full of energy and so the minute we settled ourselves in our seats he started telling jokes and I don't think he stopped until we reached Los Angeles! We had a break and then, once we were back on the plane, the jokes started up once again. Both of us fell asleep over Honolulu and woke up ready to take on the Antipodes suitably refuelled by sleep.

We played the concert at a 2,000-seater hall in Auckland and everything went really well. The following night, a friend of Tommy's, who was a guitar player himself, invited us to a gig where he was playing in a small club. I didn't really want to go because the words "small" and "club" to me meant a smoky late night and I'm not keen on either. But at the last minute, I thought I'd go because I wanted to hear Tommy play.

I went and sat at the bar with a couple of people I knew and listened to the band. Tommy played with them all evening, but at one point there was a lot of commotion and I looked around to see the whole place full of police – and they didn't look like they'd come to listen to the music. Before anybody knew what was happening, we were in the middle of a raid. Apparently the club was in the middle of a residential area and there had been some trouble in the past about the noise. So now the police were here – and they were confiscating instruments and carting them off "down town".

Fortunately for Tommy and me, we hadn't gone down there with our own instruments, otherwise they would have been seized along with everything else. I hadn't even taken part – I didn't play a note, I was just enjoying listening to Tommy playing with the band and having a few drinks with a couple of friends.

Meanwhile, things in the club were beginning to get rough. There were fights and scuffles breaking out all over the place and a couple of people were arrested. I just sat there. Once again, I found myself playing the role of an unwilling extra on a movie set and, in the end, the police arrested the owner of the club and I got a lift back to my hotel from one of the guys I'd been sitting with.

The newspapers got hold of the story and made quite a thing out of it, linking both Tommy's and my name to the incident as if we were the main instigators. I guess I should have stayed with my instincts on that one and had an early night.

After the festival was finished, I flew on to play some dates in Hong Kong. I was booked to play solo in a club there for five nights, which is usually quite a comfortable gig. You don't have to travel anywhere, you get to know the place you're playing in quite quickly and there's plenty of time for a bit of sight-seeing in between gigs.

I'd played in Hong Kong many times before and was really looking forward to doing so again, but after the first two nights, things began to go terribly wrong – at least from a gastric point of view.

On the third day I began to feel really ill. I don't know whether I caught a bug or whether it was the euphemistic "something I ate", but I felt absolutely terrible. As I've mentioned before, there's no way you can call in sick when you're a soloist. If you cancel a gig, you feel that you're letting the audience down and so, where humanly possible, I'll play no matter how bad I feel. I've played before when I've had flu or even food poisoning, because I consider it's the professional thing to do – the right way to behave.

So I struggled on stage that night feeling really dreadful, but I was determined to play the gig if I could. I played about three tunes, but it was no good, I could hardly stand, let alone play and so I had to apologise to the audience and get off stage. I crawled backstage and collapsed in a heap. I felt really, really ill and all I wanted to do was get home where I could go to bed for as long as it took for the bug to get out of my system.

The management of the club didn't appreciate my plight in the least. They thought I had been grossly unprofessional and refused to pay me – and yet I thought I had been consummately professional by even attempting to play that night! I was just glad to leave. I rescheduled my flight home and caught an earlier plane and went straight to bed. I've always prided myself on my professionalism, but that was one time it really backfired on me.

There was another occasion where my sense of professionalism backfired. I was doing a solo tour of Australia and Wally Wrightman had arranged this gig for me in a vineyard – which sounded good to me. It was a private party and I was to do a mini concert in this beautiful outdoor setting. It really was a lovely location but things went off on the wrong foot almost immediately. I always try to dress well when I'm on stage and when I was introduced to the guy who ran the place, he said, "You're a bit smartly dressed for a Pom," which didn't put me in a good mood, to say the least.

From then on, everything was total chaos. The caterers couldn't cater for all the people there and I had to sit around for ages before I was due to play. While I was waiting to go on, one of the workers there began talking to me. He was well built and looked like he'd been working out quite a lot, but there was definitely something strange about him at the same time. After a few drinks, he touched me on the bum and that really was the last straw for me. But Wally said, "Look, just play the gig." By the time I was due to go on and play, things had got quite rowdy. The drink had been flowing for a while and the people there were well on the way to becoming quite a raucous crowd.

Somebody announced me and the audience came through to where I was playing. I played the first tune but they just talked all the way through it. I tried speaking to them, introducing songs and so on, but nobody was taking a blind bit of notice. I played for a while, but halfway through a number I just gave up and walked off. I refused to go back on stage. I think my actions that night surprised Wally a bit, but there are times when actors and musicians have a really humiliating experience like that and I just decided that I didn't need any more of it in my life.

Another musician I worked with in Australia was James Morrison, the great multi-instrumentalist. Like Tommy, James is a great showman. We did a number of concerts together, including an outdoor show up in Cairns in the grounds of a hotel. The hotel itself was horseshoe-shaped, with a pool in the middle and a stage where the evening's performance was to take place. I went on and did my thing and eventually it was time for James to make his appearance. He was the last act on and when they announced him, his band started playing and the lights hit James playing trumpet from one of the balconies in the hotel. He carried on playing, came down in the lift, walked on stage, played trombone, tuba, sang, played piano and ended the show by jumping in the pool. I'd defy any rock 'n' roll act to compete with that level of showmanship. He was brilliant.

I met Gordon Giltrap during the 1980s when I was working with Stephane. He was enjoying huge success at that time with his tune, 'Heartsong', at the top of the pop charts, and making a big impact in the UK where mainstream success for instrumental music is almost unheard of. I'm a big fan of his; he has such a unique and distinctive style. Gordon had been along to a gig and we'd met briefly a couple of times afterwards, so when I saw that he was playing at the Civic Theatre in Ayr, with Ric Sanders from Fairport Convention, who I also knew, I went to see the show.

I rang Gordon shortly afterwards and said that it would be good for us to do something together – we just had to work out how to do it. He said that he didn't play jazz, but I said that it was OK because I'd written some tunes which weren't jazz at all and I was sure that we could play them together. We decided that if we were going to do a tour we'd make an album first so we went into a studio very near where he lives and made *A Matter Of Time* and then we followed that up with an extensive tour which was put together by Gordon's wife, Hilary. Meanwhile, another guy had taken charge of Linn Records who didn't want any of the Linn artists to make follow-up albums, so, as far as I was concerned, I had been dropped by the label. We offered them *A Matter Of Time*, but they weren't interested.

One of the dates Gordon and I did on the *Matter Of Time* tour was at London's Purcell Rooms on the South Bank in London. After the gig

Gordon introduced me to his publisher, Mark Rowles. Mark had run the publishing side of Andrew Lloyd Webber's Really Useful Company before forming his own publishing company, MRM Ltd. I had a few compositions which were all registered with the Performing Rights Society, but I'd never had a publisher taking care of that side of the business for me. So Mark became my publisher and remains so to this day. He's done a great job for me in handling royalty payments and looking out for opportunities composing for people. It was actually Mark who instigated the record deal with Sony – but more of that later.

# 18 In Bangalore When The War Ended

I was soon heading off to exotic parts again, this time thanks to my old friend Charles Alexander. I've known Charles for a long time. He has his own company called Jazzwise Publications and we first met back in the '70s. He is a guitar player himself and has always been involved with the British Council and so, through him, I started going on trips organised by them.

The first, as I've already mentioned, was the Indian visit I undertook during the Gulf War. Bangladesh and Pakistan were out of bounds, but Sri Lanka and India were considered neutral and safe – as long as we had those bodyguards.

I was travelling with Dave Newton and Brian Sheils and they agreed we should go ahead with the trip. I'd played Bombay before with The Jazz Yatra, which was run by a guy called Nerinjin Javeri, and it was a good opportunity to revisit India and practise my Hindi again.

It has to be said at this point that Dave Newton always dresses like an executive. It doesn't matter where he is or what he's doing, he's always got a suit and tie on. Dave took to being in India almost immediately – I can still see him sitting there with his suit on, sipping a gin and tonic like some old colonial.

After we played the concert in Bombay, Nerinjin said, "I'd like to invite you to my club tonight." This turned out to be the Willingdon Club, one of the most exclusive in India. We drew up in the car outside and you could see Dave's face light up – he'd got his blazer on and the air of Roger of the Raj. Inside it was like stepping back in time. Wicker chairs, punkawallahs – everything. And there was Dave, sitting there with a gin and tonic, looking like he owned the place.

"You know," he said, "I'd really like to join this club because it would be great just to be able to say that you are a member of the Willingdon." We thought that it couldn't cost that much and so Dave asked one of the officials. He was, of course, given the price in rupees, so he said, "How much is that in pounds?" "Around £10,000, sir..." the official replied. You could have heard a pin drop.

We were meant to fly between some of the places on the tour, but, as often happens in India, this would suddenly become not possible at the last minute and so we were introduced to the bizarre nature of some of the country's roads. The drive from Bombay to Bangalore is the same distance as London to Inverness, but it's mainly via dirt tracks. Suddenly, though, from out of nowhere you'd find yourself on a beautiful three-lane motorway and it would carry on for a couple of miles and then stop. There'd be what felt like a three-foot drop and you'd be back to dirt tracks again. Very interesting.

On the way we stopped at a tiny village and Dave got out of the car to get some air. It was roasting hot, but he still looked as if he'd just stepped out of a menswear shop window. Immaculately dressed in a suit and tie, as usual, he looked a little out of place in this dusty Indian village. All of the women from the village ran out when they saw him, not quite able to believe their eyes. I stood at the side of the road crying with laughter as around 60 women in saris started singing to him. Dave's face was a picture; it was a cross between horror and bewilderment. Meanwhile I was in agony laughing at the spectacle. Dave got his revenge the next day, however, when I was chased through a market by a sacred cow. He found that hilarious.

We were in the dressing room after the Bangalore concert when someone came in and said, "I've got great news – the Gulf War has ended." Everyone agreed that it was indeed good to hear, but the last word belonged to Dave. Standing there with the G&T, the blazer and the cigarette, in his best Noel Coward accent he said, "How wonderful. Now I can say, 'I remember I was in Bangalore when the war ended...' Marvellous!" Dave is one of the best jazz pianists and composers in the world, and a splendid character with a very sharp wit. It's always good fun to be around him.

Around the same time we heard the news that Slim Galliard had died. Slim was a singer, guitarist and piano player who did all those great recordings with Slam Stewart as Slim And Slam. Slim had come to live in London and had really become part of the jazz scene there. He used to have a kind of scat way of talking – the sort of thing you'd hear in Duke Ellington's 'Satin Doll' where the band goes, "Der da da der der derbaroony."

Anyway, David and I were sitting in the dressing room when Nerinjin Javeri told us the news of Slim's death. "Oh, what a shame-arooney," said

Dave, which I think Slim would have appreciated.

From Bangalore we went on to Sri Lanka, which was a country I'd always wanted to visit. My father had been there when he was in the Navy and told me many stories about the place. But also, I'd always had an interest in Buddhism and so I wanted to visit some of the temples there.

We were met by our representative from the British Council, a lovely lady called Ranmali Merchandani and her husband Kumar, who was a local businessman. They've both since become very good friends of mine.

We played a number of concerts in Sri Lanka; one in Colombo and another up in the hills in Kandy and then we went down to a place called Ahungala, which was just like a tropical paradise. We had been invited there for three days and asked to play for an hour and so the schedule was far from hectic at that point.

We had a young driver who didn't speak English, but he managed to tell us that his wife was expecting a baby. So every day when we saw him, I'd ask him if his wife had had the baby yet. I managed to get this across by gesturing to him, but he'd always say, "No, no, no..."

One day I asked my usual question and he said, "Yes, yes – at hospital," and he ended up taking me, Terry Gregory, Dave O'Higgins and John Goldie out to the hospital. He'd been trying to tell us that his wife had gone into labour. As I've mentioned, I'm a bit squeamish and I found myself in a ward full of pregnant women all at various stages of giving birth and it was pretty terrifying. I made a hasty retreat to the sound of women screaming and yelling.

I was interviewed by a local radio broadcaster called Arun Dias Bandaranaika, who was related to Sri Lanka's prime minister of the time. It's another friendship I've had ever since.

When I was in the British Council offices there, I mentioned that I would love to meet the science fiction writer Arthur C Clark, who lives in Sri Lanka. Ranmali said, "No problem, I'll ring him." Unfortunately he was unable to meet me on that visit, but we had a long chat on the phone and I sent him an album. I met him on a subsequent trip when he launched his book *3001*, the concluding part of the *2001* saga.

On another British Council trip I went to Ghana with Gordon Giltrap. We were supposed to go on to Cameroon but Gordon ignored the traveller's golden rule of not drinking the water and became very, very sick. So we had to return to the UK.

I have since been on further trips for the British Council, playing the Zagreb Jazz Festival through their sponsorship in the mid '90s, and have always been grateful to them for the opportunities to play in some of the more far flung corners of the planet.

The first time I went to India on my own I was playing once again at The Jazz Yatra. Max Roach was out there, too, and he was playing a set on solo percussion which was quite incredible. That was the first time I met Max and I'll always remember coming back with him on a plane from Delhi and asking him if he practised much. He'd been playing so long, I was just curious. Max just smiled and said, "No, I figure at my age that would be cheating." I thought that was quite a good answer. Since then we've recorded together on an album with Shannon Gibbons and Rufus Reid called *A Jimmy Van Heusen Song Book*.

On another occasion, Max and I were in the States together and I asked him to take me to church in Harlem. We picked one and it was absolutely fantastic, the place was packed. We only got in because Max was there and people knew who he was. They asked Max to take a bow and I found it very moving and the whole thing had a lasting impression on me. They realised what an important man Max is to the African/American community in terms of being a major figure in the jazz world and also a campaigner for human rights. He's an incredible guy. After the service he took me round the corner to Minton's, the legendary jazz club that was reopening. We went on to the stage and he showed me the spot where Charlie Christian used to sit and play and I stood there for a while, just trying to soak up some of the atmosphere and taking in the place's immense jazz history.

I've played a few times at the Django Reinhardt festival at Samois sur Seine. The first time I was on my own and so I played solo, but the next time I played with a Gypsy guitarist called Romane, Django's son, Babik Reinhardt, and an American guitarist from San Francisco called Jim Nicolls.

That first time I was first on the bill and it was pouring with rain. It had rained all the previous day, too, and so you could say I was given a bit of a duff spot. Very often soloists are asked to play at the beginning of something like that because the organisers don't think you could follow a band. But I don't mind going on first – it usually means that I can get away early, have a nice meal, a glass of wine and an early night.

Just before I went on stage, it stopped raining and so I went on and played for about an hour. At the end, Babik came on stage with tears in his eyes and embraced me and spoke to the crowd over the mike, which is something he never usually does. When I came off stage there were various members of the Reinhardt family gathered there who promptly whisked me off to the place where they had camped just outside Samois. I met Django's half-sisters, Carmel and Victoria, and I stayed for dinner – it really was a great evening.

One of my favourite Gypsy guitar players is Fapy Lafertin, who is a Dutch Gypsy. Fapy gets a great sound and he's got the real feel for that music and we've played together a few times.

Another great Dutch Gypsy guitarist is Stocholo Rosenberg, who quite often played with Stephane in the later years, after I'd left. Stocholo's cousin, Jimmy, and I have played together, too. The first time I met him was at Samois when he was about eleven years old. He was also on the bill at Stephane's memorial concert at Carnegie Hall and he simply blew the audience away.

I played at the Israel Guitar Festival, again through the British Council, in 1993, playing places like Tel Aviv, Bethlehem and Jerusalem. Their road system came as a surprise. The motorways there are incredibly similar to those in the UK, but instead of seeing signposts to Stoke on Trent, you see signs saying "Galilee" and other names familiar from the Bible. It amazed me, just being there.

While I was in Israel, I met Marcel Dadi and he invited me to play at his guitar festival in Issoundon, France. Dr Mark Pritcher, who is the president of the Chet Atkins Appreciation Society, was in the audience that night. He'd seen me play once before with Stephane in Knoxville, Tennessee, which is where he lives. After the gig we got talking and I asked him how Chet was and said that I'd like to see him again. So Mark invited me over to the Chet Atkins Convention in Nashville and I met up with Chet again, around the time of his 70th birthday.

In Nashville they have a TV show called *Music City Tonight* with phenomenal viewing figures of around 20 million. Both Mark and Chet said it would be really good if I got on to the programme. I believe that Chet pulled some strings – not that he'd admit it – because a little bit later I received a phone call from the show, asking me to appear.

It was a live TV show and one where you not only play, but get interviewed, too. There's a live band, a couple of presenters and a live audience of around 1,000 people. Because it was Chet's birthday, he came on and started talking to the audience and said, "I want to introduce you to a friend of mine from Scotland who is one of the world's greatest guitar players and I just love his playing – Martin Taylor." I came on and played 'I Got Rhythm' and the response was fantastic. After I finished I went and sat on one of the sofas on stage with Chet, ready to be interviewed.

Everyone loves the guitar in Nashville, although a lot of the people just play what we call "cowboy chords" in the first position. I guess that's where the money is! They appreciate it when someone like me comes on and plays up the dusty end of the fretboard – and they certainly loved it that night. I got a great response.

Sitting there, talking with Chet and being interviewed on this huge American TV programme with Chet saying all these nice things about me, I started thinking, "What am I doing here?" I had a flashback to my childhood and it was a moment of complete and utter bewilderment. But somehow I managed to keep myself together and I've watched the video since and I can't really tell where it happened.

While I was in Nashville I met up once again with David Hungate, who had produced my *Sarabanda* album. David likes a lot of the old style jazz guitar players, like Carl Kress, Dick McDonough and Eddie Lang, and so we get on together really well. We would often sit together and play through some old tunes on a couple of guitars.

After the TV show David said to me, "You know, you and Chet really ought to record together." Chet and I had actually recorded once before when I was going to record a follow-up to *Sarabanda*, and so I said, "Well, let's ask him." David had just finished producing an album for Chet and so we went up to Chet's office and just sat and talked. I didn't want to just come out with it and pop the question about us recording together, so just before we were about to leave, David, sensing I wasn't going to ask, said, "How about you two guys recording together again?" Chet said, "I'd love to do that – really love to – but the trouble is I don't have time." But after a couple of moments' thought he added, "You record your parts and I'll put mine on after."

So I went into a studio in Brentwood, Nashville which was run by Tom Bruner, and I recorded my parts. I was so thrilled by the sound that David had got for me in the studio that I decided to carry on playing. I played loads of tunes and brought the tapes back to Linn Records and offered it to them as an album. Chet did his parts and put them on a tape, but the album wasn't long enough and so I went into another studio while I was on tour in Hamburg and recorded some more.

I had just recorded some tracks for a radio show and so we tagged the session for the new album on at the end. Then I went back to Scotland and handed the tapes over to Calum Malcolm, who had engineered my previous Linn albums. We had Chet's tape there, but when we put it into the machine, it got chewed up and so there was a real panic. I thought, "Well, that's the end of that..." but we found that the machine hadn't chewed up the bit of the tape we needed. We phoned the manufacturers of the offending piece of studio equipment in order to free the tape from the machine, then Calum got on with assembling the album and I went out for a beer to calm my nerves. I was really pleased with the end result.

As I said, the first time that Chet and I recorded was supposed to be a follow-up to *Sarabanda*. I went over to Chet's house and we sat down together and were about to begin recording when the phone rang in the studio and Chet's engineer said, "Chet, I think you'd better take this call." Chet picked up the phone and I could see his whole face change. He just said, "I'll be praying for you," and put the phone down.

It turned out that his best friend was in hospital having a major operation with only a 50/50 chance of getting through. Chet just started crying in front of me and there was nothing I could say to him – he was my great hero, crying in front of me and there was nothing I could do for him. After a while he composed himself and we recorded 'Here, There And Everywhere'. Chet played it beautifully. That was one of those moments in my life that stand out as being special.

People are amazed when I say that I'm afraid of flying, bearing in mind how many flights I take in a year. But it's true. I just knock back a few drinks and try not to think about it. I used to go over to Nashville every year in July to play at Chet's Convention. Marcel Dadi was always there and usually we used to all fly back together to go to France to play the festival there. There would be Romane, Tom Bresh – who's Merle Travis's son – and Buster B Jones, all making the trip every year.

One year in Nashville I met a guy called Fred Kelly, who is an Indian chief and medicine man from Canada. He told me that he hadn't intended to come to the festival that particular year but something had led him there because he had dreamt that he had to give Marcel an Indian name. There is a tradition among American Indians which states that only a medicine man can give anyone their real Indian name, and this process is brought about through deep meditation and dreams. So every night Fred would go to bed with an eagle feather over his head so that Marcel's Indian name could be revealed to him while he slept. But every time I asked him, he just shrugged and told me, "It hasn't come to me yet…" I don't know whether it ever came to him either, because of the tragic incident which followed shortly afterwards.

On the last night of the festival I spent a few hours in the bar with Marcel and Tom Bresh, just sitting around telling jokes and laughing. This particular year, 1996, I didn't fly back with Marcel because Liz had come with me and we'd flown there via Detroit, whereas Marcel went to New York. We bid each other farewell and Marcel boarded the plane for Paris. It turned out to be the infamous TWA 800, which exploded in mid-air just after taking off from JFK. It gives me chills even now, thinking that Liz and I could have been on that flight and it gave me nightmares for ages afterwards. There were 230 people on board TWA 800 that night and nobody survived.

It was very sad. Marcel left his wife and two young sons. Guy Dupont, who was travelling with him and who was the editor of the French *Guitar Magazine*, also had a young family. Originally Marcel's wife was coming to the festival, but decided not to at the last moment and so Guy had taken her place.

As I said, I really don't like flying, but it's no good encouraging a phobia about it because I'd be well and truly stuck. I won't fly in small planes or helicopters, though; I'll only go on planes with an aisle down the middle with flight attendants who bring you drinks. I'll sit there and have a few drinks and that way I can fly without a problem.

Scott Chinery once wanted me to play at a private concert at his house in New Jersey. I was free on the day, but because of prior commitments I didn't have time to fly there and back. Scott came up with a solution. He said, "I'll book you on Concorde." I thought it would be a great experience to fly on Concorde, but then he added, "I've hired a helicopter to fly you from New York to my house…" I hesitated for a while, then said, "Thanks, but no thanks." You won't get me in a helicopter.

On one of my annual trips to Australia I went over to New Zealand to play a solo concert at the National Library Auditorium in Wellington. The following night I was booked to play at the Theatre Royal in Hobart, Tasmania. I was there with Ian Date, a wonderful jazz guitarist from Australia, James Morrison and his brother John. James has his own plane in which he flies his band around to gigs, but I refused to go with them. It meant that I had to fly by commercial carrier from Wellington to Sydney, Sydney to Adelaide and then Adelaide to Hobart, but there was no way I was getting on that small plane.

# 19 *Spirit Of Django*

After playing solo concerts for a while, I wanted to do something a bit different. A lot of people were saying, "Why don't you play with a band again?" but I didn't want to go back to playing straight-ahead jazz. I was missing the buzz I used to get from playing with Stephane, working with a group that was really tight and so I decided that if I was going to do anything at all, I'd put together a band with very tight arrangements, but enough room to improvise at the same time. Some people suggested a Hot Club-type of outfit, but there are guitar players around who can do that sort of thing far better than I can and I didn't want to copy anyone. It had taken me this long to develop my own individual style and I felt that that would represent a huge step backwards. I wanted to put together something more like a contemporary version of the Hot Club.

By this time I'd met John Goldie who used to come and see me play regularly. If I was playing in Glasgow or Edinburgh, John would be there and one day after the gig he asked me if I gave lessons. I said I didn't but invited him to the house to play together. He came over and I could see right away that he was a really good player, but he'd never really played jazz before. He used to come over to my house quite regularly and our two wives, Liz and Marie, used to get together and we all became very good friends.

When I was thinking about the group, John was at the house and I started running over ideas with him. I began feeling out who I could get to play in the band and so I phoned a few people, including Alec Dankworth. I started to think more about what the band would sound like and put a few demos together at home. I played them to my dad and he said, "That sounds good. I look forward to hearing the band when it's all together." Sadly, this was never going to be.

On 7 February 1994, I went out at lunchtime to pick up Stewart from primary school. We were all going to have lunch together at home, but when I came back, there was an ambulance outside the house. I parked at the back of the house as usual and, as I got out of the car, I saw Liz coming out of the back of the house. Somehow I knew.

I said to Liz, "What is it?" and she said, "It's your dad," and just shook her head. Mum and Dad had their living room upstairs and so I ran up the two flights to their room and my dad was just lying on the floor. My mum was kneeling next to him with the nurse and they told me that he had been watching the midday news and had had a massive heart attack. He'd had a minor heart attack before, back in 1977, but this one was much bigger and they told me that he wouldn't have known anything about it. He was only 65 and I remember I started crying and I knelt over him, sobbing, "No, not now, not now, it's too early, you're too young..."

My sister, Sue, was at work and I had to go and tell her. A neighbour of ours, Kay, drove me to where Sue worked – there was no way that I could have driven there myself. I told Sue that Dad had died, but it was such a shock that she wouldn't believe me and kept saying, "No, he can't have, he can't have."

We both handled the shock in our separate, different ways. I cried my eyes out, but Sue was calm and showed no emotion on the surface. In fact she found the loss very difficult to deal with later. We went back in the car and, by the time we got home, they had put Dad on the bed and Sue went and sat by him, held his hand and whispered, "Come on, stop mucking about, Dad. Come on." She was in shock and it took days for her to fully take things in.

Bob, my brother, came up from Newark a few days before the funeral. I was adamant that there was no way that they were going to take Dad out of the house until the funeral and so he stayed with us, with the coffin open all the time.

I spent the whole time keeping the candles around the coffin lit and sitting and talking to him. We had a neighbour, Mr Glover, who was a Church of Scotland minister, and I went to tell him the news. He was very kind and put his arm around me and said a short prayer. I sat down and wrote to everybody I knew to tell them what had happened and, looking back, I think it was my way of working things out for myself. It was strange because, despite being the youngest of the family, everyone looked to me all the time and so I was incredibly busy. I didn't really sleep or anything and I was working towards total emotional and physical exhaustion. I felt I couldn't leave my dad upstairs on his own and so I spent hours over the next few days just sitting with him, talking to him and when I got tired I just laid down on the floor next to the coffin and grabbed a little sleep.

Eventually, it all caught up with me and I had to rest. I went to lie down on my bed and the strangest thing happened. As I lay there I began to feel like I was being enveloped by something I can't describe. My first reaction was to move, but then I thought, "No, I'll stay with this," and I felt that my father was with me, that he had surrounded and enveloped me and was saying, "It's okay, everything's all right." I had this overwhelming feeling of being immersed in my father's love and, although I was crying, it was a comforting and healing experience. I believe it was the Conyach being given to me by him.

Bob, meanwhile, dealt with things differently. He is a really good cook and so he cooked for us all the time and generally kept busy. In the evenings, we would get some wine, have something to eat, drink some more wine and talk about things. There was laughter and tears and even the occasional sing-song – it was a really emotional few days, but certainly not all doom and gloom. Everyone felt that Dad wouldn't have wanted that.

At the funeral, my mum, brother, sister and myself went in the car that followed the hearse. Because my dad came from Lambeth, I spontaneously started to sing 'The Lambeth Walk' and everyone joined in, including the driver. It seemed a funny thing to do, but it made us feel quite uplifted.

The organist who played at the funeral was a former bandmate of my dad's called Jim Cosker. I told him, "No hymns. We're not big on hymns," and gave him a list of my dad's favourite jazz tunes. Stephane's driver, Eric Carrington, was sitting right at the front of the crematorium and he told me later that when Jim started to play 'Poor Butterfly', a Black Admiral butterfly flew out from behind the radiator and started flying around, which is really freaky in mid February. The funeral service was led by Mr Glover, the local Salvation Army Captain, and two Buddhist monks, Ajahn Vipassi and Tan Mahesi, who are friends of ours. Nobody had ever seen a funeral like that in Ayr before – Buddhism and jazz!

I put the band together and called it Spirit Of Django, a name which I got from Stephane. When he first heard the band, he said, "Martin has really captured the spirit of Django, yet he has done it in his own style. Bravo, Martin!"

Alec Dankworth was the original bass player on the first CD, but due to his many commitments he couldn't do the touring. So my old school friend Terry Gregory joined us along with Dave O'Higgins on sax and John Goldie on rhythm guitar. The album was recorded in June 1994, just four months after my dad died.

I invited Jack Emblow into the band and met up with him the night before we recorded the first album. It was Jack's birthday and when I arrived he was sitting alone in the hotel dining room having a meal and a bottle of wine to celebrate. I joined him and we had a few drinks together, then a few more drinks and then Jack remembered he had a bottle of brandy in his room and so we went up there and continued our small but lively party together. We talked about some of the things that he had done, including playing the accordion on the Henry Mancini theme to the Elizabeth Taylor movie, *Two For The Road*.

Next morning, we both had thumping headaches as we headed for the studio in Jack's convertible. We had the top down in the car so that we could get some air and blow away the cobwebs.

The first thing we recorded that day was 'Chez Fernand', a tune I'd written. I asked Jack to play the French Musette Accordion, which is a really loud instrument and not one you want to be within twelve feet of when you've got a hangover. I'm sure I saw tears in Jack's eyes as he struggled to play the tune that day.

On the second day we were in the middle of recording 'Minor Swing', which was one of the Hot Club tunes my dad played me as a kid, when I started to feel ill. I felt my dad was pulling me and he was holding me and saying how much he missed me and it was as if he was unhappy. It was awful.

In the middle of the take I just stood up and said, "I can't play any more. That's enough." I'd turned a grey colour and I could see everyone was looking very worried. I cleared the studio and lay down. My heart was thumping, I was shaking and my body felt heavy. I honestly thought I was dying. After about 30 minutes I started to feel better, but it really shook me up. My dad appeared to me in lots of dreams for months after he died, telling me things and giving me advice. In one of the last dreams we were standing together, he had some papers in his hand and he said, "Everything's fine, son. I've taken care of everything."

After my father died, Liz and my mum said that the house we had in Ayr was too big and that they really wanted something smaller. So I bought a four-bedroom farmhouse about ten miles outside Ayr. It had a garage which I converted into a small studio, and stables for our horses. I bought a few acres of land as well, and I also had all the property fenced off. Very private.

It was a good move and I'm really glad we made it. It's a beautiful spot, with panoramic views of the hills. After a short time, though, my mum decided she would like a flat of her own and got a place back in Ayr near my sister. I've never regretted the move and I love waking up there in the morning and looking at one of the best views in the south of Scotland and it's good to walk out into our fields and see our horses. I feel very fortunate to live in such a beautiful place.

One day, completely out of the blue, I decided to ring up David Grisman, who I hadn't spoken to for a long, long time. He told me that he'd just started up his own record label, called Acoustic Disc. He'd become really disillusioned with the record industry and had decided to go out on his own. He'd already released one album with Jerry Garcia and one with Tony Rice, called *Tone Poems*, on which they played vintage guitars and mandolins. David had the idea for a follow-up album using jazz guitars and I agreed to do it.

I went over to California to Mill Valley, which is just over the Golden Gate Bridge, and met up with David and Dexter Johnson. We assembled all these guitars and mandolins and paired them off year for year – if a guitar was built in a certain year in the '20s, we'd find a mandolin built in the same year, check what tune was at the top of the charts that year and record it.

I started off by playing this huge 1911 Gibson harp guitar which had about 40 strings on it. David played a mandolin from the same year and we recorded 'Swanee', the Al Jolson hit. We found instruments and songs from the '20s, '30s, '40s and so on, ending up with Chick Corea's 'Crystal Silence' on contemporary instruments.

A little later I was working in Nashville and I got a call from Steve Howe to tell me that he'd been asked to do an album for the guitar collector, Scott Chinery. The plan was to make a recording using some of the guitars in the collection and so I flew up to New Jersey to meet Steve and Scott at his house in Tom's River. Scott was once a body-builder but then he formed a company called Cybergenics which makes nutrients for body-builders. He'd recently sold up for a lot of money and had sort of semi-retired to enjoy his hobby of collecting guitars.

I'd been picked up from Newark airport by limo and when I arrived at Scott's mansion, the first thing that caught my eye was the Batmobile from the original TV series parked just outside. My WG Barker guitar had actually been used on some of the music for the '60s show – somehow I knew we were going to get on before we had even met.

Scott was a giant of a man. He greeted me warmly and took me to see his collection – which was absolutely unbelievable. There were vintage Gibsons, D'Angelicos, Stromburgs, Martins – you name it, they were all there. I was absolutely speechless for quite a time. Talk about a kid in a sweetshop, I'd never seen so many great guitars in one place before.

Scott told me that his plan was to get different guitarists to play some of the guitars on different tracks of an album, but I played a couple of tunes for him and he said he wanted me to do the whole album myself instead. Steve said he wanted to produce it, rather than play on it extensively, and so it would be mainly me playing the guitars on the CD.

Scott had had a guitar built for him by Jimmy D'Aquisto just before he died. He'd asked Jimmy to make him something a bit different and so Jimmy had built him a jazz-style guitar with a blue finish. It was one of the last guitars he made before he died and so, as a tribute, Scott decided to commission 26 guitar-makers to build blue jazz guitars. They all had to be something different, though, and that was the start of the Blue Guitar Collection.

Later that year I returned to the USA and once again went out to Tom's River and met up with Steve. We spent some time going through all the guitars, just finding those that would record well together. We ended up with about 65 in the end.

A project like this takes time to put together and so I flew back to Scotland and got on with whatever I was doing at the time. Eventually I went back to the US once again and Scott had the guitars shipped down to the studio by a security company. One of the guitars, the D'Angelico Teardrop, had been valued at half a million dollars and so nobody was taking any chances. In view of the guitar's value I was nervous about handling it and so I insisted that the curator hand me The Teardrop while I was sitting and then take it away when I'd finished playing. I didn't feel that I even wanted to try to stand holding it.

We recorded the album in a place called Lidditz, in Pennsylvania. We locked ourselves away for a couple of weeks and, by this time, the Blue

Guitars had begun to arrive, too.

Steve has an amazing way of working. We would start at around ten in the morning and he would carry on until about two the next morning. I can only go from ten until about seven and then that's it. It starts to bug me after a while and I just need to get out.

So I would record all day and at seven o'clock a car would come and get me, take me back to the hotel and Steve would carry on doing his thing, recording his tracks and editing stuff together. He has amazing energy and is a really hard working guy.

Blue Guitars were arriving every day and so I started to record those as well. I recorded 'Blue Bossa' with the accompaniment on the D'Aquisto and then a chorus each on the Benedetto, Hollenbeck, Monteleone, Manza and so on. After the recording, all the Blue Guitars went to The Smithsonian Institute as they are considered part of America's heritage – along with Bill Clinton's saxophone!

Subsequently, Steve and I were hired to play a concert in Washington DC, at the Carmichael Auditorium, playing both our own guitars and some of the Chinery Collection as well.

Another performance around the same time was The Blue Guitar concert at the Wolf Trap in Virginia, celebrating 100 years of jazz guitar. The Wolf Trap is an amazing venue, I played there many times with Stephane. It holds around 3,000 people in a covered area at the front, but behind that are grassy banks where people sit and have picnics during the summer and so you can fit in a few thousand more that way. That night, the cast of jazz guitarists present included Kenny Burrell, George Benson, Larry Coryell, Tuck Andress, Ron Afif, Andy Summers and myself. Johnny Smith came on and was presented with a lifetime achievement award by The Smithsonian.

Because I was playing solo, I went on first – everyone else was playing with bands. I didn't mind in the least, I hit the audience with four or five of my best and they seemed to really like it. A little later George Benson came on and just blew everyone away. He is the most incredible guitar player, just amazing.

A couple of days later, I played in a tribute concert to Herb Ellis at the Danny Kaye Theatre in New York, and the line-up was just about as stellar as the one at the Wolf Trap. Andy Summers was there again, too, and he called me at the hotel the next morning and suggested we went to see

Playing a solo concert in 1996, during my long-hair days

With Max Roach at Sony Studios in New York, November 1996

At Tom's River, New Jersey, with Scott Chinery and Steve Howe. I'm holding the D'Angelico Teardrop, valued at $500,000, which I played on *The Chinery Collection* album

With David Grisman. (Picture courtesy of Sue Storey)

Receiving the Freedom of the City of London in 1998, with Liz, Stewart and Mum

Dr Martin Taylor receiving his honorary degree from the University of Paisley, Scotland, with Professor Gordon M Wilson (l) and Sir Robert Eason, OBE (r)

My annual pilgrimage to Appleby Horse Fair, 1998

Rehearsing with my pal, Jack Emblow, in 1998, on a mission to make mandolin and accordion duets hip! (Picture courtesy of Sue Storey)

Relaxing in 1998. (Picture courtesy of Sue Storey)

L-r: Eddie Gomez, Matt Rollings, Martin Taylor, Al Foster, Randy Brecker, Steve Buckingham. Taken at Quad Studios, New York, during the recording of *Kiss And Tell*, 1999. (Picture courtesy of Gary Paczosa)

With my fellow Rhythm King, Albert Lee, at the Kirkmichael International Guitar Festival, which I founded in 1999. We raffled these two Aria guitars, which raised money for the local community

At the house of my friends, Barry and Sue Storey, 1998. They've always been keen supporters of jazz. (Picture courtesy of Sue Storey)

1999, Santa Cruz, California. L-r: David Grisman, Jim Kerwin, Julian Lage, George Marsh, Martin Taylor. (Picture courtesy of Dexter Johnson)

Sony publicity photo for *Kiss And Tell*, 1999. (Picture courtesy of Allan Titmuss)

Live at the Wigmore Hall, 1999. (Picture courtesy of Allan Titmuss)

On stage with one half of the greatest rhythm section in rock 'n' roll, Bill Wyman, 2000

Taking a curtain call with The Rhythm Kings. L-r: Janice Hoyte, Beverly Skeete, Martin Taylor, Bill Wyman, Albert Lee, Terry Taylor and Gary Brooker

Les Paul play at Fat Tuesdays. I know Les and we've played together a couple of times, but whenever anyone goes down there, the guitar Les has for guests to play is a real beast. It's virtually impossible to play, has a really thin sound and it's much quieter than the one Les himself plays.

Anyway, Andy wanted to go the following night and so I said I'd meet him there. I had a dinner date beforehand and afterwards, as I was walking towards the club to meet Andy, I thought, "I'm too tired – I don't think I'll bother," and so I returned to my hotel and went straight to bed.

The next morning Andy rang me and said, "Where were you?" and so I explained about feeling too tired and everything. I asked him how it went and Andy said, "It was the most humiliating night of my life." I winced and said, "Sorry – I should have warned you."

Les has done the same thing to many guitar players in the past and it can be a terrifying experience if you're not fully prepared. Les still plays really strong. He's well into his 80s, but he still loves taking you on for a good duel. Andy had to try and play on the "guest guitar" that night and didn't have a good time doing so. I really like Les, though – he's a lovely old devil!

I used to play at the Jersey Jazz Festival in the Channel Isles quite a lot. The first time I played there was with Stephane. It was at the Opera House in St Helier at a gig put on by Ernie Roscouet. I subsequently got to know both Ernie and his wife Pam really well. Pam used to make a traditional Jersey dish called Jersey Beanjar, which is basically pork strips, potatoes, onions and many different varieties of bean, cooked together in a stock for hours and hours on end. It's delicious. Whenever we were in Jersey Stephane would insist that we visited Ernie and Pam to sample the delights of the Jersey Beanjar. He used to refer to Pam as "Madame Haricot" because he was so impressed with the dish.

I went back to Jersey for the Jazz Festival more or less every year from the late '80s to the mid '90s. It was held at the Pomme D'Or Hotel in St Helier and I really enjoyed it. I took Liz and the boys with me and it became more like a holiday than anything else.

A couple called Mr and Mrs Mauger always used to come and see me at the festival. I could always rely on them being there whenever I played. One year, I turned up at the hotel and there was a message from Mr Mauger which said that they wouldn't be there this year because his wife was ill in hospital. I spoke to Pam about it and she told me that Mrs Mauger had cancer and wasn't expected to live for too much longer. I spoke to her husband and asked him if it was all right if I went to see her in hospital.

I turned up at the hospital with my guitar and the nursing staff confirmed that she was terminally ill. When I went into her room she looked very sick. She'd lost a lot of weight and her skin was grey, but I said to her, "Look, if you can't come and see me play, I'll have to come to you." Her eyes lit up. The nurses sat her up in bed and I got my guitar out of the case and asked her what she'd like me to play for her. She said, "I love 'I'm Old-Fashioned'..." and so I played it for her. It was very hard to play it under those circumstances, a very emotional experience. In the end I played about three tunes for her and when I left she was sitting up in bed with a rosy complexion and a big smile on her face. It's amazing what music can do, it touches everyone and has enormous power. It was a proud moment for me, being able to do that – I think it was one of the most meaningful things I've ever done. If you play from the heart it will definitely touch people.

# 20 For The Price Of A Glass Of House Red

I came quite late to composing. I wrote my first tune, 'Ginger', in 1978 and that set the ball rolling. I'm not the kind of composer who writes every day, in fact I can go months without writing. The problem is, once I get something going in my head I get very obsessed with it and have difficulty switching off. When I'm in the middle of writing something (which can take anything from one day to six months) I go off into a world of my own and can barely hold a conversation with anyone because of all the music going on in my head. Also, to be honest with you, I'm fairly lazy and composing is quite hard work. I write best if I'm given a commission, if I have to write something for TV or an upcoming album. I've written a lot for Spirit Of Django and some of those tunes I'm very proud of – 'Chez Fernand' in particular.

Strangely enough, I have written very few "jazz" tunes. I like to write music that just creates an atmosphere. I wrote 'Chez Fernand' in a cafe of the same name at Samois sur Seine, in France. It's just around the corner from Django's old house and he spent a lot of time there. They still have his piano in the bar. It's one of the few occasions when I wrote a tune without any hard work involved. I was just sitting there, having a glass of wine during the annual Django Reinhardt Festival and it just came to me. I don't know where it came from, I just sang it through in my head – even the harmonies were there. I didn't have to do any of the usual work you do when composing, like shaping the format and finely tuning the melody and harmonies, it was just complete. When I left the cafe I turned around and said, "Thank you very much," to the front wall! That place gave me a really good composition for the price of a glass of house red and it turned out to be a perfect tune for Spirit Of Django.

The only other occasion that a tune came to me from nowhere was in 1997. When James was at school, he played drums in The Ayrshire Fiddle Orchestra, a local group of school children playing traditional Scottish fiddle music, led by a gentleman called Wallace Galbraith.

Through James I met the MacKay family who all play traditional music in Ayrshire. All of the children played in the orchestra, and I got to know them quite well. Tragically, one of the daughters, Lorna, contracted meningitis at the age of 18 and died. It was a heartbreaking experience to see the family devastated by the early death of such a gifted and beautiful young girl. In Scotland it's traditional to have what is called "the funeral tea", which involves everyone going back to a local hotel after the service and having tea – or something stronger – and sandwiches.

After the funeral everyone went to the Savoy Park Hotel in Ayr and I went to the bar with my friend, Mick O'Brien. As I sat there thinking about young Lorna, a Scottish waltz came into my head. It kept going round and round, so I asked Mick to get me a napkin from the bar. On the top of the napkin I wrote "Lorna Mary MacKay" then drew some staves below it. I wrote the melody out and some chord symbols and sang it through in my head. Not knowing a great deal about Scottish music, I started to think that maybe it was an old tune that I had heard somewhere. I showed it to some of the fiddle players who were there and expected them to say, "Oh, that's such and such a tune written in the 18th century," but they didn't. They all said what a good tune it was, though, so I gave the napkin to Lorna's father, David.

A few months later, David did a beautiful arrangement of 'Lorna Mary MacKay' for the orchestra and I recorded it with the kids in Kirkmichael Church with Lorna's brother, David, playing the melody on the fiddle. Shortly after that I performed the tune with David and The Ayrshire Fiddle Orchestra at Ayr Town Hall at a charity concert. Wallace announced the tune and explained that I had written it for Lorna. David and I shared the melody with the orchestra behind us, and at one point I looked up and saw 600 tearful people, all grasping handkerchiefs. I felt terrible, some people were crying their eyes out and I was getting a bit tearful myself.

David played the melody beautifully and when we finished the tune I turned round and a lot of the kids in the orchestra were in a bad state, very upset and crying. I walked off stage and sat in the dressing room shaking. I didn't realise my tune would have that effect on people and I felt really bad about it.

After the concert lots of people, including Lorna's family and kids from the orchestra, came up to me and thanked me for writing the tune for her. They were all smiling and said it had helped them to come to terms with her death. Young David still plays it regularly, as do other fiddlers in Scotland. I can't play it any more – I just think that you should never underestimate the power of music.

I'm often asked about my influences when it comes to my solo playing, and of course I tell people that it's been mainly piano players in general and Art Tatum in particular. But somebody who did influence me – and people think I'm joking when I say this, but I'm not at all – was Harpo Marx from The Marx Brothers. I remember in the film *A Night In Casablanca*, there's a scene where Harpo is in a lift which gets stuck between floors and so he climbs through a door in the roof of the lift and finds a secret room full of treasure. In the room there is a harp and Harpo goes over to it and plays 'The Hungarian Rhapsody'. I can remember watching that movie as a kid and practically being reduced to tears thinking that it was the most beautiful thing I'd ever heard in my life. Consequently, there is a harp-like quality to a lot of the solo pieces I play, but that is actually where it came from.

I'm often asked to do masterclasses or to teach privately, but I do neither. I don't enjoy doing masterclasses and I really don't rate myself as a teacher because I don't think about playing from an academic point of view – it's not the way I play. I know this comes as a disappointment to a lot of people, but I honestly wouldn't be much good to any of them from a teaching point of view. But, having said all this, since the mid '90s, I've had a regular tuition column in a couple of the British guitar magazines. Firstly in *Guitarist* magazine and subsequently in *Guitar Techniques*.

Now this might seem a little bit of a contradiction, but what happens is the editor of *Guitar Techniques* (and my co-author on this book), David Mead, flies up to see me in Scotland every so often and we record about six months' worth of material. He then explains it all in the magazine on my behalf.

I have been asked to make some teaching videos which proved a bit difficult for me – like I say, I'm not a teacher. I did an early one for a company called Star Nite through Gordon Giltrap, Gordon already having done one for the same company. But then, Stefan Grossman asked me to do one and so I went over to the Manchester Craftman's Guild in Pittsburgh and recorded a performance video. The two people involved in the Craftsman's Guild are Marty and Jay Ashby. Marty plays jazz guitar and Jay plays trombone and has worked a lot with Astrid Gilberto – I knew him from the Emily Remler days, as well. More recently, I've done videos of Duke Ellington's and Jimmy Van Heusen's music, too, for Stefan Grossman's company.

David Grisman asked me to join his band several times during the '80s. It would have meant moving my family to California while the kids were still very young and, what's more, I was still touring a lot of the time. I didn't think it would be fair to move them all out there where they knew absolutely no-one, and then almost immediately have to leave to tour.

Being away from the family so much can be quite hard. It puts a lot of strain on any relationship and, as I've said, I think I'm very fortunate to have had all the love and support from my own family during my career. It's always hard to say goodbye to the kids when I leave, but many musicians I've known have had far worse experiences on that front than I have.

When I was touring with Stephane, the bass player, Jack Sewing, had a very young son and daughter. His son was OK about him coming away on tour, but his daughter used to get very upset and, while we were in America, Jack would call home every day and sometimes she would cry on the phone.

I was very lucky in that I didn't have any of that. I guess it might have been the fact that I had sons – I've heard other touring musicians with daughters say that there is this tendency for big emotional scenes sometimes. But I never had the kids crying down the phone.

Far from it, in fact. Once when I was off on tour, Liz took me to the airport with James, who was about five or six at the time. I'd got my guitar and suitcase out of the car and loaded them onto a baggage trolley, when James wound the window down and shouted, "Hey, Dad." I thought he was going to call out something like, "I love you," or "I'll miss you," but instead he said, "When you die can I have your fishing rods?"

A little bit later on, when he was eleven, James took up the drums. We were living in Ayr at the time and there was a guy who lived locally who used to play with my dad, called Dougie McDonald, who taught drums at the local ex-servicemen's club. I took James along one evening and Dougie gave him a pair of sticks and ran through a few rudiments with him. Dougie asked him if he wanted to come back the following week and James, never one to show too much enthusiasm for anything, said, "Yeah, OK..."

He took the sticks home and practised all the things Dougie had shown him and really took to it. We got him a drum kit and put it in the garage, which had been converted into a small studio, and he spent hours and hours down there practising. I had thought, because I had got into music so young, that James wouldn't get into it because he hadn't really shown any signs up to that point. But he really worked hard at it, like he worked hard at everything.

He drummed up a ridiculous number of GCSEs and then went off to Stow College in Glasgow for a year to study music business management and administration. While he was there, he put together a record company within the college and recorded a local band and also founded a local *What's On* magazine. He was a real entrepreneur, even at the age of 18.

In 1997 I made him my manager. I'd had various management deals before but things had never really worked out the way I thought they should and so I asked James to take over. He was only 20 at the time and I think a lot of people in the business thought that he'd be a pushover because of his age. It was nice to sit back and see them find, to their peril, that he isn't – he's a very astute businessman. It was James, along with my publisher Mark Rowles and lawyer Mark Wilkins, who negotiated my record deal with Sony.

My younger son, Stewart, loves horses. At the age of four we took him to Ayr races and he turned to Liz and me and said, "That's what I want to do. I want to be a jockey." So he started having riding lessons straight away, first on a little Shetland pony, then moving on to a horse of his own. After my father died and we moved out to the farm, we had space where we could keep horses and so Stewart started to compete in competitions and has ridden for Scotland at the Peterborough Show. He's also represented Scotland at Wembley and so his enthusiasm for riding hasn't diminished at all since he was four. He has just started at the British Racing School in Newmarket and so he's well on his way to realising his dream.

One thing I did for my sons when they were little was to turn them both on to The Marx Brothers. I'm a really huge fan and I've got all their films on video. I don't know if I've been a good father in other respects, but I did that for them. The kids would sometimes say, "Dad, can we have a Marx Brothers night?" and that would be Liz's cue to go out for the evening, because she doesn't like them. The boys and I would get the videos out and they would both have to sign our Marx Brothers Book, swear allegiance to "The Brothers Marx", then I would make them go out of the room and knock on the door to get back in. I would say, "What's the password?" and they would say, "Swordfish!" It got to the point where we can recite all the film scripts, practically word for word.

It's difficult to be a good father when you are away from home so much, but I have tried my best and they seem to like me!

One night in 1996, I had an incredibly vivid dream that I was with Ike Isaacs in his homeland of Burma. The colours were unbelievable and it really was the most wonderful place I had ever seen. Ike and I were standing high upon a hill looking down into a valley, there were trees there I didn't recognise and everything was so clear, peaceful and really beautiful. I turned to Ike and said, "Where are we, Ike? Is this Burma?" and he said, "No, but it reminds me of Burma. I think I'm going to be very happy here." Then, turning to me he said, "But you have to go now – don't worry about me, I'll be fine…"

At that point I was woken up by the phone ringing. It was Ike's nephew, Mark, calling from Sydney to tell me that Ike had just died. So I suppose it wasn't just a dream. I believe I really was there with him and it will always stay with me. I was very sad, obviously. We knew that Ike was seriously ill and that it didn't look like he'd make it, but I shed many tears when I heard the news all the same.

The dream was very uplifting, though, and I think about it often. It's given me a more optimistic outlook on life and it affected me in a way I can't even begin to describe.

Although I made a long study of Theravada Buddhism, I don't claim to follow any religion. But I have had a few spiritual experiences that have made me believe in "God" or something. I think it would be very egotistical of we humans to think that we are at the top of the ladder, spiritually speaking. There are other living forms here on Earth which couldn't begin to grasp our level of consciousness, and I believe that there are, in turn, higher forms of being that we cannot even begin to contemplate. But we just don't know – and that's really what it comes down to.

Any religion claiming to have the sole rights over all this is equally egotistical, too. Obviously the great prophets have had more insight into these matters than we can ever lay claim to, but none of us can really ever be sure.

There are so many musician jokes – usually told to musicians *by* musicians

– which are focused on one instrument in particular. Take the banjo, for instance; my favourite banjo joke is:

Q: What's the difference between a banjo and a trampoline?
A: You take your shoes off when you jump on a trampoline.

Or:

Q: What do you call 20,000 banjos at the bottom of a lake?
A: A fine start.

Trombone players usually come in for a lot of abuse, too. When a horn section needs to be trimmed down, it's quite often the trombone player who gets to be the first guy to go. And so...

Q: What do you call a trombone player with a pager?
A: An optimist.

Q: How do you know when a trombone player is at your door?
A: (Knock, knock) "Pizza!"

Jazz guitarists don't escape entirely unscathed, though:

Q: What happened to the jazz guitarist who won the Pools?
A: He just kept on playing until it had all gone.

A jazz guitarist had been told by his doctor that he only had two weeks to live. "Two weeks?" he said. "What on?"

Jazz guitarists have a reputation for being intense creatures, often obsessed by the instrument and very monomaniacal. So that kind of thing gives rise to jokes like this:

A woman was told by her doctor that she only had six months to live. The woman said, "Six months? Isn't there anything that can be done?" The doctor said, "Well, you could always go and live with a jazz guitarist." The woman, somewhat puzzled, said, "What good will that do?" and the doctor replied, "Oh, absolutely nothing medically-speaking. But it will make six months seem like a lifetime."

Or consider this quick jab at a jazz guitarist's earning potential:

Q: What's the least-used sentence in the English language?
A: "Wow, look at that jazz guitarist's new Mercedes..."

Jazz guitarists are always perceived as living in a basement on cans of beans, practising all day and getting the occasional gig that pays next to nothing. But someone told me that last joke just after I'd made an album for Chrysalis called *Acoustic Guitar Moods*. It was recorded for the Woolworth's easy listening market and produced by Ric Lee, the drummer from Ten Years After.

It had taken two days to record and was part of a series of records. Time was limited because I was about to fly out to Australia and so we didn't have too long to record the album's 40 tracks. The sessions were quite fraught, too, because it was all pop tunes and I hardly knew any of them. So what they had to do was play me a tape of the tune whilst getting the sheet music faxed to the studio so that, between the tape and the music, I could figure out what I was going to play. As I recorded one track I could see the music for the next coming out of the fax machine.

The resulting album sold in fairly considerable numbers and the first thing I did was go out and buy myself a Mercedes with the royalties. So when one day a wealthy friend of mine asked me, "What's the least-used sentence in the English language?" just as we were leaving a restaurant, I had great pleasure in getting into my brand new Mercedes. I could see him laughing and shaking his head as he drove off, his little joke having, for once, backfired.

Apart from my own recordings and videos, I made a couple of library albums with John Fiddy for TV films and commercials, etc. It gives me a good steady income through royalties, mostly from use in the USA and Japan. I hear our tunes played all the time on American TV shows and commercials.

In 1998, South Ayrshire Council gave me a Civic Reception to mark 25 years in music. The following year, Tony Harrison and Ivor Mairants nominated me for the Freedom of the City of London. I think Ivor saw it as me taking his place in some ways. He was very frail at this point and wanted me to record a jazz suite he had written in 1997. I had to decline and confess that I still hadn't learnt to read music well enough to do it, despite my promise to him in his shop 30 years previously.

The thing I'm always asked about the Freedom of the City of London is exactly what it entitles you to. It's a very ancient tradition, going back to the early 13th century. With the Freedom come several entitlements that haven't been changed in 700 years. So, apparently I am allowed to walk sheep over London Bridge, can be hanged using a silken noose and I'm allowed to pee in public as long as I give an audible warning first. When I told this to my friend, Sue Storey, she said, "What kind of audible warning? Do you mean like a fart?" which brought me right back down to earth.

In 1999, I was awarded an honorary doctorate by Paisley University which was a tremendous honour. I wondered if I should have a sign made up saying "Doctor On Call" so I can leave my car parked on double yellow lines when I play gigs...It's quite something for someone with such an abysmal school record as mine to be made a doctor – I'm very proud to be Dr Martin Taylor.

From the late '80s onwards, I started winning The British Jazz Award. I got it three years in a row before they decided that, because I was winning it every year, they would ban me from being nominated every other year, which they did. So I won it every other year – and now they've banned me from nomination completely.

# 21 A Very Kind Boy

The last time I saw Stephane was in Australia in February 1998. He was staying in Sydney at the hotel next door to the one I had booked. I was on a solo tour and had just played in New Zealand, so I stopped at the Duty Free at Auckland airport and bought two bottles of Chivas Regal, his favourite drink.

By this time, he was very frail, but we opened one of the bottles in his room and had a couple of drinks together. He was laughing and saying that he didn't think he had too much longer to go because he was finding it so hard. He had a tremendous sense of humour and, despite the fact that what he was saying sounded very grave, he still put it across with the sparkling wit which I knew from our long years on the road together. All the same, I couldn't believe he could still be out there touring considering his age and obvious fragile health.

As I was leaving, he kissed me on both cheeks and said, "You are a very kind boy." I felt very choked. It was the best compliment I'd ever received from anybody, and they were his last words to me.

When he returned to France after the Australian tour, he had a stroke and I was told that he couldn't play any more as a result. As soon as I heard this, I knew the time must be drawing near because he'd had heart attacks and had been really quite ill before, but he could always still play. Even when he was really tired on tour he would always come alive when he started to play. I think it's just the amazing power that music has to rejuvenate people.

The day that Stephane died I flew into London for a week's residency at the Pizza Express in Dean Street. When I got there, James phoned to tell me the news and then the telephone rang constantly for hours afterwards. Newspapers and radio stations started to call me and I appeared on Channel 4's *Seven O'Clock News*, just to say a few words about Stephane.

The funeral was a couple of days later and so, as I was playing in London that evening, I took the train through the Channel Tunnel to the

Gare Du Nord in Paris and walked to Stephane's apartment on the Rue de Dunkerque. Stephane's friend, Joseph Oldenhove, his daughter Evelyn, grandson Giles, plus three or four close friends were all there at the apartment.

Joseph said to me, "Would you like to go and see Stephane?" I said that of course I did. So I went through to the bedroom and he was lying on the bed with one of his flowery shirts on which he'd bought in Hawaii, and it looked just like he was asleep. I was very sad that I would never again have the chance to sit beside him on stage and watch him create magic every night. Or laugh at his stories as we sat backstage drinking whisky before we went on.

I remember when I first started to play with him how I thought, "This is a special moment and I must remember it because it won't last forever..." And here, right before me, was that end.

It was just a month away from his 90th birthday, but he'd had an incredible life, doing what he wanted to do, playing music. He had travelled all over the world and given pleasure to so many people through his playing. Audiences really loved him and he'd left behind him an incredible legacy and made an indelible mark on music that would last forever. I went over to the bed and, through teary eyes, looked at him and left the room once again to join the people outside.

It's strange how different cultures regard death – I guess we all see it in different ways. Another guy who was there, an American, was asked if he wanted to see Stephane, too, but he couldn't quite understand what was being said to him. Right from the time I was a child, I'd been taught that, when someone dies, you always paid your last respects. I was always told that there is nothing to fear from the dead – it's the living you've got to watch out for. But the American said, "What do you mean, 'see Stephane'?" He couldn't grasp the fact that Stephane was still there in the apartment. I guess he had come from a culture where you have drive-thru undertakers and things like that – a very detached way of dealing with death. So I said, "Would you like me to take you?" and he hesitantly said he would. I went back into the bedroom, but the guy wouldn't come any further than the door. I knew that this would be the last time that I saw Stephane, so I went over to the bed, touched Stephane's hand and kissed him on the forehead. The American came over faint and retreated to the kitchen. I saw him later, drinking his body weight in coffee. It was just obviously something that came as too much of a shock to him, but that's my culture and I was so glad I was able to say goodbye to Steph.

The church where the funeral was to be held was just down the road from the apartment. It wasn't like musicians' funerals I'd been to where music is played and maybe some records of the person who had died. It was a very traditional Catholic ceremony, very simple and straightforward. I'd been asked to sit with the family, along with Babik Reinhardt and Sacha Distel. Michel Le Grand was there, as were Michel Chaunard and Ed Baxter. There was John Etheridge, Christian Ecoude and the Irish violinist, Frankie Gavin, who had worked with Stephane for a couple of years. It was a surprisingly small gathering. Stephane didn't have a very large family.

There was one poignant moment at the end of the funeral. The only piece of Stephane's music they played was an improvisation that we had recorded for Louis Malle, 'Milou En Mai'. I remembered that when he recorded it, I was sitting next to Stephane in the studio and so that moment had very special significance for me.

I had toured with Stephane for eleven years and I often tell people that the time amounted to one year of actual playing and ten years spent having dinner. He was very fond of eating in hotels and restaurants and we often found ourselves in the situation of ending lunch by discussing where we were going to have dinner!

There were some amazing times on tour in all parts of the world and I'll always regard the time I spent sitting next to him on stage as being full of extremely precious memories.

When I was on the train back to London after Stephane's funeral, I thought to myself, "Well, Dad's gone, Ike's gone, now Stephane's gone. The three major influences on me have all gone now." Sitting on that train I felt that I was on my own, but I didn't feel lonely or isolated because I still felt – and continue to feel – their presence. I've been fortunate to have these people guide me during the early part of my life.

Some of the memories I have from my time alongside Stephane include playing a Royal Command Performance on the same bill as Paul McCartney. We did a number of concerts with Michel Le Grand, one at the Royal Albert Hall with The London Symphonia. We also did *The Tom O'Connor Show* – and I hadn't seen Tom since the Morecambe days.

On another occasion, I was recording with Stephane at Abbey Road studios at the time when he was collaborating with Yehudi Menuhin.

During the sessions a young lad came in wearing a tweed jacket. Stephane introduced us and the boy said, in a very polite accent, "Pleased to meet you, Martin." It turned out to be Nigel Kennedy. We sat in the cafe for quite a while and talked at length and agreed that we should get together at some point and play. A number of years later, I was at home and Liz suddenly shouted, "Quick, come and take a look at this." Nigel was on TV, complete with his trademark punk haircut and I couldn't believe it was the same person. He is a great violinist and is doing some very interesting things, but I haven't seen him since his pre-cockney days.

In 1988, we played at the Wolf Trap Centre for the Performing Arts for a special Bastille Day celebration. We shared the bill with Yehudi Menuhin plus Mstislav Rostropovich and The Washington Symphony Orchestra. Menuhin was conducting a performance of Vivaldi's *Four Seasons*, but he came on and played some of the things that he and Stephane had recorded together.

I'd met Yehudi before, having played on three of the Menuhin/Grappelli albums, including *Top Hat* with Nelson Riddle. I have a huge admiration for the man; he'd done wonderful things with the Menuhin School and, of course, was a virtuoso violinist. When you met him you just knew that this was a very special person indeed.

I shared a taxi with Yehudi to the concert. I had my Benedetto, which is a very valuable guitar, and he had his priceless Stradivarius violin on his lap. When we got to the venue neither of us had any money to pay the taxi driver. It certainly is a world of contrasts and contradictions.

At the concert, he'd memorised the charts for two of our tunes that we were playing in our set, which is an incredible feat. Unfortunately he wasn't that familiar with the material and so he managed to get about three bars out of sync with the rest of the band. Like a trouper, he carried on – but things were seriously out of whack.

Menuhin absolutely worshipped Stephane, but he didn't really know him that well. When Stephane died I was really surprised to see Yehudi make a TV tribute to him. He certainly didn't know Stephane as well as he said he did on television – he always thought that Stephane was a Gypsy, for instance, which he most definitely wasn't. However, it was a very warm and heartfelt tribute.

On Stephane's part, he looked up to Menuhin but felt that jazz musicians had the edge over classical musicians because of our ability to improvise, which in most cases they don't have.

The day after the concert we were at Washington airport and I could see Stephane was holding a local newspaper and I couldn't understand why. He was walking around with a grin and sat down and began searching through the newspaper. Then he obviously found what he was looking for and started laughing. It turned out that Menuhin had received a terrible review for the concert he played with us and Stephane was gloating.

He called me over and I read the review, which ended up by saying, "When Menuhin tried to play jazz I didn't know whether to laugh or cry." Stephane cut that review out and kept it in his violin case and would occasionally take it out, read it and start giggling. He really was a bit of a devil!

When you play a musical instrument you get invited to a lot of parties, but the invitation is often followed with, "Don't forget to bring your guitar..." or whatever instrument you happen to play. I rarely accept such an invitation because I feel you're not really being invited as a guest, but more as a performer. Still, it's always an embarrassing moment when you have to decline. Stephane came up with what I think is the perfect rebuff. One night, we were playing in France and after the show a very wealthy French guy came up to him and said, "I would like to invite you to a party at my house. I'm having drinks with a few friends and I would be delighted if you would be my honoured guest." Stephane said he would love to come, but the guy added, "Oh, and don't forget to bring your violin," to which Stephane replied, "My violin doesn't drink."

I've played a few times with Nils Henning Østed Pedersen, the great Danish bass player who worked for many years with Oscar Peterson. We've done duo concerts together at various festivals and we've also played together with Stephane. Last time I saw him he told me a lovely story about when he recorded an album with Stephane, Larry Coryell and Philip Catherine back in the '70s. The album was called *Young Django* and they all toured Europe together to promote it. One of the dates was in Bavaria and when they arrived at this small town, they found that the atmosphere there was really uncomfortable. There appeared to be some sort of neo-Nazi rally going on and there were flags everywhere in celebration of the somewhat dubious political stance of those in attendance.

The band checked into the hotel the night before they were due to play and the following morning met at breakfast. The owner of the hotel came into the breakfast room and for no apparent reason starting shouting at them in German. Nils can speak German and determined that the hotel owner had found out that they were jazz musicians and was chucking them out of his establishment. There was no reasoning with him at all and this was clearly some sort of political gambit and so the band didn't bother to argue, and left breakfast to go upstairs and pack.

A little while later Nils walked past Stephane's room and saw, to his total amazement, that Steph had completely trashed the room. He'd put the plug in the bath and sink and left the taps running, pulled down the curtains and thrown most of the furniture out of the window as a protest against this particular hotelier's extreme right-wing political persuasion. I think it's great that he actually did something that many rock 'n' roll musicians only pretend they've done – and Stephane was in his 70s at the time. I'm quite proud of him for that.

A lot of people ask me what advice Stephane offered me while I toured with him. Certainly the best advice he ever gave me was something that he passed on from Maurice Chevalier – "start well and end well, the middle will look after itself". I think that's great advice for any musician and it's something I try to apply at every opportunity.

In the early '80s, we were playing at a theatre in Luton and, as we were coming off stage at the end of the set, Ed Baxter said to Steph, "How would you and Martin like to do a gig tonight at Claridges?" Stephane obviously thought this was a bit of an odd request, but then Ed added, "You've been asked to do it by the Duke and Duchess of Marlborough." So we said we'd do it, went back on stage and played an encore, jumped in the car and drove down to Claridges.

We were shown into a suite where it was obvious that a party had been in full swing all evening. There were the Duke and Duchess of Marlborough and a few other people, all in very good spirits and having a good time. Steph was introduced to the Duchess as "Stephane Grappelli from the Hot Club of France" and she shook his hand and smiled graciously. But then she turned to someone else and said, "This is Stephane. Grappelli from the Rotary Club of France." I don't think she had a clue who we were, but the hospitality was marvellous and we stayed for two or three hours and played a few tunes together.

It turned out that an American banker had heard Stephane's name come up over dinner and had told everyone that he could get Steph to come and play that same evening. He obviously managed to track the band down and it was just a lucky coincidence that we were playing nearby. But it turned out to be a great evening. All night the Duke was saying to me, "Would you like another drink, Martin?" and pouring me large whiskies.

A strange thing happened when we were on a tour of Spain. We were in Granada and during the day Stephane and I went for a walk around town. We were walking along a street where all the guitar-builders have their workshops when Stephane suddenly stopped and turned as white as a ghost. He pointed into a shop and said, "I don't believe it. It's Django…" Inside was a man who was Django's double. It really shook Stephane up.

One of the last albums I recorded with Stephane was called *Years Apart*. Among the tracks on the album, I chose to record the song 'Undecided' and, as I really loved the way the Hot Club had recorded the track years earlier, I wanted to recreate it as near as possible to the original. It's not something I usually do, but I even decided to play Django's original solo practically note for note.

I got Claire Martin to sing Beryl Davies's part and most of the parts were in place when Claire and I flew over to Paris to finish the album there. Stephane arrived at the studio in a wheelchair, looking really frail. He said, "I'm really tired, I've not been well," and got his violin and placed it under his chin and put the bow to the strings. Only a creaking noise came out and I thought, "Oh, no." I hadn't seen him for a while and his health had really deteriorated and I wondered if he'd actually be able to play on the track after all.

A couple of the guys from Linn Records had come along, as well as Clive Davies from *The Times* newspaper, who was writing a piece about the making of the album.

Stephane asked his friend Joseph to go out and get him a beer and began warming up. The first track we played was 'Chicago' and Stephane was to play on the fifth chorus of the tune. But when we played back the track in the studio, he couldn't find the spot to come in at all. He began to get annoyed with himself and I began to think that everything was about to go horribly wrong. In the end he did it and played really well and so we moved on to the track 'Undecided'. We played it back over the studio's monitors and when my solo came in at the beginning of the tune, Stephane said, "Ah, that's Django…" But I said, "No, it's me!" and thought I must have done the job of recreating the solo properly.

We decided to get Claire to record her vocal part at the same time as Stephane was laying down his. I stood her in front of him and, as the track rolled, she started to sing. Stephane was absolutely mesmerised by her performance and was able to see what a great singer she is straight away. After the take, he said, "I'd like to do it again." So I said, "OK, we'll do another one." During the second take I could see Steph staring at Claire and beginning to come to life, starting to sway backwards and forwards in the chair in time to the music. The second solo he recorded was much better than the first, but he still insisted that he'd like to do another. This was very unlike him, because usually it was one-take-and-out as far as he was concerned, but I could see that he was really beginning to enjoy himself enormously.

So we did a third take and I thought we'd got it in the bag – we'd got the solo we were after. But Steph had other ideas. "Let's do it again."

Each time he got Claire to sing the song all the way through while he watched her and played his part. We must have rolled the tape at least a dozen times and with every subsequent take, you could see him come more and more alive. He fell in love with Claire's voice then and there and said that they should work together in the future. This was, sadly, not to be.

So this particular session, which had started off as being quite worrying, turned out to be absolutely magical. When I listen now to the original recording from 1934 and compare it to the one we did that day in Paris, it still makes the hair stand up on the back of my neck. It was something I really wanted to do and I'm glad I managed to achieve it.

# 22 Kiss And Tell

By the mid '90s I was in a position where I was earning quite a bit of money in royalties so I wasn't having to worry so much about touring, although I was still touring a lot.

In 1997, my publisher, Mark Rowles, started to speak to Adam Sieff, who is the head of Sony Jazz UK, about the possibility of signing me. Adam started his career in the music business in a rock band called Jaded, back in the '70s, which was promoted by none other than future British Prime Minister, Tony Blair. He started Pebble Beach Sound Recorders – a studio in Sussex – during the '80s, producing people like Alexis Korner and Big Country. He plays guitar, too, having been an active session musician working on many TV projects including *Spitting Image*, *Who Dares Wins* and *The Harry Enfield Show*. In 1991 he managed the jazz department at Tower Records in Piccadilly, joining Sony Jazz UK in 1995.

I'd recorded eight albums for Linn and really felt that I had gone as far as I could go, so after eight years, I figured I needed something new. It turned out that Sony UK hadn't signed a British jazz musician to the label for 30 years and so this was a new venture for pretty much everyone involved. Inevitably it meant a lot of to-ing and fro-ing with lawyers, contracts and meetings, but James, Mark Rowles and lawyer Mark Wilkins handled all the negotiations. It took two years to come together, the final stumbling block being that Sony wanted my website – martintaylor.com – whereas I wanted to keep it. Record deals always seem to come down to one thing in the end and the website was the thing for me. As much as I wanted to be with Sony, it would be a deal-breaker for me. The website had served me well during the previous few years it had been up and working and I didn't want to relinquish control.

Eventually, we got everything ironed out and I signed the contract with Sony's Tony Clark on 22 April 1999, in London. In fact I signed on the dotted line while Tracy Bass, my old friend Sam Bass's daughter, was filming me for a forthcoming documentary.

The next thing was to make arrangements to record the new album. I contacted David Hungate and asked him to produce it – previously, I had produced a lot of my own albums for Linn, but I had the resources of Sony behind me now. Sadly, David had too much going on in his life at that point and so I had to look elsewhere.

A few years previously, David had introduced me to Steve Buckingham, who has a very impressive track record, and who is one of the most respected producers in the States. Steve had started out as a session guitarist in Atlanta, Georgia before going on to produce some R&B and country albums. When I approached him, he was at the point of turning his attention to jazz. I'd worked with him before on an album with Melissa Manchester in Nashville, and so I called him and said that I'd really like him to do my album. He agreed immediately.

I flew to New York shortly after signing and Steve and I went over a lot of material. I told him some of the tunes I wanted to record and we discussed how we'd go about doing them. Then we went into a studio just off Times Square, with Al Foster on drums, Eddie Gomez on bass, Randy Brecker on flugel, Matt Rollins on piano and George Garzone on tenor sax. We then moved the sessions to Nashville and recorded a lot of the album down there. We managed to secure the services of the legendary George Massenburg to mix the record, too.

For possibly the first time, all I had to do was think about playing and let the guys the other side of the glass in the studio worry about everything else. It was fantastic.

During the recording sessions, Steve asked me to record a solo track so I picked 'Mona Lisa' because it had been a favourite of my dad's – everyone knows the Livingston/Evans classic composition that Nat "King" Cole had a huge hit with. When *Kiss And Tell* was released, Mark Rowles received a fax from Los Angeles from the song's co-writer, Ray Evans, who had heard my version. I was thrilled to read it:

This is one of the most imaginative and lovely interpretations of 'Mona Lisa' I have ever heard. If Nat Cole and Nelson Riddle were still alive – the great artists who guided the song to fame – I think they would agree with me that this is a beautiful extension of the melody and not a "cold and lonely" work of art.

Ray Evans (Livingston/Evans)

I like the reference to the song's lyrics at the end of the message. Being a jazz musician I just can't stop myself from messing about with the tune and harmonies. I always feel a big responsibility to the composer, though, so to get the seal of approval from the great man himself was very important to me. I poured my soul into that recording and I'm delighted Mr Evans enjoyed it.

After I signed to Sony, a lot of people thought that there would be some attempt on their behalf to "restyle" me in some way. Many people hadn't seen me with short hair until they saw the *Kiss And Tell* album cover and they naturally assumed it was all at Sony's insistence. In fact, I'd had my hair cut two years beforehand because I just got fed up having hair down to my waist.

When most people get their hair cut, it's a hair cut; but in the music business, it's a "new image". I've been asked, "Did they make you kiss the guitar in the cover shot?" and I've told them that no, it was my idea and that I did it as a joke but it turned out to be a great shot. I chose the musicians, the producer, the material, the order the tunes are in and I also wrote the sleeve notes. I certainly wasn't forced to do anything. *Kiss And Tell* is the best album I've made so far.

A few of my British fans turned their backs on me when I signed to Sony, accusing me of selling out. They thought I was now allowing myself to be manipulated by a major record company. I've even received some hate mail – one email saying, "You used to be a great guitar player until you sold yourself to Sony. Goodbye, from an ex-fan." It was nothing to do with the music, it's just that some British people hate to see someone (especially one of their own) enjoying success. They prefer to celebrate failure, for some reason. It's very sad, especially as the truth is I had been enjoying success for quite a few years anyway.

*Kiss And Tell* was released in the UK in October 1999 and went to the top of the jazz charts. It was released in Australia and Hong Kong and New Zealand shortly afterwards. The USA release was in May 2000, with 'Midnight At The Oasis' released as a single and getting extensive airplay. I recorded 'Midnight At The Oasis' for Liz, keeping a promise I made her back in the '70s when it was her favourite song. I always said that I would record it for her one day.

Due to the success of *Kiss And Tell*, Sony have taken up the option for me to make a second album which I am currently working on. As I write in Summer 2000, I am due to go to the US to make a PBS TV Special which I will host with special guests.

My last dates of the previous century were in November 1999. I was touring with David Grisman, Jim Kerwin on bass and George Marsh on drums. We'd recorded an album together called *I'm Beginning To See The Light* and this was the tour to support the album in theatres up and down the west coast of the USA. The very last concert was in a club called Palookaville in Santa Cruz. David had told me about a young guitar player who lived there, called Julian Lage and so we met up with him and his father, Mario. At only eleven years of age, Julian was already an incredible guitarist – and one of the nicest kids you could wish to meet.

It was just incredible to hear playing of such maturity coming from one so young. We played for hours together in their front room and he just sat there, smiling and laughing, just a happy kid and, to my mind, something of a genius. It was a really uplifting experience. Julian later came to the gig and we invited him up to play with us and he just played out of his skin. We did a lot of trading choruses and everything I threw at him he threw straight back at me only more so. It was such a wonderful way to end the 20th century. Julian has something very special about him. Apart from his guitar playing, he is a wonderful kid with a charismatic personality and, watching him play that night, and seeing the smiles on people's faces, was a real joy. When he finished playing, the crowd went wild. I found it very emotional and pretended to wipe my face with a towel on stage – in truth I was shedding a tear or two, I felt so proud of him.

The next day I went back to San Francisco because I was flying out from there later on. It was early December and I was walking along the street wearing a long black overcoat which I had bought for Stephane's funeral. In San Francisco you see a lot of people begging in the streets and very often they turn out to be Vietnam veterans who have had various illnesses, either physical or psychological, and of course medical help in the States isn't free like it is in the UK. A lot of them are in wheelchairs and look really sick and really should be in hospital or in some kind of care, but they're out on the streets for whatever reason.

As I was out walking on this cold December day, I saw this black guy sitting in a wheelchair. As I walked past him, he said to me, "Hey, you couldn't give me that overcoat, could you?" I kind of smiled at him and kept on walking. I had got a bit further down the street when I remembered something that Stephane gave me and that I keep in my guitar case to this day. It's a picture of St Martin, a Roman soldier who saw a beggar in the street and cut off a part of his tunic and gave it to him. On the back of the card, Stephane had written: "To my dear Martin, may your patron protect you – Stephane." I thought, "I've got to give that guy my coat," and so I walked back to where he was sitting and said, "Do you really want this coat?" The guy nodded, so I took it off and gave it to him. I thought that it was a very small thing for me to do, but it was the first time since Stephane died that I felt a presence, like he was telling me to do it somehow. Incidentally, I'm no saint, as you will have already figured out by reading this book!

I went back to the hotel and the people behind the desk said, "Didn't you have a coat?" I told them the story but they had no compassion whatsoever, saying, "Why did you give your coat to a bum?" I shouted something at them and left for the airport. I was sad about the incident, but felt good to feel Stephane's presence again.

I've lived in the south-west of Scotland for 20 years and I suppose I feel more like a "local" these days. Because I occasionally play in theatres nearby, do a bit of radio here and there and make records, I've achieved a sort of minor celebrity status in the vicinity. I sometimes get asked to open the odd village fete and, a few years ago, I was asked to crown the gala queen for Gala Day in Kirkmichael. When I did, I was overwhelmed by the sense of community in the village and so I thought, because I live nearby, why don't I try to get a guitar festival happening there?

I went to see Les Hannah, whose wife Brenda runs the local post office. Les is a keen guitar player himself and so I talked the idea over with him and we decided that there was enough local interest in music to warrant taking the idea a few steps further. I also spoke to Mick O'Brien, who runs Ayr Folk Festival, and he put me in touch with Councillor John Cree to see if we could get backing from South Ayrshire Council. We had a meeting in the village hall with various people from the community – the Reverend Gerald Jones, the minister at the church, Isabel McCrory, who is the head teacher at the primary school, and various people from local businesses – and we decided to pursue the idea.

We held the first festival in 1999 and invited Tommy Emmanuel,

Acoustic Mania, Richard Smith and Simon Dinnigan to play. The idea was to cover as many styles of guitar playing as possible, the intention being to celebrate the instrument itself and not any one particular type of music. We put a marquee up on the village football pitch and there was a tremendous response to it, people coming from far and wide to attend.

So, duly encouraged, we held the festival again in 2000 and it was a huge success with an attendance of over 2,500 people. Part of the festival was filmed for the BBC's Music Live project and the BBC have expressed an interest in making a documentary about the festival soon. We plan to expand things for 2001 still further by adding summer schools which will look at various styles of guitar playing, and we also hope to open a guitar museum.

The festival is backed by South Ayrshire Council and all the profits are fed back into the festival itself. But we also donate money to local causes, the local boy scout movement and for senior citizens to go on outings. We've also purchased guitars and given them to the three local primary schools to encourage children to take up music – not that we're planning on creating a master race of guitar players in the vicinity, but just to offer some of the kids a chance to experience different styles of music for themselves. We've also arranged for guitar teachers to visit the schools once a week and teach the kids and so I hope we've managed to preserve the community spirit of the whole venture.

It's a very time-consuming but thoroughly worthwhile project and we'd be absolutely nowhere without a team of dedicated volunteers who fuel the project with their enthusiasm and hard work. It certainly couldn't have happened without Les Hannah and James's hands on the wheel at all times.

The festival is already a major event in Scotland and so I spoke to the local council about designating Kirkmichael as Scotland's Guitar Village. It was an idea they took up and now, if you drive into the village, you'll see a sign proudly proclaiming the fact.

I think it is very important to support and contribute to our local communities. I've got a lot out of playing music and it feels good to give something back, especially when I see young kids taking up music and having such a good time doing it.

One of the other group projects I've become involved in is Bill Wyman's Rhythm Kings. I got a call from Terry Taylor at Ripple Records telling me

that Bill had formed a band and that they'd been recording with Georgie
Fame, Gary Brooker, Albert Lee, Eric Clapton, Mick Taylor, Peter
Frampton and Chris Rea. Now they wanted me to play on some of the
jazzier tracks.

Terry had heard one of my tunes played on Jazz FM when he was in his
car one day and actually gone out and bought one of the Yamaha guitars
that I co-designed, too. So I went down to The Mill Studios at Cookham,
which used to belong to Jimmy Page from Led Zeppelin but are now
owned by Chris Rea, to do some overdubs.

First of all I met Stuart Eps, who has been Elton John's engineer for
many years and had recently recorded 'Millennium' for Robbie Williams,
as well as having edited most of Billy Connolly's albums. Then Terry and
Bill arrived. From the moment I met Bill, I knew we were going to get on
– he's a real down to earth guy, with a passion for music.

They played me one of the two tracks I was due to work on and Bill
said, "Any ideas?" I played along to the track and some things he liked and
others he didn't, but we were able to decide what should go on there and
so we recorded it.

I recorded sitting in an armchair in the control room over a cup of tea
– it was a really relaxed session – and then we went outside and stood by
the river. The studio is on the River Thames, near Marlowe, and Stuart
remarked how rivers rejuvenate themselves with the tide, although sometimes they can get this green mould all over them. Bill said, "Yeah, I get
that on my moat..." His magnificent house up in Suffolk was built in the
time of Henry VIII and actually has a moat! I've played with bassists who
haven't got a roof over their heads, so to meet one who had a moat struck
me as really funny.

The first album I played on was *Struttin' Our Stuff*, followed by *Any
Way The Wind Blows* and *Groovin'*. We also brought out our own bootleg album called *Bootleg Kings*.

Peter Frampton played on the first tour and then I subsequently took his
place. Now, Albert Lee and I share lead guitar roles. Because the band covers a wide area of music, I'm featured on the jazz and blues tunes and Albert
covers the more country and rock 'n' roll numbers. I love Albert's playing –
his ideas are so inventive – he's the Charlie Parker of country guitar!

Terry Taylor also plays and is really Bill's right-hand man in the band,
putting everything together. The wonderful Georgie Fame is a key member.

In fact Bill says, "I'll never go on stage without him." Georgie is one of the most talented performers I've ever worked with.

Gary Brooker, who came to international fame with his group Procol Harum, also sings and plays keyboards in the band, and it's always a thrill when he sings 'Whiter Shade Of Pale' – he's got such a great voice.

It's a pleasure to stand next to Bill every night. He's seriously underrated as a bass player, but everything he plays is absolutely perfect and it's no surprise that people used to refer to The Rolling Stones' rhythm section of Bill and Charlie Watts as the best in rock 'n' roll.

We're very fortunate to have Beverly Skeete in the band, too. She has such an incredibly distinctive voice and makes a great team with our other backing singer, Janice Hoyte. Frank Mead and Nick Payn are on saxes. Frank can really turn on the fireworks when he comes up front to play a solo, and Nick is a tremendous player who also contributes a lot to the band. The drum chair is shared by Graham Broad and Henry Spinetti, both tremendously solid drummers with years of experience behind them.

What started out as a bunch of friends getting together to do a few gigs once a year, has grown and grown due to public demand. More tours are scheduled for Europe and America in 2001.

The Rhythm Kings have become like a family and I enjoy playing with them all, it's a great band. To some people it may seem a little strange that Martin Taylor, the jazz guitarist, should be playing in a band that plays blues, rock 'n' roll, R&B, swing, jump jive and even the occasional reggae tune, but I've always seen all forms of music as being connected, and in this music I can hear the common thread running through. I learn all the time from playing in The Rhythm Kings and I think over the past two years it has made a major contribution to me becoming a better musician – thanks, Bill!

Bill and I share a lack of knowledge of guitar amplifiers. One day when we were rehearsing at Nomis Studios in London, Bill's amp developed a rattle every time he played a low G. We both messed around with the amp for about 15 minutes, trying various things to fix it. Finally our tour manager, Tony, realised the problem – he lifted Bill's ashtray from the top of the amp and the rattle went!

It turns out that Bill and I share similar interests in history. He's a really interesting guy and knows a lot about archaeology, his big thing being metal detecting, going all around Suffolk looking for Roman remains. Maybe I'll get him to help me find those old irons in the River Lee one day!

When Bill Wyman opened his Sticky Fingers restaurant in Manchester I was seated at the same table as Professor Stanley Unwin. He is unique in that he has invented an entirely new language which he used on stage and TV. He would do things like read the weather forecast and, while it was possible to get the meaning of what he was saying, the words would all be twisted and turned around into his own version of events. He once did a commercial for beer on TV and he would start off by saying, "Down the throatload, gurgley, gurgley, oh much joy…" and things like that.

I had always been a great fan of his and so it was a delight to meet him at last. I used to listen to him on the radio as a kid, and when I mentioned it to him he said if I gave him my address he'd send me a tape. I thought he meant he was going to send me a tape of one of his old radio broadcasts, but a couple of days later I received a parcel through the post and in it was a tape he'd recorded specially for me. It was absolutely wonderful, starting off, "Ahhhhh, Martin Taylor, plucknee, plucknee…" I laughed all the way through it. It was an incredibly kind gesture from an extremely generous man.

Having been on the road for practically all of my life, I don't really have the desire to travel any more than absolutely necessary and so it's always a problem when Liz says to me, "Where shall we go for our holiday?" I usually think of the nearest place where the weather is half decent. The thought of spending hours on a plane is not exactly a spellbinding aspect for me any more. That's the downside to spending an awful lot of your professional time travelling from place to place. But Liz had always wanted to go to Singapore and so as a compromise I once agreed to meet her there on my way back from Australia. Possibly the only form of travel left that interests me is time travel. If it were ever possible, then I would love to travel in time. It would be absolutely marvellous.

Sometimes I find my name cropping up in the oddest places. For a start, both "Martin" and "Taylor" are very famous makes of acoustic guitar and people in America often ask me if I changed my name to this end. I usually say, "Yes, my real name's Gibson Rickenbacker." I wish I had come up with a stage name at the beginning of my career. "Smoky" Taylor just didn't seem to fit.

My mum attends a regular book club with a few of her friends and one of the ladies there found a romantic novel, in the Mills And Boon sense of the word, where a young lady is preparing her flat ready for her boyfriend to come round a little later. She's decking the place out with candles and trying to create a really romantic atmosphere. Anyway, the book goes on to say that she searches her record collection for the correct mood music and ends up putting on a CD "by the jazz guitarist Martin Taylor". This has since become one of my favourite stories.

By 1997 I had been playing guitar for 37 years. It had been 33 years since I'd played my first "gig" in the music shop back in Harlow, and I had been a professional musician for 25 years. My silver anniversary had been celebrated with a civic reception, I had received the Freedom of the City of London and I been made an Honorary Doctor of the University of Paisley. I felt very flattered and honoured to receive all these accolades, but underneath it all, deep down, there was something really bothering me. After so many years of working non-stop, through thick and thin, sometimes struggling to provide for my family, and having to deal continually with all the bullshit that this profession throws at you, I felt that the music business had just worn me out. I didn't want anything more to do with it. I was burnt out.

I was still enjoying playing, and I was playing better than I had ever done, but I just felt that I couldn't deal with the music business any more. James had just come on board as my manager; he was young, enthusiastic, full of energy and raring to go, but personally I'd had enough. Liz and I seriously talked about selling our house and hitting the road in our caravan, but I decided to continue a little longer just to help James get on his feet and establish his business.

I left everything in James's hands and said that if the Sony deal came off then I would go for it 100 per cent, but if it didn't, I would go into semi-retirement and not really pursue my career any more.

After all the negotiations I signed with Sony and, knowing that I couldn't let everyone down after all the hard work they had put in (and all the money I'd spent on legal fees!), I set about recording the best album I could possibly make.

Once again it was music that saved me. Once I started making that record I came to life again and any thoughts of retiring disappeared completely. I can never thank James enough for giving his old man a good kick up the backside, or Adam for having the faith in me and giving me the opportunity to make *Kiss And Tell.* I'm now raring to go again and I'm enjoying every minute of it.

Whenever I pick up the guitar and play, whether it's in a large concert hall or sitting at home on my own, I still get the same thrill as I did all those years ago when my dad gave me that little red ukelele. The guitar never ceases to amaze me and teaches me something new every day. It's a very humbling experience. Just to hold the guitar, play a few notes and feel the Conyach come to me makes me realise how fortunate I am. I've come a long way since that dark day at Loch Doon and look forward to writing Part Two of this book in 25 years' time.

There have been some good times and some bad times, but, as Ronnie Scott would have said, "You can't have everything – where would you put it?"

# Discography

TAYLOR MADE *Wave Records*
Martin Taylor with Peter Ind & John Richardson
Recorded in London 1978

TRIPLE LIBRA *Wave Records*
Martin Taylor/Peter Ind Duo
Recorded in London 1979

SKYEBOAT *Concord Records (CJ-184)*
Martin Taylor, Peter Ind & Jimmie Smith
Recorded in San Francisco 1980

STRICTLY FOR THE BIRDS *EMI (EMD5533)*
Yehudi Menuhin & Stephane Grappelli
Recorded in London 1980

WE'VE GOT THE WORLD ON *EMI (EMD5540)*
A STRING
Stephane Grappelli & The Martin Taylor Duo
Recorded in London 1980

AT THE WINERY *Concord Records (CJ-139)*
VINTAGE 1981 *Concord Records (DJ-169)*
Stephane Grappelli featuring Martin Taylor
Recorded in California 1981

TOP HAT *EMI (EMD553)*
Nelson Riddle, Yehudi Menuhin & Stephane Grappelli
Recorded in London 1981

ON THE ROAD AGAIN *Doctor Jazz Records*
Teresa Brewer & Stephane Grappelli featuring Martin Taylor
Recorded in San Francisco 1981

DAWG JAZZ/DAWG GRASS *Warner Brothers (23804-1)*
David Grisman Quintet with special guests Stephane Grappelli, Earl Scruggs &
Martin Taylor
Recorded in California 1982

LONDON REPRISE *Capri Records*
Spike Robinson Quintet featuring Martin Taylor
Recorded in London 1984

GROOVIN' *HEP Records (HEP2030)*
Buddy De Franco & Martin Taylor
Recorded in London 1984

BRINGING IT TOGETHER *Symekob Records (CYK 801-2)*
Stephane Grappelli & Toots Thielmans featuring Martin Taylor
Recorded in San Francisco 1984

TOGETHER AT LAST *Flying Fish Records (FF70421)*
Stephane Grappelli & Vassar Clements featuring Martin Taylor
Recorded in Nashville 1984

A TRIBUTE TO ART TATUM *HEP Records*

Martin Taylor
Recorded in Edinburgh, Scotland 1984
ACOUSTIC DUETS                                          *Jardis Records Germany*
Louis Stewart & Martin Taylor                           *(JTCD 9613)*
Recorded in Dublin 1984
DAVID GRISMAN'S ACOUSTIC                                *Rounder Records CD 0190*
CHRISTMAS
David Grisman featuring Martin Taylor
Recorded in California 1986
INNOVATIONS
John Dankworth conducts The London Symphony Orchestra
Featuring Martin Taylor & Peter King
Recorded in London 1986
SARABANDA
Martin Taylor Band featuring John Pattitucci, Paulinho Da Costa, Sal Marquez & Pete
Cristlieb
Produced by David Hungate
Recorded in Los Angeles 1987
JUST ONE OF THOSE THINGS                                *EMI Records*
Stephane Grappelli featuring Martin Taylor
Recorded in London 1987
STEPHANE GRAPPELLI PLAYS JEROME KERN                    *GRP (GRD-9542)*
Recorded in New York and London 1987
ALL MY TOMORROWS                                        *Linn Records*
Carol Kidd with guest Martin Taylor
Recorded in Scotland 1988
OLYMPIA 1988                                            *WEA Music (243977-2)*
Stephane Grappelli's 80th Birthday Concert featuring Martial Solal, Svend Asmussen,
Martin Taylor, Marc Fosset, Patrice Caratini
Recorded in Paris 1988
JAZZ BASS BAROQUE                                       *Wave Records*
Peter Ind with guest Martin Taylor
Recorded in London 1988
GARDEN OF DREAMS                                        *Projazz (CDJ 661)*
Buddy De Franco/Martin Taylor Quintet
Recorded in London 1988
MEMORIES OF YOU                                         *Tee-Jay Reocrds (102)*
Barbara Jay featuring Martin Taylor
Recorded in London 1988
MILOU EN MAI                                            *CBS (466285 2)*
Stephane Grappelli featuring Martin Taylor
Soundtrack to Louis Malle movie *Milou En Mai*
Recorded in Paris 1989
DON'T FRET                                              *Linn Records (AKD014)*
Martin Taylor Quartet
Recorded in London 1990
THIS TIME IT'S LOVE                                     *Reference Records*
Eileen Farrell with Robert Farnon Orchestra & Martin Taylor
Recorded in 1990
CHANGE OF HEART                                         *Linn Records (AKD016)*
Martin Taylor Quartet
Recorded in Scotland 1991
WHERE EAGLES FLY                                        *BBC Enterprises (BBC CD 771)*
Moira Kerr featuring Martin Taylor

Soundtrack from BBC TV's *Where Eagles Fly*
Recorded in Scotland 1991
GLENCOE GLEN OF WEEPING                    *Mayker Records (CD MAYK 1)*
Moira Kerr featuring Martin Taylor
Recorded in Scotland 1991
ARTISTRY                                   *Linn Records (AKD020)*
Martin Taylor
Recorded in Devon, England 1992
A MATTER OF TIME                           *Prestige Records*
Martin Taylor & Gordon Giltrap
Recorded in England 1992
JAZZ HOT                                   *Bruton/Zomba Music BRS*
Martin Taylor & Jean Pierre Fabien (John Fiddy)   *14 (166)*
Library Music
Recorded in London 1993
REUNION                                    *Linn Records (AKD022)*
Martin Taylor with special guest Stephane Grappelli
Recorded in Mireval, France 1993
JAZZ HOT 2                                 *Bruton/Zomba Music BRS*
Martin Taylor & Jean Pierre Fabien (John Fiddy)   *19 (213)*
Library Music
Recorded in London 1994
SPIRIT OF DJANGO                           *Linn Records (AKD030)*
Martin Taylor's Spirit Of Django
Recorded in Scotland 1994
GUITAR MOODS                               *Hit Label Records (ULTCD*
Martin Taylor and Academy                  *023)*
Recorded in England 1995
TONE POEMS II                              *Acoustic Disc (ACD18)*
Martin Taylor & David Grisman
Recorded in California 1995
CALANAIS                                   *An Lanntair (CD001)*
Compilation CD Celebrating 10th Anniversary of An Lanntair Art Gallery in Stornoway,
Scotland. Featuring original compositions by Martin Taylor, Tommy Smith, Phil
Cunningham & others
Recorded in Scotland 1995
BEGINNING TO SEE THE LIGHT                 *Dawg Records (ACD 36)*
Martin Taylor/David Grisman Jazz Quartet featuring Jim Kerwin & George Marsh
Recorded in California 1995
PORTRAITS                                  *Linn Records (AKD048)*
Martin Taylor with special guest Chet Atkins
Recorded in Scotland, Nashville & Hamburg 1995
YEARS APART                                *Linn Records (AKD058)*
Martin Taylor's Spirit Of Django
Recorded in Scotland 1996
GYPSY                                      *Linn Records*
Martin Taylor's Spirit Of Django
Recorded on tour in the UK 1997
MARTIN TAYLOR GOLD                         *Linn Records (AKD064)*
Compilation CD 1997
TWO'S COMPANY                              *Larrikin/Festival (LRF 484)*
Martin Taylor with guests
Recorded in Sydney, Australia 1997

ANDROMEDA HEIGHTS                                    *Columbia (KWCD30)*
Prefab Sprout with guest soloist Martin Taylor
Recorded in England 1997
JIMMY VAN HEUSEN SONGBOOK                            *Degga Records*
Martin Taylor, Shannon Gibbons & Rufus Reid
Produced by Max Roach
Recorded in New York 1997
MARTIN TAYLOR IN CONCERT                             *Stefan Grossman's Guitar*
Martin Taylor                                        *Workshop*
Performance video
Recorded in Pittsburgh 1997
CELEBRATING GRAPPELLI                                *Linn Records*
Martin Taylor's Spirit Of Django, Stephane Grappelli, Claire Martin & Gerard Presencer
Compilation CD 1997
JOY                                                  *Angel (7243 8 33305 22)*
Melissa Manchester with guest soloist Martin Taylor
Recorded in Nashville 1997
STRUTTIN' OUR STUFF                                  *BMG (74321 51441 2)*
Bill Wyman's Rhythm Kings
Recorded in London 1997
ANYWAY THE WIND BLOWS                                *BMG Classics*
Bill Wyman's Rhythm Kings featuring Martin Taylor, Eric Clapton, Albert Lee, Georgie
Fame, Chris Rea & Gary Brooker
Recorded in England 1997
THE MUSIC OF DUKE ELLINGTON                          *Stefan Grossman's Guitar*
Martin Taylor                                        *Workshop*
Tuition video and CD
Recorded in Pittsburgh 1998
THE MUSIC OF JIMMY VAN HEUSEN                        *Stefan Grossman's Guitar*
Martin Taylor                                        *Workshop*
Tuition video and CD
Recorded in Pittsburgh 1998
BOOTLEG KINGS                                        *Ripple (RIPCD 001)*
Bill Wyman's Rhythm Kings
Recorded in Denmark, Germany & Norway 1998
KISS AND TELL                                        *Sony Jazz*
Martin Taylor featuring Randy Brecker, Kirk Whalum, Eddie Gomez & Al Foster
Recorded in New York and Nashville 1999
GROOVIN'                                             *Papillon (BTFLY CD0003)*
Bill Wyman's Rhythm Kings
Recorded in London 2000

*For more information, or to purchase Martin Taylor records, visit www.martintaylor.com*

# Index

# also available from sanctuary publishing

FOR MORE INFORMATION on titles from Sanctuary Publishing Limited visit our
website at www.sanctuarypublishing.com or contact Sanctuary Publishing Limited, 32-36 Telford Way,
London W3 7XS. Tel: +44 (0)20 8749 9171 Fax: +44 (0)20 8749 9685.

**To order a title direct call our credit card hotline on 0800 731 0284** (UK only) or write to
Sanctuary Direct, PO Box 2616, Great Dunmow, Essex CM6 1DH. International callers please ring +44 (0)20
8749 9171 or fax +44 (0)20 8749 9685. You can also order from our website www.sanctuarypublishing.com